DESOLATE HEART

Sidney Archer

Ecanus Publishing

Ecanus Publishing
Ramsgate
Kent
United Kingdom

Published by Ecanus Publishing 2013

Sidney Archer asserts the moral right to be identified as the author of the work.

All rights reserved. No part of this publication may be reproduced, stored in a retrieval system, or transmitted, in any form or by any means, electronic, mechanical, photocopying, recording or otherwise, without the prior permission of the publisher.

ISBN 978-0-9574126-7-5

"Dedicated to my cubbies in the Lounge. Y'all know who you are. Mama Bear loves you."

PROLOGUE

August, one hundred years ago

Hester Kyle shook out the money she had stashed in the toe of an old stocking. She could count it all at a glance; she hoped it would be enough.

Clutching the money in one fist, she slipped from her room and through the house then darted out the back door. It wouldn't do for any of her family to know she had cash. Pa would demand it, Ma would cry for it, or one of the brats would steal it.

No sirree, nobody was taking what she'd scrubbed floors to earn. She had planned to buy herself a new dress, a fancy one with ruffles and lace in which to marry Andrew Wade, but all that had changed. Now she had something else she needed to do with her earnings, and Mr. High-and-Mighty Andrew Wade would rue the day he had turned away Hester Kyle's love.

The air smelled of baked earth and dry, sunburned grass. The early afternoon sun seemed to broil her in her skin, and there was not a whisper of a breeze. Hester hurried on her errand. It was too hot to be rushing like this, but she had to get to Granny Hodge.

She entered the woods. It was cooler there, and shady. She toyed with the notion of stopping for a moment in the dim shadows, just to catch her breath, but the memory of Andrew's rejection goaded her onward, in search of the old woman, in search of revenge.

Hester hated Andrew Wade. Hated him with the same blind, burning passion which, until this morning, she had loved him. How dare he turn her down when she had poured out her heart to him, confessed to years of yearning, and openly offered herself to him? Couldn't he see she would have been perfect for him? He was the handsomest, smartest man on the ridge, and everyone said she was the prettiest girl in these parts. She was built for having babies; she and Andrew could have had a lot of them. But he had other dreams, and his dreams could take him far away from Sumac Ridge if he took the notion to leave for good.

He had been kind and gentle, of course, when he turned her down. That was Andrew's way. But he also had been so stubborn that no amount of her crying and begging moved him.

Her anger exploded then. Exploded with such fury that she had lashed out, kicking and clawing, screaming every foul name she knew. Andrew had effortlessly restrained her by holding her wrists, and when she had finally quieted, she read pity in his eyes. Pity, not love or desire.

Just the memory scalded her to the very bone.

"I'll get even with you, Andrew Wade!" she had screamed at him. And she would. He would be sorry for the day his mother had pushed him from her belly, and when he realized there was no hope for him, Hester would laugh as she had never laughed before, because he would get what he deserved and she would have her payback.

She was near Granny Hodge's cabin now, eager to reach the old woman who was reputed not only to cure all manner of ailments and disease, but was capable of casting monstrous dark spells. Hester felt she could not reach the old woman soon enough.

She broke out of the trees and into a small clearing where the harsh sunlight met her again. Shading her eyes with one hand, she looked across the meadow at the cabin on the other side. The old woman she sought was in front of the cabin, hoeing a garden patch.

Hester hurried toward the bent figure in the faded blue dress and sunbonnet; anticipation pumped frantically through her blood. By the time she reached Granny Hodge, the older woman had stopped her work, clutching the wooden hoe handle in one gnarled hand. She stared hard at Hester.

"I need your help, Granny."

The woman spat a stream of tobacco juice in the dirt near Hester's bare feet. She did not move her rheumy gaze from the younger woman, and for a long time she did not speak.

"It's a man what's brung you here," she said at last.

"Yes," Hester said with eagerness. "Andrew Wade. Do you know him?"

"Reckon ever'body hereabouts knows Andrew, or knows of him."

Hester winced. Of course everyone knew Andrew. Everyone liked him, respected him. That's why she wanted him so much. In her dreams, she would not be the drunkard Etcyl Kyle's daughter; she would be Doctor Andrew Wade's wife. She would live in a big, fine house with servants and everybody bowing to her like she was somebody. But that dream was gone now and replaced by something devious and destructive.

Granny still had not taken her eyes off Hester. She worked her tobacco and spat again.

"You ain't wantin' no love potion, but it would sure be a heap better than what you got in mind."

"It's done too late for love potions!" Hester snapped. She flung back her thick, dark hair. "I tried everything I could think of to make him want me, but he ain't got no heart. Nor anything else, I reckon, 'cause I couldn't even get him to lay with me." She pulled herself up straight and shook back her hair again. "Look at me, Granny. Ain't I got what it takes to make a man want me?"

Hester had high, full breasts, a small waist and round hips. Her arms and legs were long and supple, her skin dusky and smooth. Thick, black lashes framed deep brown eyes. Her full lips were as red as fresh berries. Granny Hodge looked at her.

"You're right pretty," she said finally, "but you'd best forget Andrew Wade. He's never made it a secret that he's gonna be the ridge's first doctor. He don't want to be tied down with no woman and young 'uns for a long time. You'd best set your cap for somebody else or wait for him to finish up his studies and training."

Hester's renewed fury rang in her ears. She stomped one bare foot on the hot earth.

"No, no, no! I don't want no one else, and I ain't gonna wait for him to get done at that university. I want to fix him good. Look here." She opened her hand where the money lay in her sweaty palm. "This here is all I got, and you can have it, every bit, if you'll put a spell on him."

The old woman's eyes brightened at the sight of the coins and crumpled bills. Granny's greed was almost as legendary as her healing skills.

She shifted her eyes up a moment.

"Sounds to me like you ain't wantin' a spell; you're wantin' a curse."

"Call it what you want to. I just want him punished for what he done to me!"

Granny Hodge looked at the money again.

"That all you got?"

"I done told you. And I been saving for months."

The old woman did not hesitate again. She scraped the money from Hester's palm. Hester stared at the dark, crescent-shaped birthmark on the old woman's left hand. Everybody said it was the devil's mark, and that it was the devil himself who gave Granny her powers. Hester feared the devil, but he didn't scare her bad enough to keep her from using him when she thought he'd help her. She watched Granny tuck the money into the deep pocket of her apron.

"Come with me."

Hester followed, but at a distance. Once the money had changed hands, the old woman seemed to have changed, becoming more misshapen and peculiar, somehow evil. Granny leaned the hoe against the side of her cabin and went inside without looking back. Hester paused just outside the door then gathered her courage and determination. She stepped across the threshold.

The odor of herbs and stale wood smoke met her immediately. Every available space inside the cabin was filled with jars and vials. Drying herbs hung from the low ceiling. There was barely room for the bed, table and chair, cook stove and two rocking chairs. Paintings done by the old woman hung on the walls. They were ugly paintings, mostly trees and rocks, without much color or light in them. Hester liked paintings of big houses and people dressed in jewels and fancy clothes. Granny's dark pictures made her feel strange inside her skin. She looked away.

Granny Hodge had removed her sunbonnet, revealing flattened, sweat-damp gray hair in a wispy bun. She spat her wad into a rusty can then drank a dipperful of water from the bucket on the table.

She sat down in one of the cane-backed rockers and fixed her eyes on Hester who continued to stand without moving in the doorway.

"Git yourself a drink of water. It's right hot today. Then set down." She pointed at the other rocker.

Hester declined the water but sat on the edge of the chair, tipping it forward. She twisted her fingers while waiting for Granny to do something instead of rock in her chair and stare straight ahead.

After a minute, Hester said impatiently, "Well, ain't you gonna do anything?"

The silent old woman kept rocking, her chair thumping a slow, hypnotic rhythm. After a short span of time, Hester jumped up. She prowled the room like a restless cat, but she kept glancing at Granny who seemed to have forgotten all about her.

"Look, if you ain't gonna do anything, I want my money back."

"Sit down."

Hester returned to her chair, again perched on the edge like a hungry bird.

"Sit back."

"But—"

"I said sit back."

The voice was strong, commanding. Hester sat back, tense, out of patience with Granny Hodge as the old woman continued to rock and to stare at her. She felt uneasy, being watched that way, but found she couldn't take her eyes from Granny's gaze. In a couple of minutes her muscles began to feel heavy, her joints liquid. Now she could no longer keep her eyelids open, no matter how hard she tried. She settled back into the chair, drowsy and comfortable. The thump-thump of Granny's rocker was soothing, like a mother's heartbeat.

"Tell me what you want for Andrew."

Hester heard the question from a great distance. She no longer felt her fury burning out of control at the mention of his name. She tried to open her eyes and found she could not.

"Punish him," she said thickly.

Granny Hodge grunted. "So what's that mean? He didn't do nothin' wrong."

"Make him pay for what he did to me." The words came more easily that time, as though her tongue and lips were waking up while the rest of her body napped.

Granny heaved a deep sigh.

"You want him to be ugly? Poor? Sick or mangled or blind? You want him…dead?"

The word hung heavily between them, like a dense black curtain. Hester felt a tiny shiver of fear, but in her relaxed state, she dismissed it.

"Not right off," she said. "First, he oughta want somethin' so bad it's all he can think about, even when he's sleepin'. I want him to try and try to have it, 'til he's sure he's done gone crazy, like he's all locked up with his wantin' and can't never get out. He oughta be so lonesome it's like his heart's gonna bust from it, 'cause that's how I been feelin'. And then, after a long, long time, he can die."

Her request, for all its passion, had been delivered coolly and simply. It seemed now to linger in the air all about her, like a smothering cloud of smoke. It became hard to breathe. She could not move, could not speak.

The thumping of Granny's rocking chair suddenly ceased.

"You go home now."

Hester awakened, coming out of a thick fog of panic and confusion. The day seemed far advanced although Hester had not been aware of its passing. Granny Hodge was at the small table, her back to Hester. She stirred something in a pot.

"Did I sleep?" she asked, her unease subsiding. Granny either did not hear or did not want to hear. She kept working as if Hester was not there.

"Are you making a potion for Andrew?"

The old woman did not turn.

"I'm fixin' my supper. You go now."

Hester got out of the chair, hesitated, then slowly moved toward the front door of the tiny cabin.

"When…when will Andrew get what's coming to him?"

Granny turned slightly and looked at her from rheumy eyes.

"Everybody gets their reward…or punishment."

"But…"

The old woman carried her pot to the stove and said nothing else. Hester knew Granny would not speak again.

She left the cabin, surprised that daylight was no more than an orange smear along the western edge of the woods. Darkness greeted her as she entered the trees, and it grew denser as she plunged farther into the forest. But Hester had been born and raised on Sumac Ridge; neither the black shadows which leaped and shivered nor the shrill night sounds frightened her.

Her earlier detachment had faded. Now she felt joyous. Andrew Wade would get his comeuppance, sure enough. Him and his highfalutin plans to be the first doctor on the ridge. He'd be needing a doctor before Granny's spell was finished with him, yes sirree—

Falling headlong over a tree root which her keen eyes had failed to see, she crashed hard against the earth. For a minute she was sure her chest had exploded, and she knew a moment of panic when she thought she was dying. A few seconds later air rushed into her lungs, and she lay without moving for a bit, simply breathing.

After a minute or two, when she was certain she was all right, Hester pulled her legs up under her and started to rise. A weird, prickly feeling brushed across the back of her neck, as if she were being watched. She looked around, eyes straining to see through the darkness. What she saw froze her blood: not three feet away, its long sleek body poised to strike, a huge snake had fixed its unrelenting stare on her.

Unable to move, Hester watched the snake until it began to inch forward. She screamed, tried to scramble to her feet. Fear made her clumsy, and she sprawled on the ground again. Awkwardly, she clambered to her feet and started to flee.

The serpent lunged, sinking its fangs into the soft, pulsing vein in her throat.

Venom poured into her blood like a river of fire. She grabbed the thick, lashing body and tried to yank it free, but the more she tugged and fought, the more deeply the fangs settled.

She screamed again and could not stop screaming until her throat swelled shut, and she collapsed, her rapidly bloating body turning blue. When her heartbeat ceased, the snake released itself and slithered away into the night.

***

Granny Hodge, enjoying her pipe on the front porch before going to bed, stared across the meadow at the woods. Hester's cries were far away, but the night air had carried them clearly. When the screaming stopped, Granny heaved herself out of the porch chair and knocked her pipe against the rough-hewn support post.

She gazed at the woods again.

People did not realize the force of Granny's curses. Sometimes, if there was enough hatred in the one who had come begging for a curse, the power spilled over on them, and they got caught in their own black deed.

She could tell them, of course, but most folks wouldn't pay for a spell if they thought something bad might happen to them. Granny reached into her apron pocket where the bills and coins were.

She could tell folks, of course, but she never would.

Once in a while, some good would come along to break a curse. But it didn't happen very often, more's the pity, because Andrew Wade was a good man. He did not deserve what was going to happen to him, and Granny regretted what she had to do. But a pact was a pact, and she had to keep her part of the bargain. If she didn't, she'd suffer a worse fate than that selfish young woman who now lay dead in the woods.

The ancient woman took the money from her pocket and looked at it. The amount was pitiful, but it was more than she had this morning. She stumped into the cabin and pulled out the intricately carved ebony chest from beneath her bed. She took a key from her pocket, unlocked the chest and pushed back the lid. Gold and silver shone in the lamp light while bright jewels winked and sparkled. Granny added Hester's pittance to the store then locked the trunk and hid it once more. Maybe someday, if she saved enough, she could buy back what she had lost so long ago.

Until then, there was nothing to prevent her from making a way out for Andrew Wade, if the right person came along. And if that person came in time.

The old woman went out into her yard a few steps and looked up at the sliver of moon, a crescent-shape like the one on her hand. She began a chant:

"Passion spurned; hatred burned.

A curse of thirteen hundred moons must pass.

Then death will come, unless love breaks the curse and sets the prisoner free."

The dark night shivered around her as Granny heaved a sigh of sorrow. She turned and went back into her cabin to prepare her canvas and sort her paints.

***

Andrew carefully arranged his two new shirts in his valise and looked around the small, sunny bedroom to see if he forgot anything. This would be the last time he would be leaving for the university because this was his final year. At the age of thirty, most medical students had finished with their studies and were already practicing medicine. Andrew had worked and saved his money to pay for that education long after others of his age were in their final years of study.

"Don't forget to take your dinner," Ruby Jean Wade said as she came into the room. In her plump, work-worn hands she carried a small, brown-wrapped parcel containing fried chicken and thick slices of buttered bread. "It's a long train ride back to your school."

Andrew stopped adjusting the straps on his valise to turn to her.

"Thanks, Mama," he said, accepting the food. "I'll think of you when I eat this."

Looking away, she nodded and blinked hard. Her lower lip trembled. He put his arms around her, hugged her and stood back.

"Now, Mama, how many times have I left? Don't I always come back? This will be the last time. Next summer, when I return, I won't have to leave the ridge again."

Ruby Jean crimped her lips into a hard, straight line for a minute as she looked up at her son.

"I know that, Andrew. Don't never think I doubt it for a minute." She reached up and laid one calloused palm against his cheek. "But I'm gonna miss you just the same. Can't a-one of you kids leave home without leaving a empty place in the house."

"Mama, you got seven young 'uns to take care of. Here I am, over thirty. It's time I'm out of your house."

The hand that lay against his face gently pinched his cheek.

"Don't matter if you're three or thirty-three. Ever' last one of you kids is still my baby, and will be 'til I'm moldering in my grave."

"I know that, Mama." Andrew smiled at her. "We all know that."

"See that you remember it, too. When you bring some fancy young wife from the city, see that she understands it, and we'll get along just fine."

Andrew laughed as he packed up the books he had not sent ahead to the university. He closed and strapped that case and set it on the bed next to his valise.

"Mamma, how many times do I have to tell you, there is not a young woman, fancy from the city or otherwise?"

Ruby Jean, ever the vigilant housekeeper, squinted at his dresser top then wiped her hand across the invisible film of dust.

"Hester Kyle seems to think there is. Seems to think she is, way she's been hanging all over you lately. Disgraceful how she acted at the church supper last week. I hope you don't take up any notions about her."

Andrew touched a long scratch on his cheek and silently recalled his last encounter with Hester, just two days ago. She had surprised him by stepping out of the bushes near the creek as he walked home from Uncle Cy's farm. Sweat made a fine sheen on her dark skin and the top buttons of her red gingham dress were open, exposing the round tops of her breasts. He knew she had fancied him for a while and had done his best to discourage her kindly, but Hester was not easy to discourage. She had flung back her rich, dark hair and met his eyes, almost brazenly.

"I hear you're leavin' the ridge again right soon," she said.

He nodded. "That's right."

"Comin' back?"

"Of course."

"Whyn't you just stay?"

He had smiled as he answered. "You know why, Hester. I need to finish my training."

"You're a good enough doc, just like you are," she said, flinging her hair again and moved a step closer. "Folks come to you all the time for ailments and such."

"But I'm not a doctor yet."

She came close enough to touch him. He refused to look at her breasts. She ran a bold finger down the line of buttons on his shirt.

"Reckon I could make you stay."

Andrew wasn't sure if she was asking or telling. He shook his head.

"I'm going back day after tomorrow."

Hester linked her arms around his neck. She smelled of sweat and musk.

"I could make you stay," she said again and pressed

her lips to his.

He turned his face away, gently unclasped her arms and pushed her from him.

"I'm sorry, Hester."

She took a deep breath, her generous bosom swelling. She pulled her dress down from her shoulders. Andrew grabbed her hands before she could bare herself to his eyes.

"Please, don't do this," he said.

She looked at him in surprise. "Why not?"

"Because…you shouldn't."

She narrowed her eyes.

"Why not?" she asked again. "They ain't a man on the Ridge that don't want me."

He said nothing.

"You ain't no different. You got all the parts, I reckon." She looked directly at his crotch. "You like women, don't you, Andrew?" She grabbed one of his hands and put it on her breast. "You like me, don't you?"

He yanked free of her clasp and stepped back.

"It has nothing to do with whether or not I liked you. I'm leaving because I am going to finish my education and training. There is no time or place in my life for a girl. Any girl. My studies have to come first."

"Huh!" She stared hard at him then said, "Would you want me if you wasn't going back to the university?"

"Hester, I—"

"I know you would! Andrew Wade, you know I've been loving you ever since I was knee high. Ain't no man on this ridge as fine and good-lookin' as you. I'd make you a fine wife, and you know it. Let me prove it to you." Here she began to unfasten more buttons and when he tried to stop her, she fought against him.

"Look!" she shouted. "Look what I got!"

She tore open the dress, exposing her breasts to him completely. He stared long enough to realize what he was doing and turned away.

"Cover yourself, Hester. My God."

She shrieked in a fit of temper. "What kind of man are you, anyway?"

He began to walk away, not looking at her.

"Come back to me!"

"I'm going."

She caught up to him and grabbed his arm. Her fingers bit painfully into his muscle.

"You can't just leave me."

Andrew stopped walking and drew in a long breath. He turned to her, took her upper arm in a gentle grip and looked into her eyes.

"Hester, I've been working for years on my medical degree. I will not abandon my—"

"I don't care what you want!" she screamed. "I want to be your woman, and I want it now!" She stomped her grimy bare foot on the dusty path. "Now!"

Andrew fought rising anger. He reminded himself she was a poor ridge girl, the unfortunate daughter of a mean, lazy man and his slovenly wife. He knew Hester earned most of the income that went into their pathetic household by doing whatever work she could find. It made sense that she saw an opportunity for escape by finding a good man who would take care of her. But he was not the man for the job.

"Hester," he said, looking into her eyes that flashed with vehemence. "There are a lot of men on this ridge who'd be honored to have you for a wife. You're beautiful and passionate. It won't be hard for you to find a man to love you. I'm flattered that you want me, but you must understand that I'm not going to take you as my girl, my lover, or my wife."

She stared at him, breathing hard, dark eyes flashing, her face flushed. For what seemed like a full minute she stared at him, and he waited for her to understand and accept his refusal.

Then, with a shriek of fury, she lashed out, her ragged fingernails scraping the skin of his face. He grabbed her wrists before she could dig deeply enough to draw blood. She struggled, screeching and cursing, trying to kick and claw, her dark hair flying in a wild tangle.

"Stop it, Hester," he yelled above her maniacal shrieks, still holding her wrists and dodging her kicking feet. "Stop now! I'm not going to change my mind."

She kept screaming and trying to flail him until she finally seemed to exhaust herself. With one last futile attempt to launch her knee into his crotch, she quit. Her eyes were wilder than ever, her face flaming and dripping with sweat, her entire body heaved with ragged breathing.

"Let go of me, you bastard," she said through clenched teeth.

"Are you finished with your fit?"

Her eyes narrowed and she bared her teeth, hissing at him.

"Mister High and Mighty. You think you're too good for a ridge girl like me. Reckon you think you're gonna get you some uppity rich girl somewhere, don't you? Some snotty gal with silk dresses and fancy hats with feathers who'll look down her nose at us ridge girls. Let go of me, you bastard."

Watching her closely, he loosened his grip bit by bit. Hester yanked free and stepped back, rubbing her wrists. Her gaze was as venomous as ever.

"You just wait," she said. "You're gonna get what's coming to you, Andrew Wade, and I'm gonna laugh 'til the day I die. Just you wait and see."

She spat on the ground near his feet, turned and ran through the trees, away from him, back toward the scrappy, fallow farm where she lived.

Now, two days later, in the warm, sunny bedroom of his home and with the wound on his face healing and Hester an ugly, fading memory, Andrew said to his mother, "Don't you worry about me having any notions about Hester Kyle. I think she finally understands how it is with me."

"Hmm." Ruby Jean eyed him. "Stick by your guns, son. You worked too hard to let any piece of skirt ruin your life."

"I know."

"'Course I ain't sayin' you shouldn't never have a wife. You're gonna need one someday."

He smiled at her as he picked up his valise and the case with his books and the food she had prepared for the trip.

"Let someday take care of itself, Mama," he told her gently. "Today has its own concerns."

At the gate of the clean, shady front yard, his young twin sisters ran to him. From the near field one of the brothers strode toward them. His father and other two brothers were in the fields on the far side of the farm, and his other sister was in town, working as a seamstress at Miss Betsy's. They had said their good-byes at breakfast that morning.

"You comin' back at Christmas, Andrew?" Karol and Maggie asked in unison.

He put down his cases and gathered both girls to him for a long, hard bear hug.

"I am," he told them, letting go. "The two of you help Mama around the house without fussing and complaining."

"We will," they answered.

"Don't reckon you'll ever take up a winnowing hook again," Matthew Levi said as he approached.

Andrew grinned. "Maybe not, but I can stitch you up

when you get too rambunctious at the Harvest Dance."

Matthew Levi grinned back.

"Shucks," he muttered. Matthew Levi was too bashful even to go to the dance.

Andrew bent to pick up his cases again, and as he straightened he ran his gaze over his home once more as he always did before leaving. While he was away, he always kept in his mind the cheering remembrance of this rambling, gray-boarded house, comfortable in the cooling shade of the towering oak and maple trees. This image sustained him through those days when he wondered if he'd ever be finished with his studies and training. Today, however, as he took in the sight and breathed deeply the smell of fresh cut hay and Mama's summer flowers, he knew it would be the last time he'd have to do this. Next year, he would be back on Sumac Ridge for good. He would see this home and his family every day.

He kissed his mother and little sisters good-bye and nodded to Matthew Levi. "I'll be home for a few days at Christmas. Keep the home fires burning for me."

Ruby Jean futilely sniffed back a sob. Karol and Maggie began to wail. Matthew Levi shifted his feet and rubbed his jaw. Andrew gave them all a smile and went out the front gate.

***

The day was hot and still and dry. Heat waves danced

ahead of him on the scorched, shadeless stretches of dusty road as he walked to the small town of Smith. It wasn't much of a town, just the train station, general store, post office, lumber mill and Miss Betsy's Sewing Parlor where she made clothes for a big store in St. Louis. Trains stopped in Smith only twice a week. Andrew wondered if the little settlement would ever grow into a real town. Most folks in the area were farmers or worked in the timber. He planned to build his home and office in town so folks could find him easily, and he had just the location picked out across the street from Miss Betsy's and the general store.

The rattling wheels of an approaching wagon interrupted his thoughts. The big man on the seat took off his slouch-hat and waved it over his head.

"Howdy, Andrew!" he hollered as he got closer. "On yer way back to the big city?"

"Hello, Earl. I'm on my way back. I start my training with Doctor Lowell this year. You've been to the mill this morning?"

"Yep. Goin' home fer dinner. You might just as well come along. Lottie and the kids'd relish seeing you."

Andrew shook his head and set down his luggage for a minute. In this heat it seemed to get heavier with every step.

"Got to catch the train if I want to make it back by Monday. How's Lottie feeling today?"

Earl pulled out a ragged, limp handkerchief and wiped his face and neck.

"Oh, tolerable, I reckon. She says this weather is right hard on her, says this is the last young 'un she wants to have. Said as how she wished you was back fer good 'cause she knows you'd take care of her if things get... well, you know how it was with the last young 'un. Granny Hodge did her best, but...."

"I don't think I could have done anything more, Earl. Babies sometimes just don't grow right in the womb. Not the fault of anyone, it's just the way of things."

Earl shook his head and stared in the distance at nothing.

"Reckon you're right. Still I can't help but believe that having an educated doc will make a heap of difference in these parts." His gaze rested on Andrew. "You took right good care of me last Christmas when I broke my leg."

Andrew smiled.

"It was Granny who taught me how to set a broken bone, Earl. Trust her to take care of you. I'm hoping that when I set up practice, she'll assist me. She's too old to be way out there in the woods by herself. Assisting me would give her a good reason to move closer to folks."

"Boy," the man said, squinting at him, "don't you know Granny has been old since I was kid? Pop said she was old when he was a young man." He mopped the back of his neck again. "I've always thought they was something peculiar about that old woman, with all her potions and tonics and the way she can look at you outta her eyes. And that mark on her hand? Folks say it's the devil's mark."

"Granny's got a reputation," Andrew agreed.

Earl scratched a whiskery jaw.

"She learn you how to cast spells and whatnot?"

Andrew laughed and picked up his suitcases.

"No. She keeps all that to herself. Earl, it was good to see you. I need to get going. Tell Lottie to rest some every day and eat a good diet. Get those kids to take on more of the chores. She's not as young as she used to be."

"No, she ain't. I wish she wasn't havin' to go through this again."

"Well, it takes two, Earl."

The man looked down, his face red. "I know it. I get ashamed sometimes."

"No help comes from being ashamed. Just remember what we talked about, and the time of the month when conception is most likely to happen."

"I'll do that."

"I need to get to the station now. Don't want to miss my train."

The other man looked up.

"Want me to take you into town? Be glad to do it, Andrew."

Andrew shook his head and started to move away. "Thanks, anyway. You just get on home to Lottie and the kids. She's probably got dinner already waiting for you."

As the wagon resumed its clattering way down the road, Andrew continued his walk in the opposite direction. The last stand of woods before reaching town was just ahead. Eager to leave the hot glare of the August sun for the cooling shade, he quickened his step.

He heard a distant moan and stopped. Had he really heard the sound of someone in pain, or were his ears playing a trick on him?

"Hello?" he called. "Is someone there? Do you need help?"

When no one answered, he began to walk again. At the edge of the woods he heard the sound again, louder this time and most definitely a groan of illness or pain.

Once more, Andrew put down his cases. He pulled his watch from his pocket. The train was due shortly. If he missed it today, he would have to get Matthew Levi or his father to take him in the wagon to the next train station, a day's ride from where he stood. Otherwise, he would have to wait until next week. He would not ask his father to miss two days of work, but he didn't want to be late for the start of classes.

The groan came again, more intense, more desperate. Miss the train or not, he could not walk away and leave someone who needed help. Settling his cases under a scraggly blackjack tree just off the road, Andrew Wade hurriedly followed the sound into the woods, seeking the one who needed him.

He saw nobody, but the groan came again when he called.

"Here," a weak voice spoke from a dense thicket nearby. "Please, please help me."

Andrew crashed through the woods toward the thicket.

"I'm coming. Help's on the way."

Then, as he neared his destination, an unexpected cool, almost chill wind blew over him. He pushed aside a thick bush. The next step he took seemed endless as he felt himself fall into a cold darkness.

ONE

August, one century later

The shop smelled of dankness and neglect. It was not the kind of place Abigail Matthews liked to frequent. In fact, she usually limited her shopping to places like Saks and Neiman-Marcus. But, for the next two weeks, Abbie planned to step out of the usual and look for a missing piece of herself, something that would restore her trust and banish the self-doubt that seemed to have taken over. Four years of criminal law practice without a break was more than enough. And after what had happened just last week, she might very well be making a major life change in the near future.

So there she stood, on the threshold of the open doorway into the dismal little junkorama, feeling a bit fidgety and more than a little out of place. In the back of her mind, Abbie gave into the notion that something had drawn her here, tugging mentally at her skirt like a persistent child. She had pulled into the rut-filled, unpaved parking lot of the Lost Treasures Shop a few minutes earlier with a nagging sense of anticipation—or was it a sense of foreboding? She found the parking lot deserted except for her pearl Lexus and an old van parked with its rusty grill facing the peeling white paint of the building. Scraggly weeds grew around rotted, flat tires.

Abbie curled her nose at moldy odor of the dismal interior, and though her first instinct was to turn around, go back to her car and return to the highway, she found herself unable to do so. So many wrong decisions lately that now the simplest of them eluded her. She stood, clenching and relaxing her fingers, trying to rid herself of this anxiety.

She saw no one, heard no one, and decided the place was deserted and deservedly so. Who could stand to shop here, let alone work in such a morbid little establishment?

"You'll find what you seek below."

Startled by the voice, Abbie whirled and searched the dim interior with straining eyes.

"Hello?" she called, still seeing no one.

She nearly jumped out of her skin when a tiny, gnome-like figure in a dark, shapeless garb, stepped from behind a shelf and into the aisle few feet away. It was impossible to tell if the person was male or female.

"You'll find what you seek below," the figure repeated.

"Oh, but I'm not really—"

"Below." It was almost a command.

The person turned, drifted away into the murky shadows. The silence was complete: no shuffling steps, no whisper of clothing to mark the passage. It was as though the creature had never been.

Abbie took a few steps toward the back of the store, pretty sure the person had gone that way.

"I'm not really looking for anything," she called. "Actually, I don't know why I even..." She let the words evaporate into the musty, empty air.

I don't even know why I stopped here, she finished in her head.

She sighed and glanced around, telling herself she should leave right now. There was something weird and spooky about this whole situation. Besides, her friend, Lefty - whose real name was Linda Richardson but dubbed "Lefty" because of her powerful left-handed softball pitching in junior high - lived at least another hundred miles down the road and was expecting Abbie to arrive before dark.

She really should leave. But she walked toward the back of the store, toward an open doorway, compelled to follow the narrow steps leading down into a shadowy cellar so dark it looked black. What was down there? Trolls with long, gnarled fingers reaching for her? Maybe demons with grotesque red eyes and fiendish grins? If she went down, would she be able to return to the world of sunlight and air? Abbie was not given to such foolish imaginings and she wanted to turn away, but the temptation of the unknown abyss was too powerful.

She knew she was being ridiculous. The only menace down there would be spiders— she shuddered at the mere thought— and maybe rats.

Abbie stood on the first step, unaware that she had actually gone that far. More than ever she wanted to turn and flee; instead, she followed the urge to continue downward. Slowly, with fingertips barely touching the grime-covered railing, she descended, one foot, pause, the other foot, pause, until she reached the final step.

She waited for her eyes to grow accustomed to the darkness. The cellar, after all, was not completely without light, as she first had thought. One small window on the back wall allowed a bit of daylight to seep through its dirt. A single dim bulb, suspended from a filthy cord, was the only other source of illumination. The odor of mildew and decay nearly made her retch.

She jumped as something small and furry scurried past her feet. How many more small, furry "somethings" might she encounter? Abbie was a city girl, accustomed to her clean, spacious apartment in a clean, bright high-rise. She worked in another gleaming building. A dark, secretive cellar was as foreign to her taste as eating dirt.

She wanted to escape, to forget her bizarre need to be here. She turned and looked up the stairway. Her heart stopped. The grotesque little body was etched against the gloomy light behind it, every detail outlined, from the misshapen head and humped shoulders to the stumpy legs. The unblinking eyes, riveted on Abbie, glittered eerily although no light shone to reflect from them.

Abbie tried to swallow but choked on the dryness in her throat. A coughing fit brought tears to her eyes, and by the time her vision cleared, no one stood at the head of the stairs. For a moment, Abbie wondered if the figure was nonexistent, some part of a weird hallucination brought on by last week's horror and her subsequent sleepless nights.

She stood in place, motionless, hardly breathing, wary of going forward into the cellar, terrified of returning upstairs. At some point, she realized she would rather face the shadowed unknown of the cellar than the dwarfed, menacing figure above.

A shudder ran through her, a sudden chill that did not

come from the dank air but rather from deep inside her. Abbie knew if she did not move soon, the frozen tremors which crept through her body would render her immobile, unable to do anything but stand in place like a ninny. She would die, quaking like a dry leaf on a dead limb, in that black hole. Through sheer willpower, she turned and walked one deliberate pace after another until she was away from the steps and out of sight if the creature upstairs returned to stare down at her.

Looking around, Abbie momentarily lost her anxiety as she took in the collection the basement held: a pile, waist high and six feet wide, of plastic flowers in assorted faded colors, two old rusty bicycle frames without wheels or seats, a huge three-legged metal desk with one side smashed in, several boxes of moldy books and magazines, and heap after heap of old clothes that indisputably were congested with mildew.

How could anyone find anything down there? Surely no lost treasures existed in that nasty junk. And she wasn't looking for anything, anyway, no matter what that old person had said.

Abbie took in a deep breath, exhaled through her mouth, hating the odor that surrounded her.

"I'm getting out of here," she muttered. Gathering her courage which seemed to have ebbed in the last few minutes, she drew in another breath of foul air and turned with resolution. Her teeth were clamped against each other, her fingers clenched into tight knots around her purse.

It was then she saw the light. A muted light, as if it came from a small candle burning in the farthest corner of the room. It was a strange radiance, soft and beckoning, like a love call. Abbie approached the corner with an unease bordered by wild hope, as though the light were a promise unborn.

The light diminished as she approached, and by the time she got there, only shadows lingered. Squinting, searching for the lost source of brightness, she found nothing. Had it, too, been a trick of her fear and imagination? Maybe her eyes, straining to see in the dark room, had conjured a ghost light to trick her brain.

Her gaze fell on the nearest pile of junk. She saw the corner of a blackened picture frame jutting above everything else.

That's it! She thought wildly.

But if she truly had not been actively seeking anything why did she feel as though a long search was nearing an end? Rather than hash the notion in her mind, she gingerly plucked away the debris of dank cardboard boxes and ragged books mottled with mildew. She stifled a cry when a large and particularly ugly spider ran across a brittle plastic raincoat the color of a rotten orange and retreated into a crevice in the rubble. Shoving aside her natural antipathy of eight-legged creatures, she continued to clear away junk surrounding her target as her excitement grew. What was she about to find?

It was in following a path toward purpose that had led Abbie into practicing law. As her career thrived, her name became well-known, her bank account grew fat. She cultivated friends, gave to charities, but she remained unsatisfied, knowing deep inside that there was some special thing she needed to do, some act that would touch more than just her own life. She had made a difference in a lot of peoples' lives, but not in the way wanted. She had argued and won most of her cases, watched her clients happily leave the courtroom free to return to society.

Lately more than just her innocent clients were acquitted. Now, because of Abbie's decision to defend a man she knew kept his violent nature masked behind an expensive suit and a cool, professional smile, five-year-old Madison Tyler would never grow up. Abbie shuddered and tried to shove away the bleakness that yawed at her like an open grave. Could she ever reclaim her own soul after this?

Her gaze rested on the corner of the painting. Holding her purse strap between her teeth, Abbie lifted the painting from its miserable corner, ignoring the cobwebs that came with it. It was caked in dust so dark and thick she could hardly see the subject: a large house with a mansard roof and arched windows surrounded by trees and thickets, all under a sky so ominous she could almost feel the approaching storm.

There was something about it that embodied how she felt, some sort of darkness and desolation. As primitive and disturbing as it was, she had to have it.

Relinquishing her apprehension of the bent figure upstairs, Abbie held her purse in one hand and her find in the other and carried both to the cluttered, shadowy room above, pausing only long enough to locate the cash register near the dusty window at the front of the shop.

The sound of shuffling footsteps preceded the appearance of the gnome-like person.

"I see you found it." A smile creased the misshapen

face, revealing stubby yellow teeth.

"How did you know I would want this?" Abbie asked her. "What is it about this painting that draws me?"

The person went behind the counter and stepped into a full shaft of dusty sunlight. In the brightness, Abbie realized the little figure was not grotesque shrunken fiend at all but an elderly woman, crippled by advanced arthritis. On her face were the deep creases and folds of time; in her dim eyes lay wisdom. Abbie felt like an utter fool with a runaway imagination. It was unlike her to be so uncharitable without cause.

"Did it call to you?" the old woman asked.

"Yes." Abbie looked at her closely, trying to read the expression in the old eyes. "How did you know I'd find something I wanted...something I had to have?"

The woman smiled an odd smile.

"I only directed you downstairs. You found it on your own."

Abbie leaned the painting against the counter and opened her purse.

"How much do I owe you?"

The old woman eyed Abbie's ash blonde hair in its neatly coiled chignon, her wheat-colored linen sheath dress, the Louis Vuitton purse, and her manicured nails. Abbie braced herself for an astronomical figure.

"Since you need it, maybe you oughta just take it."

"Take it? I couldn't do that. Here." She handed over her credit card.

The other woman ignored the card and looked into the dark shadows of the shop.

"Greed is right costly," she muttered. Looking at Abbie again, she said, "One dollar for every minute you were down there looking for that painting."

Abbie blinked.

"I have no idea how long…but surely it's worth more than the short time I was in the basement."

The old woman rubbed a deformed thumb across a dark, crescent-shaped mark on the back of her thick hand.

"Time's a funny thing," she said. "Sometimes hours seem like minutes and minutes like years. Years can feel like eternity, like forever."

"Yes, but I still don't know—"

"Time's very important."

Maybe the woman was senile; maybe she was just eccentric. Either way, Abbie wanted to pay her something. She put the credit card back in her wallet and pulled out a checkbook. She filled out an amount she thought was fair.

"Will you accept this?" she said as she tore it out and handed it over.

"Yes."

The old shopkeeper did not even look at the scrap of paper in Abbie's hand. Finally, Abbie laid the check on the counter near the cash register.

"Remember what I said," the woman told her. "Time is real important for some people. A matter of life and death." Here she peered straight into Abbie's eyes. "Others must find what they come to the earth to do, or die trying."

Abbie swallowed hard. The old woman seemed to pluck statements out of the air, or maybe out of Abbie's thoughts. She shivered.

"I'll remember," she replied at last. "'Bye now."

Abbie got as far as the door when the old woman's voice stopped her:

"Passion spurned, hatred burned.

A curse of thirteen hundred moons must pass.

Then death will come, unless love breaks the curse to set the prisoner free."

Abbie stared at her.

"Hurry," the woman urged as she moved away from the sunlit corner and blended into the shadows again. "Time grows short."

***

Granny Hodge watched the young woman drive away. She smiled sadly.

Would it work, this counter-curse? Andrew Wade's time was almost over. If he was unable to fulfill his own destiny because of the curse, it would be one more wicked deed committed by an old, old woman who only wanted to be released from her dark power.

Granny closed her eyes. Behind the lids she saw the old chest, full of coins and jewelry, ancient currency as well as new. These uncounted years of saving; what had it all brought her? She could never buy her freedom from the dark power. What did the one who gave her the power need with earthly riches, anyway? He had her and others like her, to do his awful work. They would do anything he asked them to do just to receive the desires of their hearts.

For Granny, the desire had been immortality, life without end. But foolishly, she neglected to request that youth and health accompany her immortality; therefore, she continued to grow older and more infirm, and by now she had passed centuries in this crippled, pain-filled body.

Having exhausted every bargaining notion she could imagine, Granny wondered if doing good deeds were the antidote for the black actions of her past. The problem with good works is that the recipients always had questions for which Granny had no reply. The deeds had to be accepted with blind faith.

Turning from the window, the old woman wondered how many people had the courage of blind faith. Not many. But maybe this time…

TWO

Abbie punched in Lefty's number on her cell phone and waited for her friend to answer. The phone rang once.

"This better be you, Abigail Jane Matthews."

"It's me. And I'm late."

"No kidding. Is everything all right?"

Abbie hesitated a moment. She had driven these last three hours of her trip, contemplating the daunting knowledge that life as she knew it would never be the same. Not that it was a bad thing, but the unknown yawned before her.

"Of course," she replied. "Everything is… it's fine."

Lefty never let anything get past her. "It doesn't sound fine, Abbie," she said. "You don't sound fine."

The glaring late afternoon sun broiled her through the windshield.

"Let's save this conversation until later. I'm in Tomville, sitting in front of Shelby's Shop 'N Go where you told me to stop and call you. So if you'll tell me how to get to your house from here, and give me good directions, please. I do not want to get lost back here in the sticks."

"Oh, Abs, I wish you could forget being lost in the Appalachians."

Abbie had tried and failed more times than she could count to shove aside the memory that continued to haunt her more two decades later.

"You weren't there," she said, "lost, alone, while the sky and the woods got darker and darker. I was a scared little kid, Lefty. To this day I have dreams about that night."

"I understand, Abbie," the other woman said softly. "I really do. But I promise that today you will not get lost."

Abbie replied with a nervous, "Hmm." She added, "This is my first time in the Ozarks, you know. I didn't realize there were so many..." she glanced at the landscape "... steep hills and big trees."

Lefty laughed at that. "Well, you are in one of the oldest mountain ranges in the world, hon, and you're going to find thick forests and rugged hills. Millions of years have worn away the sharp edges of the Ozarks, but they're mountains nonetheless."

"Dear God," Abbie said. "What have I got myself into?"

"Tell you what. If you're not here in fifteen minutes, I'll come looking for you, so don't worry. OK?"

"Promise?"

"Absolutely."

The hard knots of tension between Abbie's shoulder blades lessened a little.

"Lefty, you're the best friend in the world."

"Aw, shucks, ma'am," her friend drawled like a cowboy in an old television show. "Just do me a big favor, all right?"

"What's that?"

"Do not, repeat, do not call me Lefty in front of anyone else. I'm a respected recovery room nurse; it wouldn't do for a slew of patients, not to mention doctors and co-workers, to start calling me 'Lefty'. It might damage my credibility or something. Would you want someone named Lefty taking your blood?"

Abbie laughed with her, although she thought the woman was only half-joking.

"Don't worry, Linda. I'll not spill your dark secret."

"Great! Now, listen, girl, hurry yourself along now, because I have supper cooking."

Ten minutes later, following Lefty's detailed directions, Abbie pulled into the driveway of the shadiest yard she had ever seen. It was so dim and cool that air conditioning might seem redundant.

From a deep front porch, fragrant and dim with red climbing roses on a white trellis, Lefty emerged and came down the steps. Abbie jumped out of her car almost before she killed the engine. She ran and flung her arms around her friend.

The two women had been friends since second grade, were roommates in college, and had been inseparable until a law office and a hospital took them in different directions. Abbie offered the comfort of her home when Lefty's Aunt Sally, her only living relative, passed away, and Lefty never ceased to cheer on Abbie's upwardly mobile climb.

There was very little they did not know about each

other. Although nine hundred miles and three years had separated them when Lefty moved from Ohio to Arkansas, the women kept in close touch through phone calls and e-mail. Therefore, it was Lefty to whom Abbie had turned this past Monday when she realized she could not return to life as she knew it.

"I need to get away…from here…from everything," she had said on the telephone to her friend that night. "I need time to think. And I really need to talk to you."

"By all means, get yourself down here," Lefty had replied. "But there's a little conflict. I'm scheduled to speak at a conference in Savannah next week. I'll be gone several days. I'd try to get out of it, but this has been scheduled for months. And, of course, I'll be driving, not flying. You know me and my need to be firmly grounded to the good earth. You said you're leaving Dayton in the morning? That'll give us a few days to visit before I have to leave."

Abbie had been bitterly disappointed, of course. Lefty was the only person she knew and trusted well enough to listen to her story without making judgments. And the woman had a remarkable knack for being objective in spite of their close friendship.

"I'd be more than happy for you to go with me, Abbie. You know I'd be gone all day, but we could run around Atlanta in the evenings. See the sights, do the town. You know."

Abbie took in a deep breath and let it out slowly.

"I need to get away from the city. I need peace and quiet and time to think. That's why I thought…"

"At the risk of repeating myself: come down here.

It's quiet and bucolic. You can tell me what's going on, and we'll talk about it. While I'm gone, you can have the place to yourself with time and solitude for thinking."

It was not the ideal situation, but it would do. And maybe having time to herself, away from everything familiar was exactly what Abbie needed.

"You're the best friend ever," she had assured.

Now, two days later, the friends were laughing and hugging after their lengthy separation.

"Three years is too long!" Abbie said.

"Much too long. Let's not let it happen again." Lefty linked her arm with Abbie's. "I've missed you! Come into the house. You must be starved."

"Yes, I am." Abbie said as they walked across the shady lawn toward the house. "And tired. And travel-stained." She stopped when they reached the steps and looked around Lefty's home. "This is absolutely beautiful."

"Thank you." Lefty squeezed her arm. "Knowing how you like glass and steel and busy sidewalks, I hope this spot in the back of beyond won't be a disappointment to you. It's very quiet here; not much excitement, I'm afraid."

"I need the quiet and the peace. I need to do some serious soul-searching."

"Here's the place to do it." Lefty gestured to the front porch, the roses and the towering trees beyond them. The lowering sunlight gilded everything they looked at. "I've prepared a room upstairs for you, and it has a beautiful view over the back yard and the pond. Perfect for deep thinking. It was my room years ago when I came to visit Aunt Sally in the summer. One year I pretended I was Emily Dickinson."

"Oh, I remember that!" Abbie said, laughing. "You wrote bad poetry."

"Bad, nothing. It was terrible."

"Well, at least you gave it up for softball."

"Thank God for small favors."

They giggled like schoolgirls as they went inside. Abbie eyed the blue and white décor, the collection of patchwork quilts, and the antique porcelain. Braided rugs in shades of blue adorned the gleaming hardwood floors. Waning daylight streamed through sparkling windows.

The décor was a far cry from the sleek stainless and white leather of her apartment, but she liked what she saw.

"This is lovely," she said. "So welcoming."

"Thanks. I find my tastes are turning more toward the simple and homey these days. Remember how we decorated our dorm room in red and black?"

Abbie laughed. "*Tres chic.*"

Lefty nodded, grinning. "Very *tres chic*. Well, thank goodness those days are over! No more posters, no more tragic poetry. We've grown up."

"Haven't we just," Abbie muttered with considerable grimness.

Lefty patted her hand. "Sounds like we definitely need

to talk. But for now, why don't you freshen up then come into the dining room for dinner?"

A few minutes later, Abbie entered the cozy, fragrant dining room. The aroma of cinnamon, roasted meat, and warm bread enticed her appetite.

"Bearing in mind your picky palate," Lefty called from the kitchen, "I cooked what I hoped you'd eat. Baked chicken all right?"

"Wonderful," Abbie replied as she sat down at the table with its snowy linen cloth and blue willow patterned china. A tall cobalt blue goblet of iced tea sat near her plate, its sides beaded with moisture.

Lefty emerged from the kitchen with a feast on a tea cart: baked chicken, cinnamon apple rings, fluffy mashed potatoes, fresh garden salad, several ears of corn drizzled with melted butter, thick slices of fresh tomatoes and cucumbers, and a basket piled high with soft, warm yeast rolls. Abbie, to whom all food had tasted like cardboard for so long, stared at the dinner and felt the welcome pangs of her appetite as it returned full force. As they ate, their conversation ranged from differences in their lifestyles to people they knew who had been married or divorced, had children, moved to exotic locations.

"You haven't mentioned Michael in a while," Lefty said.

Abbie grimaced. "We broke up several months ago. I've put off telling you because I'm such a miserable failure at relationships."

"You just haven't met the right guy, that's all."

"And not likely to," Abbie said firmly. "I mean look at my record: David, who entered the priesthood after we'd been together nearly three years. There's Robert, who preferred to spend his time with a telescope looking for signs of life 'out there' rather than living the life he had here. And let's not forget dear sweet Michael, who decided an eighteen-year-old college girl was more his kind of woman."

Lefty patted her hand. "I repeat, you just haven't met the right guy. Don't give up."

"I've come to the hard-won conclusion that there is no right guy." She smiled sadly then brightened. "So let's talk about your love life, pal. You met anyone?"

"Not likely when the only men I meet are either going under sedation or coming out of it." She shrugged. "Besides, I rather like my life the way it is. If I meet someone, then fine. If I don't, that's fine, too."

"Well," Abbie said, "I can tell you right now, it'll be a cold day in August before I meet the man of my dreams."

A bit later Lefty said, "Shall we sit on the porch swing?"

Abbie's stomach knotted as she thought of the darkening woods surrounding the house. She had never liked dark, shadowy places. Lefty must have read and recognized the expression; like the good friend she was, she said nothing of Abbie's fear.

"Let's sit in the front room instead," she said.

Abbie settled into a blue-checked armchair so big and soft it almost swallowed her. The light from a table lamp gave the room a soft glow as they sipped brandy. For a while they sat quietly, listening to tree frogs and crickets. Abbie cast a look toward the darkness outside her window. As long as the country night and all its creatures stayed outside, Abbie could tolerate the sound. In the city, the lights and movement of human life fed her comfort and security. She wondered if she had made another foolish decision by coming to this isolated place.

Lefty's voice interrupted her uneasy thoughts.

"So tell me what's going on," she said. "What terrible thing has brought you to my doorstep, looking thin, worn and exhausted?"

Unexpected tears pricked Abbie's eyelids. It had to be the combination of exhaustion, alcohol, good food and a good friend, because Abbie rarely cried.

"One of my clients murdered a child last week."

"Oh, my God, Abbie! What happened?"

"I defended him a month ago on a charge of felony child endangerment. I did such a good job, he was able to walk right out of the courtroom as free as you and me." Her voice broke, and she cleared her throat. "That little girl would be alive today if it hadn't been for me."

Lefty sat forward, hands clasped around her brandy snifter. She rested her elbows on her thighs and gazed intently at Abbie.

"Don't say that. It's not your fault if some creep—"

"Yes it is!" Abbie snapped. "Yes, it most certainly is my fault. I knew what he was, right from the minute I saw him. I've learned to recognize it, Lefty, the truth from the lies, the good from the rotten. I knew he was as bad as they come, but I defended him, anyway. He walked right back into the world a free man. Then he beat his girlfriend's five-year-old daughter to death. It never would have happened if I hadn't made a bad decision, if I followed my heart's urging, if I had stood for truth instead of profit and status."

Lefty stared at her for a long time then put her empty glass on the end table next to her chair. She said nothing.

"Well?" Abbie prompted after a while. "Tell me what you're thinking, Lefty. Tell me I'm not responsible or that I'm irresponsible. Tell me I'm a good soul, or that I'm a total jerk. Tell me something!"

Her friend sucked in a deep breath and let it out noisily.

"Truthfully, Abbie, I don't know what to tell you." She met her friend's eyes. "I just don't know…" Her voice trailed and she looked away then spoke again. "I don't think I could have done what you did." She returned her gaze to Abbie. "I'm not condemning you, please understand. I realize you must have had a reason for what you did, but I just don't know how, or why, you defended someone you knew in your heart had hurt someone – a child – and was capable of doing it again." She shook her head. "How could you have defended him, Abbie? Why?"

Abbie leaned her head back against the chair and closed her eyes. She hated hearing these words from her friend but understood them. Hadn't she been asking herself the same thing a hundred times, at least, in the past week?

"I don't know," she said. "No, that's wrong. I do know. It's my job." She raised her head, looked at Lefty, trying not to see the reproach on her friend's face. "I'm a criminal lawyer. I defend people charged with crimes." She paused, listening to her own words. "My God, how awful does that sound? I defend robbers and thieves and rapists and murderers and guys who evade the IRS. It's what I chose to do." Her voice grew thick and labored. "Lefty, I don't want to do it anymore."

Her friend remained silent, waiting for her to continue.

"I got into law practice because I thought I could help. And you know, at first, I did help people. I got all the cases that nobody else wanted, like helping the jilted wife get some sort of maintenance from a philandering husband, or a tenant finally get hot water and an exterminator in his apartment. Good things. Right and just things."

"What happened to change all that?"

"I'm not sure. A combination of situations, I guess. I moved into a more expensive apartment then into a bigger one in a better part of town. I bought a new car then a bigger and better one. Clothes, friends, entertainment. I guess I fell into a trap."

"Or walked into one," Lefty said.

Abbie nodded.

"Well, do you like it there?" Lefty prodded. "I mean the apartment, the car, friends, clothes, entertainment?"

"I don't know," Abbie admitted miserably. "I thought I did; I mean it's what my folks wanted for me. But the way it is now ... it all feels so wrong. I'm sure this is not the way my life is supposed to be going. Something has to change. Not doing the things I must do to have them. That's why I'm here, in a place foreign and a little frightening to me. I need to sort this out. I'm pretty sure I don't want to continue practicing criminal law. At least, I'm through defending scumbags so they can walk the streets. But the rest of it?" She shook her head. "I don't know."

"Abbie," Lefty said, her expression serious and very earnest, "it's long been my belief that anything is possible if you want it badly enough. But it takes commitment." She paused. "Think about, my friend, then made the decision you feel is best."

Abbie let her friend's wisdom and counsel soak into her mind. Yes, this is what she needed. To ponder, to decide, to commit. But whatever she chose to do, she must be sure it was the right decision.

Again, as neither woman spoke, the night sounds took over the room. Abbie became aware of the soft ticking of the old clock somewhere in the house. It struck ten times, deep and melodious, a gentle comforting sound.

Lefty stirred in her chair. She smiled tenderly at Abbie.

"You've had a big day, Abbie. You have traveled far and eaten much. You have a lot of things to think about. But right now you need to get some rest. Leave your worries down here tonight." She stood. "Come on, and I'll show you to your room."

THREE

During the next two days Abbie and Lefty talked almost nonstop as they caught up on the years that had separated them. With her friend's undying love and support, Abbie embraced a measure of relief that she knew would comfort her in the upcoming days of her self-imposed isolation.

"Plenty of food in the 'fridge," Lefty said Saturday morning as she got into her red Jeep Wrangler. "And town isn't that far away, if you need anything." She turned the key in the ignition, and the motor purred to life. "I'll call you every day to see how you're getting along."

Abbie hesitated only a moment before she spoke.

"That's sweet of you, Lefty, but actually I'd rather you not call, if you don't mind. I think solitude is what I need. Maybe by the time you get back, I'll have had an epiphany, or something."

Lefty seemed to search Abbie's expression for a moment, as though seeking a truth she might be hiding.

"Well, maybe you will have solved your own dilemma, anyway," she said. "Being alone opens your mind, if you'll let it happen." She put the Jeep in gear. "If you don't want me to call you, at least promise that you'll get in touch with me if you need to talk."

"I will. You posted the number of your hotel on the door of the refrigerator, remember?" Right next to the number for the fire department, the sheriff's office, and the pizza delivery place, she added silently with affection. It was nice that someone was concerned for her. In spite of her many friends back in Dayton, Abbie never felt the level of true friendship from them that she and Lefty had always shared.

Lefty drove a few yards along the circular driveway then stopped to peer at Abbie through the dim light of early morning.

"I feel awful, going off and leaving you this way after you came so far. Are you sure you don't want to come with me?"

Yes, she wanted to be with her friend, not alone in the backwoods, but Abbie knew it was something she had to do. She would never have resolution in her life if she did not face her fears or change the state of her existence.

"I'll be fine," she said firmly to herself and to Lefty. "Everything will be fine, I promise."

Lefty studied her face a moment longer. "All right then, my friend. I'll see you in about ten days."

Abbie watched the other woman reach the end of the driveway. When the crunching sound of car tires on the gravel faded, a silence descended that quickly sent Abbie into the house. She switched on the television to erase the unfamiliar and uncomfortable quietude, and then turned up the sound as she showered. She dressed in a pair of khaki shorts and a soft white T-shirt and pulled her long, blonde hair back in a free-swinging ponytail.

Gazing in the mirror while she opened her make-up bag, Abbie laughed aloud. Why would she need this stuff when the only person who would see her was her own reflection? She tossed the bag into the dresser drawer and planned to leave it untouched for the next two weeks.

It took most of the day to become accustomed to the absence of traffic noise and voices of many people. By mid-afternoon, she turned off the television and went outside to sit in an Adirondack chair on the front porch. Abbie watched birds flitting from branch to branch and two gray squirrels chase each other up and down every tree in the yard. Filled with the variety of bird songs, the world around her was not as quiet as she thought. She moved from the chair to the porch swing and with a shove of her bare foot, set it in motion. The next thing she knew, she was waking up from a long nap and the sun was almost down.

Abbie stood, stretched her arms and neck to loosen stiff muscles then walked down the porch steps to the front yard. She looked up at the massive trees. Lefty had told her these trees had probably been alive when the state was young and unsettled. She touched the rough bark of an oak tree close to her.

A squirrel chattered at her peevishly from a branch not far above her head. Abbie eyed it uneasily, taking a couple of steps back.

"Go away," she said. The furry rodent twitched its bushy tail impudently, but it did not move. When she clapped her hands together, it scampered into higher branches and out of sight.

She relaxed a little and looked around the yard. Lefty had told that in this hot, dry weather the flower beds needed a generous watering every day. Abbie got the hose and turned on the spigot. While the dry ground under the purple salvia, brilliant yellow marigolds, and blue petunias soaked up the water, she thought about a small creek Lefty mentioned that ran through the woods behind the house. Maybe, before the week was over, Abbie would conquer her fears of the forest enough to find the stream. Wouldn't Ms. Linda Richardson, RN, be surprised at that?

That evening, Abbie soaked in a lavender-scented bubble bath until the water turned tepid. She dressed for bed in a short, silk nightie with spaghetti straps. Abbie loved the feel of the cool, soft fabric against her skin, like a lover's sweet touch. The midnight blue silk shimmered in the lamplight as she dried and braided her hair. A few minutes later, in the ultimate quiet of a summer night in the Ozark mountain countryside, she plumped her pillow, stretched between the soft, clean-smelling sheets and snuggled down for a good night's sleep. The soft hum of the fan muffled cricket chirps and frog songs. Sleep should overtake her with no effort.

But it did not.

In the darkness, her mind wrestled with an uneasy thought: Something was out there. Oh, not "out there," like a prowler or wild animal; nothing so tangible as that. That "something" was a feeling, a need. A need like the one she had experienced when she had felt compelled to stop and enter the little junk shop to explore the murky cellar.

The "something" hovered in the air, whispered in her mind's ear, shivered across her skin and skittered into her bloodstream. It refused to let her sleep. She sat up and snapped on the bedside lamp.

Abbie needed to see the painting. In fact, the need to

see the painting was so urgent, she felt as if she could not get to her car trunk fast enough. She slid out of bed, thrust her feet into thin, backless house slippers, got the car keys from her purse and went downstairs. She tried to switch on the porch light, but the bulb flared briefly and went out. Abbie pushed aside her unease and stepped out the front door. With no traffic lights or street lights, the outdoors was blacker than she'd had seen that horrendous long ago night when she got lost in the forest. She nearly returned to the bright safety of the house.

No! She told herself. Face down your fear.

Standing on the porch steps, she impatiently willed her eyes to adjust to the darkness. She clicked the button on her car key to unlock the trunk and light the car, and at last saw the shape of her car beneath the leaf-heavy tree branches.

The painting lay in the trunk, a great, dusty square which she was going to carry into Lefty's clean house. Ah, well. She would clean the painting then clean up after herself. Grasping the grimy, thick edge of the frame, she removed the picture, closed the trunk and carried it into the house. She leaned the painting gingerly against the banister on the lower stair, fetched some soft cloths from the tiny broom closet, found yesterday's newspaper in the recycling box and carried everything to her bedroom. She spread the paper across the floor and placed the painting on it. A hard, flat piece of wood with the canvas stretched across it had been nailed to the frame.

Abbie wiped away some of the dust from the intricate carving of the frame. She supposed the frame might be valuable, but just then she did not care about that. It was the painting itself that intrigued her.

She sat cross-legged on the bedroom floor, propped her elbows on her knees and rested her head on the interlaced fingers of both hands. She stared at the picture.

What was it about this dismal portrayal that called to her? Was it the desolation of that house as it sat strong but helpless beneath an approaching storm? Did she somehow equate her despondent state of mind to a long-neglected house? Hadn't she forsaken pleasure and peace in the pursuit of a vocation for which all her interest and passion had died? Was her heart as dark and sorrowful as that house?

With gentle fingertips and a tear stinging her eye, she touched the dusty image. Yes, this house resembled life, built with hopes and dreams to enfold her into its welcoming embrace. Somehow, she had allowed the outside world to tangle about her vitality, to threaten it with snarled overgrowth. And now the storm of an unknown future approached. It was a storm could that could destroy or a storm that could cleanse and offer a fresh start.

For Abbie, which would it be?

She reached for one of the soft cleaning cloths and gently began to wipe away years of accumulated dust, hoping to brighten the aspect of the painting. The cloth gathered the dirt, but the painting remained bleak.

Had those clouds just moved across the glowering sky? She snatched back her hand and blinked hard.

That light in the upstairs window…had it been there before?

Abbie swallowed hard.

Of course it had been, she told herself. It must have been.

But she did not remember any spot of light on the dark surface of this painting.

She stared hard at the upstairs light and at the clouds, and then blinked her eyes again. Abbie dismissed the notion telling herself that her afternoon nap must not have been long enough. She really needed to get more sleep.

But she refused to abandon this task just yet. With the cloth she wiped cobwebs and grime from the edges. She discovered the paint in the lower left-hand corner was cracked and chipped. Unlovely as the painting was, she did not want to cause damage beyond what time and neglect had done. She bent closer and gingerly dabbed the tip of the cloth against the damaged corner. To her dismay, a tiny piece of paint, wedged near the frame, flicked off.

With a fingertip moistened slightly by her tongue, Abbie picked up the fragment where it had fallen on her thigh. Leaning even closer, her face mere inches from the picture; she hoped to fit the minute chip in place, like a piece from a jigsaw puzzle.

What was that sound?

She did not move, but her body tensed as she strained to listen. It seemed as compelling as a whisper but as relentless as a roar. She straightened her spine, turned her head to look at the night outside her open window. She saw nothing but blackness. The curtain barely stirred.

Seeing things. Hearing things. She was tired.

Again Abbie bent over the painting. She was so close she held her breath so as not to exhale and lose the chip on her fingertip. She saw exactly where the tiny fragment fitted.

Looking at that small gap in the dark image made her lightheaded. The sound she had heard moments ago returned. That point on the canvas seemed to swirl, a rapid whirlpool of crystalline blue. Abbie blinked hard.

She reached out quickly to cover the spot but the moment her finger touched the marred canvas she felt her breath dragged from her lungs. In an instant she was without weight or substance.

All thought and reason slipped away. For the only time in her life, Abbie was aware of simply being.

Then there was nothing but a cold darkness.

FOUR

It was the cold that awakened her. The kind of cold that was unlike a winter's chill, but something that seemed to have soaked, stealthily, deep into her skin, penetrating muscles and organs, then settled into the marrow of her bones.

Abbie tried to move. She felt as if she had been battered without mercy then folded and crammed into cold storage. And the wind. It pounded against her without ceasing, as if heralding a storm.

Sluggishly, with an effort she did not know she could muster, she struggled to her knees as the chill wind whipped the silk nightie against her skin. She grabbed a nearby tree to help her stand without falling over, and hung onto the trunk.

Tree? Wind? Why was she hanging onto a tree in a raging, freezing wind? Where was she?

Abbie sent a bleary, panicked look at her unfamiliar surroundings. The bit of dark sky revealed through the encircling forest glowered ominously. Tree branches swayed and bowed, leaves thrashed like something caught in a trap. But it was not the impending storm that shoved the fear into her frozen bones and shifted it to full-blown terror. It was the absolute silence. No howling, no roaring, not even a rustle. It was as if she were watching a storm from inside a glass box.

Abbie could hear her own rapid breathing and the

blood that thrummed wildly in her ears. Again she shot a horrified glance around her, all haziness gone from her vision. She was not deaf, but she most assuredly was lost. And not simply lost, but lost in a thrusting, violent storm as the alien world around her remained totally and freakishly soundless.

Releasing the tree trunk, Abbie gripped both sides of her head while hysteria raged to free itself and run wild in her mind. She refused to panic. Forcing herself to take a couple of deep, slow breaths, Abbie closed her eyes. She willed herself to be calm and rational.

What was the last thing she remembered doing?

It took a moment for the memory to release itself into her conscious mind: she had taken a bath at Lefty's and got ready for bed. And after that...after that, she could remember nothing.

Abbie stared at the forest in which she now stood. Lefty's home was surrounded by woods. Had Abbie taken a walk, fallen and knocked herself out? The painful lump she touched near the top of her head testified that she may have done just that. But no. Taking a stroll, and at night, seemed a foolish notion. Abbie would never have done such a thing. The memory of being lost in the wilderness and the possibility of its happening again had always been enough to deter her from roaming freely and unaccompanied into the woods.

She looked around for her cell phone. She never went anywhere without it, but if it was there, it lay buried within the thickly tangled vegetation around her, completely hidden, lost.

She was wearing her nightie. Maybe she had sleepwalked. That was the only explanation that made any sense.

But there was another thing that did not add up. The weather. When she had arrived at Lefty's, the afternoon's temperature had reached ninety-five degrees. It had been hot and dry and still. Lefty had told her no rain had fallen for five weeks and none was predicted in the near future. Yet here she stood while the day around her was cold and dismal, like a day in November.

But it wasn't November. It couldn't be November, because in November no green leaves remained on trees. So it was August. It had to be August, because if it wasn't, where had the time gone? And where had she been as it passed?

Abbie's knees gave way, and she slid to the ground. She sat there, slumped and chilled, her mind as dull as the grayness of the day around her. Where was she? How did she get to this place? How was she going to get out?

And why, oh, why didn't the wind stop blowing? If the wind would just stop for a minute or two, maybe she could think. But it seemed the soundless buffeting was in her brain, blowing away her sanity.

She wrapped her arms around her knees, head tucked into the protection of her arms, trying to get warm, trying not to lose her mind.

"I have to think," she whispered. "I have to think!"

It took all her willpower to focus her mind on one point rather than let it run amuck. Through sheer strength of mind, her heartbeat settled, and her brain slipped into a semblance of normal, calm functioning.

Perhaps she was asleep. This was one of those dreams she sometimes had where she knew she was sleeping but had felt awake.

Sucking in a deep breath, Abbie stood quickly, thinking the sudden movement and the shock of the cold wind against her whole body would do the trick. But it did not. She tried the old cliché of pinching herself hard enough to leave bruises. She even slapped her cheek. The sting nearly brought tears to her eyes, but it did not bring her into wakefulness.

She tried to squelch her rising terror. She had to get out of there, because if she truly was lost, then she was lost in the woods. The wilderness, with all that it embodied and promised, horrified her.

"I refuse to be lost in this forest!" she shouted, looking upward, turning as though someone or something could hear and come to her aid.

Looking at the sky, or as much of it as she could see through the upper branches of the trees, she noted that it remained leaden, glowering, threatening her with storms and with darkness. Night could not be far away, and she did not want to be in these woods when night fell. She shoved aside memory; she refused to think of bears, wildcats and snakes.

Abbie stepped away from the tree and turned full circle, searching for a break in the woods, a path, anything that might lead to civilization. But everywhere she turned she saw only tangled undergrowth and huge trees with low, heavy branches bending in the wind. She saw no road, no trail, and no path. Any course she chose might be right, or could be wrong. She had to take a chance because standing like a frozen ninny in the forest was about as stupid a thing as she could conceive. Glancing around once more, Abbie chose a direction and plunged into it.

Although she worked and struggled like a mad woman in chains, she made little progress. The vines and briars beneath her feet shredded her slippers and grabbed and clung to her as if they had a sentient mind. She did not allow herself to think of whatever crawling, slithering life might exist beneath the heavy undergrowth. How long she fought the wild vegetation, the chill wind, and her terror, she had no idea. She simply kept moving, stomping down brush with each step, forcing herself to stay calm.

At one point she looked back to view a path of broken bushes in her wake. Seeing no sign of her passage renewed Abbie's terror. It was as if the hideous undergrowth had swallowed everything. She had the strangest feeling that the forest knew her, had trapped her and was never going to let her go.

She had to stop thinking this way; had to think with the rational part of her brain. She stood still for a moment, staring behind her, rubbing her icy arms, fighting tears. She swallowed hard. Squeezing her eyes shut, Abbie sucked in a deep breath, clenched her jaw muscles so tightly her face ached.

"I can do this," she muttered.

She opened her eyes and turned to face forward once more. She stomped down more bushes and advanced a few steps.

"I can do this," became her mantra, keeping her focused on the words and not on what might be lurking, watching and waiting in this terrible forest.

Hours seemed to pass before she broke into a clearing of sorts, unseen a moment ago because of the monstrous trees and brush growing around it. She stood only a moment, staring at the house a few yards away, across what may have been, at one time, a full, lush lawn but was now an unkempt, weed-choked patch of ground. The house, a dark, hulking monstrosity of Gothic architecture, stirred a chord of memory, but in a flicker of a second the notion faded. Perhaps she had seen something similar in Hitchcock's Psycho, or maybe the Munster residence at 1313 Mockingbird Lane.

The house did not exude the malevolence of the forest and the lowering sky. Something told her it was abandoned; it seemed to reek of loneliness. It looked sturdy, well able to face down the encroaching vegetation, but Abbie got the deep impression that the house was closing in on itself, dying bit by bit.

She shook her head to clear her thoughts. Just then she did not care whether or not she had seen the old house before. At that moment, all she wanted was to find shelter from the hideous silent cold wind, get to a telephone and find her way home. That was her goal.

She stumbled and scrambled toward the house. No trees or overgrown bushes blocked her way through the clearing, but the groundcover was just as snarled and treacherous as that through which she had already passed. It seemed an eternity before she reached the porch steps and labored up them on weak, trembling legs.

Her body was stiff, aching, and oh so cold. Although the thin soles of her delicate house slippers had protected the bottom of her feet somewhat, they had not held up well throughout her trek. At that moment they clung to her icy feet with a few scraps of tattered fabric. She yearned for her Nikes and thick, soft socks; she craved her comfy down jacket and jeans; she ached for the warmth and comfort of a fire. Once she was on the porch, she nearly cried with relief.

"Please, someone, be home."

Abbie grasped the tarnished brass doorknocker—a ring held in the mouth of an ugly gargoyle— and pounded it against the dark panels.

Not content with that, she pummeled the door with both fists, crying, "Please, please, open the door! Someone, please be home."

FIVE

Andrew Wade knew his treacherous mind once more played tricks on him.

Long ago, when he first came to this place, he had heard sounds. Talking, laughter, music, odd roars and strange rumblings. Back then he had sought maniacally for the owners of the voices and the source of the sounds until he exhausted himself only to find nothing.

He had wanted to hear a voice, any voice, other than his own, just so he could know that a world apart from this place existed. For a long time now, the only noises Andrew heard were the ones of his own making: his spoon against a bowl, or his footsteps as he walked from one room to another or the click of his door latch when he opened or closed the door. Over the course of time, these sounds proved that he still lived and breathed yet remained inexplicably and utterly alone. To save his sanity, he long ago had ceased to listen for any noise or voice not of his own making. He had no idea how long he had been in this God-forsaken place, but the only face he'd seen was his own image reflected in the window glass or in the dripping well bucket when he fetched water. His was not a bad face; in fact, it was quite a good face, with dark eyes and strong regular features framed by dark, unruly hair. His appearance was neither wasted by years nor dissipated by the pain of his isolated existence. The amount of time that had passed seemed an eternity to him; he should look and feel old by now, but he did not. He had never known one hour of illness or disease; his was still the same strapping, healthy body of a strong thirty-year-old man.

At that moment, when he heard a relentless pounding on the front door and a woman's voice pleading for entrance, he immediately acquiesced to the fact that it was a hallucination.

He declined to give credence to it and turned his attention to his meal of beef stew and bread. Andrew's food never varied, neither in amount nor flavor. Tea, potatoes, carrots, onions, apples, beef and bread were what he had available; tea, potatoes, carrots, onions, apples, beef and bread were what he consumed. His larder never diminished, never spoiled, was never invaded by bugs or mice. What he removed and used at one meal would be on the shelf by the next meal. Long ago, he had stopped questioning how this happened and accepted, grudgingly, the phenomenon that nourished his body.

He had almost forgotten the taste of pork or fish, the bite of fresh, hot coffee, the singular burn in his gullet from a shot of whiskey. Those sensations were a dim memory, as was nearly everything else that had once been familiar. For sanity's sake, Andrew Wade had learned to live only from moment to moment.

The shouting voice and the door-thumping ceased at last. He cocked his head slightly, listening, and then nodded, satisfied he really had heard nothing.

He cleared the table. It took only a moment to wash and dry his spoon and plate and put them in the cupboard. He stared for a moment at the collection: one spoon, one fork, one knife, a single cup and plate. They had been in this kitchen when he arrived, and he had never needed more. Andrew took in a deep breath, let it out slowly, turned and went into the parlor across the hall.

In that room, the walls were lined with books. The books, there when he arrived, had been his only friends and his salvation. He loved them with pure devotion. How they had come to be in this desolate place mystified him as much as his own presence or how his food supply never dwindled or why he never sickened or aged. Over the course of time, Andrew had learned to thank whatever good fortune had granted the books to him. Without the company of these beloved volumes, he surely would have gone mad.

The front door opened.

Andrew froze. Again he reminded himself that any sound not of his making was a trick of the mind. With some difficulty, he ignored the sensation of another presence in the house as he picked up his book from the small table next to his favorite chair. It would not do for him to acknowledge, even for the length of a heartbeat, that someone else might be with him. In that way of thinking lay insanity. It had almost happened before, long ago, when he believed he could depart this limbo and pick up his life.

"Sir? Please, sir. I knocked, but you didn't hear me. Can you help me?" The voice, frantic and breathless, was also as sweet and fresh as an April morning.

What madness was this? Those other voices from so long ago had ever spoken to him. His breath stopped. One thing Andrew valued as highly as his books was his sanity. He clung to it fiercely, for if he lost it, then he lost everything. He closed his eyes, forced himself not to look, not to hear, not to sense the sweet soft, gentle presence of a woman in his world.

After a bit, he allowed his eyes to open. He gazed down at the printed pages of the book he held. Ah, they were real enough beneath his gaze and his touch. He leafed through them, settled himself into his much used armchair.

"Sir!" she said, loudly, stepping closer. "I need help. I...seem to be lost...something's wrong and..."

Andrew fought the urge. He curled his hands into fists, tightened his jaws, clenched shut his eyes.

She is not there!

Dear God, how he fought the urge to look. He sensed her increasing nearness, and he clenched the book so hard his knuckles whitened.

She is not there, he told himself again. Not real, not real, not real.

"Sir!" she shouted, grabbing his arm. He leaped inside his skin at her touch, his heart nearly burst from his body. Her hand held his arm in a firm grip, the coldness of her fingers reaching through the fabric of his shirt. "Sir, can you hear me? I need help!"

With her touch, his resistance broke. He turned his head suddenly, sharply to view the apparition.

What was this cruel fever in his brain that conjured a beautiful woman in her shimmy – a clinging, revealing shimmy? Andrew's stupefied gaze began at the top of her head and traveled downward. She had hair the color of ripe wheat, eyes as blue as a sky he hadn't seen for an eternity, and a face, delicate enough to be porcelain, framed by curling wisps escaping from a ponytail that hung down her back. Her large blue eyes blinked at him, and he paused his perusal of her long enough to look into them. Those eyes met his straight on, without fear, speaking silently of strength and longing and passion. He forced his gaze away from those captivating eyes, over a nose that was short and straight, lips that were generous to a fault. Her shoulders and arms were bare, smooth and firm. The dark blue shimmy she wore clearly outlined the shape of her breasts.

She was fantasy although her touch was as real as the voices from long ago. He could not stop himself from staring at her the way Adam must have gaped at Eve that first time in Eden. The book he had clung to so desperately fell from his slack fingers. Andrew, who had been an eternity without a woman, stared at her breasts so long that she folded her arms across her chest and leaned toward him angrily. He dug his fingers into the armrests of his chair, swearing he smelled her perfume.

"Excuse me!" she nearly shouted. "What is wrong with you? Someone needs your help and all you do is act like you've lost your senses!"

He blinked, moved his gaze back to her flushed face and angry eyes.

"Good. Now that I have your attention," she said, "will you please let me use your telephone? I seem to have lost my cell phone out there..." Her voice cracked and she shot a fearful look out the window. "I...I don't know where I am or how I got here." She turned back to him, her eyes full of fear. "Please. Won't you help me?"

Andrew swallowed noisily, barely hearing her voice above the anthem of lust singing in his blood. He knew there was no way he could find true physical relief with an illusion, but he could no more halt his visual review than he could stop breathing.

He reached down to retrieve his fallen book, shifted in his chair so that she was not easily in his line of sight. He tried his best to discount the aching, throbbing arousal that tried to consume him. He tried to read, but the words on the page were only lines and dots to his vision.

One slender pale hand grabbed the book and yanked it from his grasp.

"If you are mad at the world and want to shut yourself off from everyone, that's fine," she said. "I'm not here to change that. I just need your help, and then I'll be on my way."

Andrew stared at her. How could an apparition pluck a book from his hands?

"Please let me use your phone. Or if you don't want to do that, at least tell me where I can find the nearest one."

He listened to her words, then realized that the very act of listening entrapped him more deeply in this flight of fancy. Perhaps she would vanish if he commanded it.

"Leave me." His voice, a commodity he no longer needed, was rusty from disuse.

She stared at him, her lovely eyes widened in obvious indignation. The color rose in her cheeks. Her eyes glittered; her ripe body vibrated with passion.

"I will be happy to leave you," she said. "In fact, I

want to leave you. But I don't know where I am or how to return to where I came from."

Dear God, she was the most beautiful thing he had ever seen! How wonderful it would be if she were real, if she were to stay with me, he thought. Someone as beautiful as this flower to look upon, to talk to, perhaps one day to touch and hold and share life. Then he came to himself, awakening as it were, from a dream. Andrew felt he was about to lose control, and by all means, he must preserve his strength of mind. Trapped in an isolated world where there was neither sunlight nor night, no variation of time or season, no challenge to meet—these were out of his control. And so was being consumed by white-hot lust for this hallucination.

He would, by God, banish the vision. He had tried ignoring her; he had tried commanding her. Maybe his analytical brain needed to hear logic to dispel this intrusive and unacceptable situation. He stood up, paced the room a moment, felt her gaze fixed intently upon him. He turned to face her. "Here's the situation," he stated, looking her straight in the eyes. "You come to me in this," he gestured to her clinging attire, "looking like that," running his eyes over her breasts, hips and legs, "so it is quite obvious that you are the invention of a brain-fever I didn't know I had. An invention beautiful enough to bring me to my knees if I was a weaker man, but you are a mere creation just the same."

Her eyes grew larger and rounder as he spoke.

"You see," he continued in his logic, "it all stems from this extended exile of mine, and after the battles I've fought to maintain my sanity, I refuse to let a seductive little piece of baggage like you destroy me. In short, my dear young woman," he concluded like a great orator, "you do not exist!"

He clasped his hands behind him and waited for her to evaporate, melt, faded away, or whatever visions did when they were banished.

The woman before him was blinking rapidly, as though someone had kicked sand in her eyes, as if she were about to burst into tears.

No, no, no! he thought. He mustn't be moved by a phantom that shed a woman's tears. Manipulative little wiles like that had never worked on Andrew Wade, and they would not work on him now.

"How dare you!" she spat at him instead of shriveling away into nothing.

Her hands were clenched at her side, her body shaking. Andrew realized then she was neither about to burst into tears nor evaporate. She was furious and ready to spend her anger on him. The last young woman he had dealt with and who had not gone away when he encouraged her had bared her teeth and unsheathed her claws. He braced himself for the same reaction, although he doubted ghostly claws would do much damage.

She stood a hair-breadth away from him before he even knew she had moved. She stood so near that he felt heat coming from her trembling body and smelled the sweet, womanly smell of her. These sensations were real, uncomfortably real.

"How dare you say such things to me when I only asked for your help! I'm lost and confused, and right now

I'm royally pissed off that anyone can be so callous."

"You do not exist," he declared again, backing away, not because she intimidated him, but because her nearness nearly drove him mad with desire.

She advanced as he retreated until he backed into a bookshelf. She stood on the tips of her toes, leaning toward him, so near he could feel her breath.

Do visions breathe?

"Maybe it's you who doesn't exist. I must have fallen and knocked myself out. I'm probably unconscious right now, and that's why I'm in the middle of this wacko, weirdo house in the middle of these spooky woods, talking to Mr. Howard Hughes the Second on a cold day in August!" Her voice rose in pitch until the last five words became a shriek.

Andrew looked down at the face a mere six inches from his. The heat of anger radiated from her, and he could feel it all over his body.

In that moment, he lost the fight, the struggle with willpower, the battle for control. He yanked her soft female body against the length of his lonely, aching one. Andrew kissed her full on the mouth. He was not gentle or seeking in the plundering of her lips; he was hot and starved, devouring a sweetness he had not known in a time untold.

In his arms, she struggled like a mountain cat, digging her fingernails into his shoulders, then pounding and shoving his upper arms. He knew he should release her. It was not right for him to hold her this way, against her will. A moment longer to hold her, to taste her, then he would let her go. His arms tightened, drawing as much of her into himself as he could.

Then, like taming some wild thing, Andrew felt the change come over her, the softening of her lips, the slackening of her body as it seemed to melt into his own. She trailed her hands upward, an exploring of his chest, his shoulders, and his throat. She looped her arms around his neck, and those same fingers, which moments earlier had tried to abuse him, now threaded through his hair, pulling his head closer to hers.

His heart almost exploded when her tongue parted his lips and entered his mouth. It was a wanton kiss; no decent girl would permit it. A second later, he forgot what decent girls would or would not do and returned the kiss deep into the sweet, warm recesses of her mouth. The ache in his loins was almost unbearable, especially now that she rubbed herself against him. He groaned deep in his throat, cupped her round bottom with both hands and held her even closer.

She broke the kiss abruptly and, breathing rapidly, yanked free of his embrace and looked into his eyes. He read his own heat and desire reflected in her eyes. Her look of defiance was a poor cover-up.

"Now," she gasped, stepping back, "tell me again that I don't exist!"

SIX

"Tell me if that was a figment of your imagination."

Abbie stared at the man standing in front of her, looking as if he had just been pole-axed. Unfortunately, she felt none too steady herself. She had intended to give in to his kiss just long enough to catch him off-guard so she could escape his hold. What she had not expected was to feel the kiss of the handsome black-haired stranger all the way to her tingling toes. In fact, she'd had to force herself to stop. She welcomed the feel of his warm, rugged body against hers and the hot, sweet taste of his lips and tongue. She loved that he smelled of the clean scent of soap and not of cologne. The raw hunger in his kiss aroused her most of all.

She was no longer cold. In fact, heat seemed to have settled into every pore of her body.

Had that really been her, the normally implacable Abigail Matthews returning the hot kiss of a man she had never seen before, a man who, for all she knew, could be a serial bomber with a passion for his own company.

But Abbie had seen killers face to face. She recognized soullessness in their eyes or glimpsed an inner coldness that no amount of smooth talking and confident posturing could disguise. This man before her was no menace, except perhaps to himself, shutting himself away from the world as he had done.

Abbie could not look away from him nor did he take

his gaze from her. If she had not broken the kiss when she did...She felt faint from the idea. Groping blindly for a chair, she found the back of one and held on for dear life.

The man closed his eyes as though taking his inner bearings, opened them again and looked at her. For a moment he appeared totally lost, and then he drew in a deep breath and let it out slowly, silently between his lips. With one shaking hand, he wiped his face.

"Haven't I lived through enough hell without you?" His voice was almost a whisper. The words perplexed her no less than everything else he had said. "Why have you done this? Why don't you leave me?"

He turned away, as if the sight of her tortured him. He went from the bookcase to the window, staring out at the dark sky and tangled vegetation which threatened to swallow the house and its occupants. With his back to Abbie, he stood without moving for so long he seemed to be made of stone.

She watched him, willing her breath and heartbeat to return to their normal, quiet pursuit of keeping her alive. Broad shouldered and tall, he stood straight and proud, his head unbowed, hands clasped behind him in an attitude of waiting or perhaps resignation. Beyond the attraction to a man gorgeous enough to inhabit her hottest dreams, Abbie felt the stirring of something deeper, more complex, even tender: An empathy with someone who seemed a bit off-center, a lost soul who needed its home. He seemed so...alone.

She crossed the room to stand beside him, looked at the gloomy aspect beyond the window. It was a grey, matted picture, unbearably depressing.

"Where are we?" she asked him. "What is this place?"

He did not answer, and after a time she tried a different question.

"Who are you?" She paused then added, "Why are you here?"

She continued to gaze through the glass, watching as the wind wildly whipped leaves and branches. She waited for him to speak.

He said nothing for a moment, and then replied slowly, "I would ask you the same thing, but I know who you are and why you are here."

The words perplexed her. She shot a glance at his face, noted an expression that seemed as bleak as the world at which he gazed. She touched his forearm lightly.

"Why don't you tell me who you think I am?"

He met her eyes, and though his gaze still smoldered with desire, it was full of hopelessness.

"At first I believed you were just my imagination. A hallucination. But I see I'm wrong." He took in and held a deep breath then let it out slowly. "I have no other choice than to believe you must be a demon from hell in the guise of every fantasy I've ever had the courage to dream. You've been sent here to torture and tempt me beyond the brink of madness." He shifted his gaze to her fingers resting on his arm. "Your touch burns me. Please remove your hand and step away."

Abbie found the agony on his face almost unbearable to witness. What had brought this man to such a tortured existence? She dropped her hand and took a couple steps back.

"You're wrong about me," she told him softly.

He rubbed his forehead as though in pain and turned to the window again.

"I think not. You are a witch, a sorceress."

Abbie chafed her arms which were growing chilly once more. She moved closer to the fire burning cheerily in the grate and held her hands toward its warmth.

"I seem to be many personalities to you. You have labeled me as non-existent, a delusion, a witch, and a sorceress." She looked over her shoulder at him. "None of which are very flattering, by the way." She smiled slightly when he slid a sideways gaze at her. "In reality, though, what I am is cold, confused, tired and very lost."

"And nearly naked," he added, flicking a glance along her length.

Abbie straightened her spine even more and lifted her chin.

"The last thing I remember is preparing for bed. I'm sorry if you're offended."

He laughed; a small sound that rasped in his throat and sent him into a fit of coughing. He tossed her a second detailed appraisal.

"Oh, I'm not offended. Quite the contrary, as you well know. After all, that's why you're here, isn't it, to make my body burn to have you, to lie with you?"

Abbie let those words sink in. She had invaded his home. She had responded to his kiss, a kiss that still burned on her lips and caused her to yearn for more.

"I apologize for my behavior a minute ago," she said quietly. "I'm not in the habit of kissing strange men. It's just that…I mean, there is…" She almost said, there is something about you. I couldn't help myself. "If you'll just let me use your telephone, I'll get out of here." She paused briefly. "You do have a phone, don't you?"

"No."

"Oh. Well, could you drive me to the nearest one so I can call for help? You at least have a car, I hope?"

A small frown flickered across his brow.

"No, sorry," he replied slowly.

She bit her lower lip. This man really was isolated. And, now, unfortunately, so was she. She tried a last, desperate and probably futile attempt.

"I assume it's too much to hope for a motorcycle? A bike, roller blades, skateboard…?" His frown deepened and she sighed. "If I had known I was going to get lost, I'd have brought my cell phone."

He regarded her with a look that was both puzzled and amused.

"Do you realize you're talking gibberish?"

"No, I'm not. Forgive me for saying this, but it seems to me that you have shut yourself from the real world for far too long. You've lost touch with what's out there."

He arched one heavy dark brow and said nothing.

Abbie swallowed her frustration and paced the room

for a moment. Perhaps it was her training that had taught her to pace. She usually found her best resolutions in that tiny pathway of walking back and forth, her mind centered, totally focused. This time, however, no solution seemed forthcoming. All that kissing nonsense had created an awkward state of affairs. Abbie realized she was stuck in this situation and was going to have to deal with it. She stopped pacing and faced him.

He had not moved except to fold his arms across his chest, a subconscious signal of self-protection, she thought. He had put on an expression of patience worn thin, though Abbie sensed a deep wariness. Was he really that apprehensive of her?

"Listen," she said, "it's not my intention to disturb you, but you really are going to have to lead me out of these woods, either to your nearest neighbor or to the highway. And I would appreciate the loan of a coat or a jacket or a robe or something."

"I can't do that."

A bright spot of temper ignited in Abbie's belly.

"For heaven's sake, I'll pay…"

"I will give you something to wear," he interrupted hastily. "God knows we'd both be better off. But I cannot lead you out of here."

She stared at him a full moment then flung her arms wide in an overload of frustration.

"You want me to leave. I want to go. Why won't you help me?"

When he did not reply, she sighed heavily. "Then at

least tell me how to get out of these woods."

He shook his head. "I'm sorry, but I can't do that."

"What do you mean you can't?" Her voice hit a shrill note. "You live here, damn it!"

He winced. "Kindly refrain from profanity."

"Profanity? You've only just begun to hear profanity unless you tell me how to get out of this place and back to the main road."

He finally moved, walked to one of the bookshelves. He appeared to peruse the titles as though she were no longer in the room. This renewed indifference infuriated Abbie to the point that she wanted to scream and throw something at him. She sensed a display of temper, no matter how well-deserved, would not benefit her. Taking a deep breath, she forced herself to speak quietly.

"If you won't help me out of here, what do you suggest I do?"

He pulled a volume off the shelf and looked at it as though he had never seen a book before today.

"I suggest you leave the same way you came."

Abbie stared at him, incredulous.

"Have you not heard one word I've said to you? I don't know how—" A wave of dizziness crashed into her and broke off her words. She swayed, grabbed for something to break her fall. He crossed the room and caught her in the time it takes the heart to beat once.

"You're ill," he said, helping her into the armchair.

"No, not ill," she murmured, swimming up out of the wooziness that gripped her. "Injured, I think." She touched the tender place on the side of her head. "I blacked out, or fainted, or something, and when I came to I was in the woods."

He was silent a moment, regarding her. "You don't know how you got here?"

"Haven't you been listening to me?" she replied with some heat. "I'm…" Just thinking the words made her shudder. "I'm lost." She clenched and unclenched her hands, trying to squelch a rise of panic. "I got lost in those woods. I don't even know…" Her head pounded; she could not continue.

He hunkered beside her chair, peering into her eyes in an attitude unlike his earlier suspicion or desire. Right now he seemed almost, well, clinical.

"And the last thing you remember?"

Abbie tried to recall, but the pain in her head increased.

"Getting ready to go to bed, I think." She closed her eyes, opened them again. "That is, I remember taking a shower and dressing for bed, but there was something else…something I was doing, but I can't…" She shook her head slightly, winced at the throbbing.

His eyes narrowed as he stared at her, but it seemed he wasn't really looking at her. A form of recognition seemed to steal across his face. He rubbed a shaking hand across his chin and jaw.

"It is possible?" he murmured. "Can it be?"

"Excuse me?"

He stared at her a moment longer then shook his head as if to clear it.

"You said you were injured?" he asked in a more brisk voice.

At last he seemed actually to be listening to her and making an effort to believe what she said. Maybe now he would help her get back to civilization.

"Yes. But a bump on the head seems minor when compared to the fact that I have no idea where I am or how I arrived here."

"Where's this bump?"

She touched the aching spot on her head, the place where all pain seemed to center and expand. He gingerly probed the area with his fingertips.

"A good-sized knot with a cut," he muttered. He picked up her right arm, examined it and did the same with her legs. "And you have considerable scratches to the skin as well. None of these look deep enough to cause you a problem." He stood. "Come into the kitchen with me so I can attend to your injuries."

Abbie blinked. Suddenly he was solicitous in manner and voice. Had she finally reached through his peculiar notions and awakened him to reality?

She got to her feet and followed him out of the cozy parlor. The kitchen she entered was not a large room, but it was comfortable with a wood stove radiating warmth. A stew pot steamed fragrantly on top of the stove. There was only one window in the room, flanked by a small table on one side and a cupboard on the other. A larger cupboard had been built along the back wall and had a long, much-scrubbed looking top. A door with a window led to the outside; another smaller door was tucked into the far corner of the room.

"Sit there, please," he said, dipping his head toward a chair at the table. "I'll be back in a moment."

He left the room, and she heard his footsteps going up stairs. A short time later, he returned, a quilt over his arm.

"Here," he said, approaching her. "Stand up and let me…"

She stood, and he wrapped the warm coverlet around her. He moved the chair closer to the stove then and indicated for her to sit once more.

She remained where she was, luxuriating in the warmth of the thick, soft quilt around her. She watched the man as he opened the larger cupboard. He removed two stone jars, and a mortar and pestle. Into the mortar he measured dried leaves from each jar and with the pestle ground them together into a fine powder. His hands looked strong, she noted, with long fingers and clean, blunt nails; his face was a study of concentration. He said nothing as he worked.

Again she was struck by his sheer masculinity. As she watched him, Abbie's eyes defined his muscular body as he moved. His renewed silence bothered her a little. She did not want him to start pondering again on whether she was real or some dark spirit sent to wreak havoc. She needed him as an ally in this strange place.

"You've not told me your name," she said, breaking the silence.

He glanced at her.

"And you haven't told me yours."

He dribbled hot water from a kettle on the stove into the powder, a few drops at a time. With his forefinger, he tested the consistency of the paste he was making until he seemed satisfied.

"I'm Abigail Matthews. Abbie." When he said nothing, she prompted, "And you are…?"

He looked up from the greenish-gray glob in the mortar bowl.

"Andrew Wade. Sit, please. Abbie." He offered her a smile, a tentative and rather endearing one, she thought. "Please call me Andrew."

She took the chair near the stove, glanced dubiously at the mortar he put on the table near her.

"You're not expecting me to eat that, are you, because I positively refu—"

He laughed, a sound that seemed raspy and ragged because laughing seemed to be something rare in his existence.

"No. This is a paste for that lump on your head. It will help numb the pain and take down the swelling."

"Oh."

"I wouldn't expect you to eat it."

"Nor would I."

"The taste would be off-putting, I should imagine," he said with a wry tone, grinning at her.

"The appearance is off-putting," she said. "Sort of like pea soup and cement."

Andrew laughed again. He brought more hot water and poured into a small galvanized basin.

"I ought to tell you, I don't have much faith in home remedies," she said. "If you'll just give me some aspirin, I'll be all right until I can get to a doctor."

He gave her a quick, sharp look then turned back to the cupboard.

"You had a bit of dizzy spell a minute ago," he said as he reached for another jar. This time he measured leaves into a cup, poured hot water over them and covered the cup with a saucer.

"Well, that's probably because I haven't eaten anything for a while."

His brow creased. "You haven't?"

"I don't think so. I don't remember."

His frown deepened as he returned to her. He tipped her head sideways, parted her hair and once more examined the tender site.

"Well," he said as he dipped a small, clean cloth in the water, "I think you'll find a combination of this plaster and the tea will be sufficient for the pain." He peered into her eyes and added quietly, comfortingly, "Now, I'm just going to clean this wound. It may hurt a little."

His touch was incredibly light and gentle, but pain shot from the cut as he dabbed it with the cloth. Abbie drew in a sharp, sudden breath and flinched.

He stopped long enough to say, "I'm sorry, Abbie." His voice was as soft as a butterfly's breath, an apology in his eyes.

"Where is your husband while you've been out getting lost?" he asked after a bit. "He should be looking for you."

She gave him a sharp look.

"I'm not married, and I can watch out for myself, thank you very much."

He paused and lifted one eyebrow. "And yet you're hurt and you're lost. You haven't eaten for a while."

"Yes, but…well, a husband would hardly change that. Besides, would I have kissed you if I were married?"

His face reddened and he smiled slightly, but said no more as he continued to clean and rinse the wound until he seemed satisfied. No doubt he did not want to remember that kiss any more than she did. She squirmed a little, wishing she had not mentioned it.

"I'm sorry cleaning that wound took so long, but I'm convinced the cleaner it is the less likelihood of infection. One thing we absolutely do not want is infection to set it. Now, I'll just apply this plaster, and I'll do my best not to hurt you this time."

Abbie hardly felt it as he daubed the mixture onto her scalp.

"You have a good bedside manner," she told him. "You would be a good doctor."

His hands stilled their task a moment, fingertips a

hair's breadth from her scalp. She ventured a sideways glance at his face; saw a peculiar, deeply sad expression in his eyes. He caught her gaze, smiled so briefly it was merely a flicker.

"Thank you for saying so. I rather fancied that notion myself at one time."

"It's not too late, you know," she said. "To be a doctor, I mean. You're still young."

He said nothing but tipped her head again, and finished applying the paste.

"Now," he said briskly as he picked up the pan of water and carried it to the door. "That will help with the pain and swelling in short order."

He stepped outside with the pan and a moment later returned with it empty. She watched as he silently scrubbed his hands in fresh hot water and dried them on another clean cloth.

He brought the cup to her, removed the saucer and indicated the contents with a dip of his head.

"Drink that. It will ease the pain and your light-headedness."

Abbie picked up the cup, held it between her hands and looked at the reddish liquid.

"What is it?" she asked, sniffing it suspiciously. It smelled bitter.

"Bloodberry and barley-thorn."

She wrinkled her nose. "Sounds absolutely vile. I hope it isn't toxic." She said this last only half-jokingly.

A scowl, darker than the menacing sky outside, settled on his face.

"Of course not! I cure, I do not poison."

She widened her eyes.

"So you are a doctor!"

He said nothing, but she did not let the subject drop.

"Why have you shut yourself off from the rest of the world when doctors are so badly needed? What good are your healing talents if you don't use them?"

He glared at her for a space of time. She watched as his scowl faded and his shoulders drooped slightly. He looked away, but not before she saw the lost expression in his eyes.

"Ah!" he said, half a sigh, half a groan. He went to the cupboard and put away the jars.

"Drink your tea, Abbie."

From the other cupboard he got a bowl, filled it with the stew from the pot on the back of the stove. He set the bowl before her and laid a spoon and a square of cloth for a napkin beside it. Next to these, he laid a plate with two pieces of crusty bread.

"Eat this. Every bite of it. I'll draw us some fresh water."

Abbie looked at him as he picked up a large bucket near the backdoor. His problems, whatever they were, lay deep inside him. She ached for him and the depth of his despair and wondered if she could get him to open up, at least a little.

"Andrew, forgive me if I'm out of line by asking this, but…is there a chance…that is, is it possible…well, what I mean is…do you suffer from agoraphobia?"

"I beg your pardon?" He paused with his hand on the door knob.

"Agoraphobia. It's when someone—"

"I know what it is," he replied. He stared hard at the floor for a moment then lifted his gaze to her. "I'm not agoraphobic, but please understand when I tell you that I cannot leave this place."

Abbie held his gaze for a long moment. She did not understand, but she knew he would offer no further explanation. His attitude plainly said that his problem was none of her business, but she felt another tremor of compassion stir deep inside her and come to life.

"Listen," she said, getting up and crossing the room to him. "I'll find my way out somehow. When I get back to town, I'll bring someone out here to help you."

She waited, half expecting another explosive protest. He merely returned her look.

"Someone to help me leave?" he echoed after a bit.

She nodded.

He gave her half a smile, a sad one. "Dear lady. Don't you realize that if I could leave, I would have done so a long time ago? There is no one who can help me. This I know."

Abbie laid her hand on his arm, felt him tense at her touch.

"I will bring help," she promised softly, giving his forearm a gentle, reassuring squeeze before letting go.

He looked into her eyes a long moment before turning away.

"I'll get the water now." He glanced at her over his shoulder as he opened the door. "Eat your food and drink your tea while the plaster dries. You'll feel better soon."

SEVEN

Abbie hungrily devoured the chunks of beef and vegetables and both slices of bread. Andrew carried in a bucket of fresh water, and the glassful he brought to her was cold and sweet, slaking her thirst. Sitting snug in the quilt, a fire burning in the stove nearby, and her stomach full of good food while the pain in her head faded minute by minute, Abbie felt closer to contentment than she had in a long time.

Watching the man who had offered these things to her brought a warm stirring to her heart. His eccentricities did not diminish the kind heart and generous spirit Abbie had glimpsed. He seemed to possess a true attitude of compassion, a trait she rarely found in her clients, and even less in her co-workers. Sometimes she was struck by the callousness of her friends whose natures seemed never to reach beyond their own needs. Here was a man who had so much to offer, so much to teach, and yet he sequestered himself into this lonely existence.

He left the room again and once more she heard his steps going upstairs. This time when he returned, he placed a tan shirt and a coffee-colored pair of trousers on the table next to her. Abbie, nibbling the last bit of crust of her bread, looked up at him.

"Whether you undertake to leave, or whether you choose to stay, you'll need to wear something other than… well, other than what you have on beneath that quilt."

His words bothered her a little, as if he believed she

might actually prefer to stay in the middle of nowhere. Maybe he hoped she shared his partiality to isolation. Yes, she wanted to be away from the city for a while, but not here in this dreary old house in the middle of the woods, and not for long.

She started to tell him so, but caught his gaze and read something in the depths of his eyes. Perhaps it was hope. In any case, she shifted her gaze to the clothes and smiled as she picked them up. While the big shirt was no problem, the pants were miles too long and too large around the waist. Certainly she would be warmer in them. Anything would be warmer than her silk nightie. She glanced at Andrew and saw he gazed dubiously at the clothing in her hands. Their eyes met. He smiled, and she laughed.

"Not to worry," he said. "I'll find something to cinch them." He left the room and returned a short time later with a length of cloth.

"An extra sheet," he told her, "but we can make it work."

He tore three long, narrow strips and knotted the ends together. He braided them tightly and tied the other end, then held out the make-shift belt to her.

"Go ahead and put these clothes on. You'll be much warmer."

She stood, clothes and belt in one hand, holding the quilt snug around her with the other.

"You may get dressed by the fire in the parlor," he said. "When you're finished, call me, and I'll bring you a cup of tea."

She wrinkled her nose. "I don't think I want another—"

His lips twitched. "Regular black tea, hot and comforting."

She returned his smile. "Thank you. That would be nice."

Abbie went across the hallway and back into the book lined parlor. The fire burned cheerfully, brightening the room. She loosened her hold on the quilt and let it drop to the floor. For a moment, she held the shirt and the pants before the fireplace, letting the sturdy fabric soak in the heat. Slipping in them quickly she sighed with delight as the delicious warmth caressed her skin. She tied the rag belt snugly around her narrow waist, adjusted the excess fabric and rolled up the pants legs and shirt sleeves.

Abbie looked down at her feet, at what was left of her ridiculously, thin slippers. She wriggled her cold toes and supposed there was no help for that. Her host's shoes would never fit.

She picked up the quilt, folded it neatly and looked for a place to put it. One chair near the fireplace looked comfortable and she decided that was probably Andrew's favorite place to sit. A second, similar chair was in the corner. She laid the quilt across its back, bringing a splash of color to an otherwise drab room of brown chairs, brown book covers, and dark wood floors.

"I'm dressed," she called and went to stand near the fireplace. The warmth trickled through the thin fabric of her slippers, but she wondered if her feet would ever feel anything other than chilled.

As if he had been reading her thoughts, he walked in and handed her a pair of socks.

"These will be too large as well, but they're wool. Maybe we can shrink them in some hot water."

Abbie accepted them with a big smile.

"Wonderful! Oh, thank you, Andrew. My feet thank you."

"Your feet are welcome," he replied with a smile.

She sat on the raised hearth, peeled off the slippers and pulled on the heavy socks. She moaned in pleasure and gratitude, stretching out her legs and wriggled toes numb from cold.

"Food, clothes, warm fire." She cocked her head to one side, studying him, her confidence in him as a decent, kindhearted soul grew moment by moment. He was obviously skilled, his manner empathetic—that is, once he understood a person was real, not a product of brain fever.

What did it all mean, then? Why would a caring, skilled physician lock himself away from a world that needed him? What had happened to him to bring him to this place in his life? What had he done?

"Andrew, why are you here?" she blurted.

He did not reply. Instead, he pulled the armchair from the corner and settled it in front of the fireplace near the other chair.

"Why don't you sit here, Abbie? You'll be more comfortable." When she moved, he went to the hearth and rearranged the burning wood with a heavy poker. "Are you warm enough now?" he asked as he turned from the fire.

"Yes, thank you. But I'm serious. Why don't you give some thought to returning to—?"

"I'll get your tea."

He walked out of the room, leaving her to stare at the spot where he had been standing. Obviously, he did not want to discuss his withdrawal from society, and she knew it really was none of her business.

Who was she to judge him, anyway? Hadn't she given in to the pressure of a world gone mad for wealth, power and possessions? Hadn't she assumed the role of a high profile attorney to earn money and prestige? Hadn't she squelched that inner voice so she could follow what appeared to be the most profitable path?

Up to this point in her life, Abigail Matthews did not serve the highest good; she served the highest pay. In many ways she had shut herself off from doing the right thing, just as Andrew had. The only difference being, for whatever reason, he was helping no one, and for the sake of gain, she was helping the wrong people. Who was she to lecture him about doing the right thing?

He returned with a cup of steaming, fragrant tea and handed it to Abbie. She bent her head to inhale the warmth.

"Thank you," she said with a smile. "And I'm sorry, Andrew. I should mind my own business."

He slowly sat down in the other armchair and looked at her as if he tried to read her thoughts.

"Please know that I understand what you're saying to me," he said. "And please understand that it was my desire to heal the injured and the sick. In fact, it was my life's dream."

He seemed to be searching for the right words. Abbie waited, but after a few moments, he simply shook his head and said nothing. She decided not to pursue the subject.

"How did you find me, Abbie?" he asked after a time.

"Honestly, I don't know. As I told you before, the last thing I remember was getting ready for bed. I know I was doing something…but I don't remember what. When I try to recall, it's like a blank spot on a video tape…" She shook her head.

"What do you mean?"

"Nothing there, but you know without a doubt that something used to be. And then I just woke up…" She shot a fearful look at the window, saw the trees shivering and bending in the wind. "…in that awful forest." She shuddered.

His gaze seared her face with its intensity.

"But you did not know this place was here before you arrived?"

She shook her head. "I'm a city girl who prefers skyscrapers to tall trees and the sounds of traffic to the sounds of crickets. There is no way I would have purposely gone into the forest."

"I see." He remained silent for so long she thought he would never speak again. "Did you see anyone else in the woods?"

"No one." She shuddered again. "I simply cannot understand how I came to be there. It's as if...as if someone slipped a roofie in my drink..." She swallowed hard. "But I didn't go anywhere, no bars or restaurants...I stayed at Lefty's place...Do you think someone broke into my friend's house and drugged me?"

"Roofie? Lefty's place?" He sounded as mystified as she felt.

"I just don't know what happened," she said, feeling helpless and panicky, "but I should go back, look for signs of a break-in. She's my oldest friend, after all, and let me stay there while she was gone. If I had my Blackberry I could call the cops, and call or text her..."

She buried her face in her hands for a bit, hating the idea of returning to a place where she'd be alone if someone meant to harm her. At least here in this gloomy old house with Andrew her isolation was shared. And yet, she owed something to friend who had generously taken her in. She needed to make sure Lefty's beautiful home was untouched. She lifted her head.

The gaze Andrew had fixed on her was perplexed and full of concern.

"I think the knot on your head has affected your sensibilities again. Maybe you should lie down, Abbie."

"No, no. I'm just fine, but when the storm is over, Andrew, will you please go with me?"

"The storm?"

She looked toward the window. He followed her gaze.

"The storm will not pass," he said.

"Of course it will. All storms pass."

"Not this one."

"Of course it will!" His words irritated her, scared her, spoken with such resignation and assurance. She glanced around. "I'm sure it's too much to hope that you have the internet out here…?"

He gave her a completely baffled look, and she knew the answer.

"Do you at least have a radio?" she said, somewhat hopelessly. "Maybe we could hear a forecast."

"I have no…radio. Abbie, really, I think you—"

"Of course you have no radio," she muttered, tamping down exasperation. "You don't even have electricity."

She stood. Andrew rose to his feet.

"I really must leave now," she said.

"Abbie, it's not possible to leave this place." He spoke with such earnestness, leaning toward her as though to imbue her with knowledge.

"Anything is possible."

He shook his head. "You don't understand! I've tried, time and again. There is no leaving this place."

"And I'm telling you, Andrew, I refuse to think that way. I need to return to my friend's house and see if it's all right. I must let the authorities know there might be a dangerous person out there; drugging women, harming them…" She let her voice trail, wondering if abduction was really what had happened to her. If so, she was extremely fortunate not to have been injured or killed.

He grabbed her shoulders, shook her gently. "Abbie, listen to me. It's not possible—"

She jerked free of his hold.

"Anything is possible!" she repeated, this time with considerable heat. She wanted neither to hear nor believe such a dire proclamation. Then she softened, knowing his deep-seated problems were his own, nothing she could understand unless he chose to share them with her. Obviously, he preferred to keep his own counsel.

"Andrew," she said quietly, "you've taken good care of me and I thank you for that. And I appreciate the loan of your clothes. But I must leave."

He made an impatient gesture.

"Please listen to me," he said, leaning toward her. "I wish I could take you out of here, Abbie, but I can't. It's foolish for you to go looking for a way back to your friend's—"

"No! What's foolish is to sit here and waste your life instead of..." She broke off, hearing the strident sound of her own voice, lashing out at him, and that's not what she intended to do at all. "I'm sorry, Andrew. I'm the last person who should be talking about wasting a life." She raked her fingers through her tangled mass of hair. "Listen. You do what you must do, and I'll do what I must." She sought his dark eyes, reading in their depths his loneliness, his hopelessness. "Are you sure you don't want to come with me?"

"Abbie, it's my heart's desire to go back with you,

even to lead you out," he said wearily, "but believe me when I say it's impossible. There is no way out."

For a long moment silence lay between them. She knew his inability to leave this awful old house in the heart of the forest was something far beyond her understanding. Her heart ached for him, and she fully intended to help him break free as soon as possible.

She laid one hand on his arm. "I'm going to leave," she said gently, "but I'll come back just as I promised, with someone to help you. Soon."

Andrew said nothing.

"Can you give me something to help me mark my trail so I can find you again?"

He shook his head. "You won't need anything to mark the trail. The vegetation will soon cover anything you use."

She frowned at such an absurd notion, but said, "Then I need a knife to mark the trees."

"The trees will heal themselves moments after you carve them."

"Forgive me, Andrew, but that's not only ridiculous, it's impossible." She went into the kitchen, located a large knife and returned with it. "I'll take this with me and cut a path like Indiana Jones."

His face registered a stoic acceptance, becoming almost frozen as she opened the door.

"Andrew, are you sure…?"

"I'm sure."

She paused just a moment longer, waiting for him change his mind. When he did not, she went outside and closed the door behind her. She crossed the porch, and descended the steps. At the bottom, she turned to see Andrew at the entry hall window. He lifted his hand briefly then stepped from view.

A hard knot settled in her throat and she fought back tears. Foolish to feel so tender toward a man she'd just met, a man who was eccentric and secretive but compassionate and tender. She turned her back to the grim old house and faced the forest that seemed more malevolent than it had earlier.

She walked into the wind that assaulted her as if she had no more substance than a withered leaf. She bore into it, thinking more about the man she had just left than finding her way back to civilization. What awful thing had happened to cause him to choose this kind of life? He had revealed no more than his dream of being a physician but some traumatic experience was surely locked in his mind and heart where his only escape was avoid the world. Had he ever tried to face his fears and conquer his pain, or had he simply back away, resigning himself to isolation? He hardly seemed the type to be cowardly or weak. Whatever had crippled him was something larger than a mere obstacle. When Abbie reached civilization again, and after she went to the authorities with her story and made sure they followed- through on their investigation, she'd find someone willing to help Andrew. She would take that person to him, even if it meant she must face this awful forest again.

Andrew Wade was man of intelligence and heart. He could start over, if he wanted to. Cut off from the world and all social interaction, he was out of touch with the times. But that could be easily remedied, because Abbie would be more than happy to reintegrate him into society.

No doubt about it, Andrew Wade was a man Abbie could fall for—if she were ever to let herself fall again. Considering her track record, she doubted that would happen. Didn't the three strike law apply to love as well as baseball and felonies?

Abbie plunged deeper into the forest, slashing the thick vegetation to mark her passage and praying she was on her way to rescue. A vine, heavily stitched with tiny thorns, almost seemed to avoid the knife then reached for her. It caught her clothes, the thorns sinking into the fabric to tear open her skin as though hungry. While the wind blew her hair around her face and eyes, she struggled to pluck the barbs free of her flesh. When she pulled back the shirt sleeves and trouser legs, she saw blood striped her limbs with thin trickles. It was odd that the fabric of Andrew's clothes did not rip or even snag.

Blundering on, Abbie clumsily hacked at the bark of a tree but the wood resisted. With both hands she wielded the knife and tried again to mark her passage. The knife slipped from her cold fingers. She saw its dull blade in the brambles and reached for it but just as her fingers touched the handle, the knife slid deeper into the undergrowth. Abbie hesitated for only a moment, envisioning life forms that no doubt inhabited the dense thickets around and beneath her. She shuddered, drew in a deep breath and plunged her hands into the vegetation. Her fingers sought the cold metal of the knife but found nothing other than stems, vines, and thorns. Her search became frantic, and she tried to tear away the plants. Everything resisted her touch. It almost seemed the forest floor might draw her in and feast on her blood, flesh, and bones.

Abbie scrambled to her feet and clumsily moved away a few steps. She pushed her hair out of her eyes and glanced toward the stormy sky, or what she could see of it through the trees. Andrew had been right about futility of marking her path. Had he also been right about the storm not breaking?

One thing about it, Abbie refused to let obstacles get in the way of her quest. She gathered her grit and determination and pressed forward. If she could not find her way out of this forest, how would anyone be able to find her? Not that anyone would be looking yet. Lefty had gone to that conference in Savannah; no one from the firm back in Dayton would be second-guessing her whereabouts. Her parents, somewhere in Switzerland these many months, did not know she wasn't home. In any case, they were likely too absorbed in their own pursuits to call her. She was lucky to receive a card two weeks after her birthday.

She struggled through the forest for a while, seeming to make minimal progress. At one point, nearly breathless with the effort of moving forward, Abbie turned to look behind her. She saw no sign of her passage. It was as if this forest was a separate world unto itself, closing around her even as she watched.

Maybe the malevolent woods that surrounded him had something to do with Andrew's inability to go farther from the house than the few steps it took to get to the well. Maybe he felt as threatened and fearful as she did right then.

She shivered in the cold, silent wind and slowly faced forward again. There had to be a path somewhere. A fence or a creek, something she could follow. Something other than trees and bushes, and briars and thorns. She fought tears and she fought the wind; she fought her rising fears, determined to get out of these hideous woods and back to civilization. Frightened or not, there was nothing she could do now but keep going.

"I'll get out of this place," she said aloud. "And I'll get Andrew out, too." That's when she saw the snake.

She froze, unable to move or look away. It was no ordinary snake, and she knew it. Bigger than any serpent Abbie had ever seen in a zoo or television documentary, it lay curled, sleek and black, around the lowest branch of a small tree near her. The snake looked Abbie straight in the eye as though it could read her every thought. The red tongue lashed out, more as a taunt than a reptilian sensory instinct.

The eyes glittered with a weird intelligence. It seemed to be more than just a reptile; it seemed to be the very embodiment of evil. Although Abbie knew the notion was foolish, she thought she detected an expression of malicious amusement on the narrow face.

Slowly, Abbie stepped back. The wind shoved her as though trying to push her toward the awful serpent.

The muscles of the huge body rippled as the snake relaxed its grip and slid without sound from the branch to the ground. With deliberate slowness, it glided forward.

Watching the snake's approach, she became lost in the gaze of those slitted eyes. Abbie became numb, almost unable to move. The tongue flicked and her blood froze.

Run! She screamed silently. Go now!

She struggled, fighting an invisible web that seemed to bind her in place, helpless, waiting to be the prey of such a terrifying predator.

RUN! Go before it's too late.

With more strength than she knew she had, Abbie broke free of that hypnotizing stare. Her scream came from the depths of her lungs and burned the soft tissue of her throat as it erupted. The snake recoiled.

Without direction or plan, Abbie fled. Legs pumping, arms flailing, she dared not turn her head to look, but she knew the snake pursued her. She ran, screaming and stumbling, heedless of the whipping wind and mindless of the briars and thorns which congested her path. Branches slapped her head and body. There was no time to acknowledge that the obstacles in her way had seemed to multiply, to thicken and grow more tangled.

She did not know if she drove herself deeper into the forest, or if she neared a place of safety. At that moment, being lost seemed a minor complication. She knew if the snake reached her, it would kill her. Abbie could almost feel it at her heels and forced herself to race even faster. She ran until her breath heaved in and out in hard, ragged gasps. The painful stitch in her side nearly doubled her over. Fear kept her body moving.

When she spotted Andrew's house ahead, relief almost brought her to her knees. Ignoring her raw throat, Abbie screamed like a banshee as she forced her legs to carry her onward.

"Andrew! Andrew!"

As she neared the porch, she dared a backward glance.

The snake's jaws opened, baring huge fangs. It lunged. Abbie leaped to the porch floor, scaling the side without aid of the steps.

The front door flew open.

"Oh my God!" she shrieked as she crashed into Andrew. "Don't let it in the house!"

She shoved him back through the doorway and kicked the door closed behind them.

EIGHT

When Abbie left him, Andrew had watched for only a moment before turning away. How could it be that her presence, which had been a mere flicker in time, had given him such hope, such deep, brief fulfillment? To see her walk away from him tore his heart so brutally he almost felt his soul bleed.

At one point, he had reached the door to call her back, but stopped himself. Perhaps, if God existed and heard prayers, Abbie would be able to leave, even though Andrew could not. Perhaps this exile was his alone. He hoped so. Although having Abbie with him would fill him with a joy unknown, he could never wish for her to live isolated in a cold, dark place with no hope of liberation. To let her go with the hope she could find freedom had been the right thing to do.

But if she could not find her way out of that awful forest, and she returned to him…

"No!" he growled at himself. It was wrong to allow even a glimmer of hope for her to come back, because her return would mean her exile.

Andrew returned to the parlor and tamped down the urge to check out the window to see if she was still within sight. Deliberately, he went to the bookshelf across the room from the window. He removed Great Expectations then replaced it, and did likewise with House of Seven Gables, Jane Eyre and Innocents Abroad.

Escaping into the familiar pages of his books offered no release this time. Nor would scrubbing the already immaculate house, or physical exercise, or working with his herbs. No amount of protest or denial could diminish the fact that the short time Abbie had spent with him had filled him with light and hope. She was all he ever desired in a companion; she fulfilled his concept of fantasy. Her touch, her voice, her kiss and her passion had proven she was more than a vision of his own design. She made him feel alive again.

And yet he had let her go away from him with hardly a protest.

Andrew cursed himself as a fool. He was a fool for wanting her to leave and a fool for not going with her. He wanted her. He needed her. He thought he would surely die now in this prison without her. Maybe Abbie had been a hallucination after all.

Better for her if she is not real, he thought as he settled into his chair. This existence is not life.

His despair bloomed again.

A second chance, he prayed desperately to the God he was no longer sure existed. Give me a second chance, and I will not toss it aside.

He heard something, and lifted his head. He heard Abbie screaming.

Andrew leaped from his chair, rushed to the door and flung it open. Abbie hurled herself against him and kicked the door shut.

Heart thundering, he stared down at her. He had

wanted her back and here she was. Had wishing for her somehow brought her back? She clung to him, her fingers digging into his arms, her face buried in his shirt. Great racking sobs tore through her body. He felt the repercussions of her violent trembling in his limbs and chest. Andrew enfolded Abbie in his arms, holding her close. He absorbed her shuddering movements and felt the wild flight of her heartbeat against him. Slowly, she quieted; her heartbeat slowed and her sobs ebbed.

"Abbie," he said softly, his head resting gently against hers. "What is it? What has frightened you so?"

She took in a deep, ragged breath and let it out unevenly.

"It came after me," she said brokenly. "It would have killed me if I hadn't reached you when I did."

She pressed even closer, wrapped both arms around him, fingers clamping his back muscles, her eyes squeezed shut as though shutting out some awful vision. As she clung to him, Andrew perceived she feared being torn from his clasp. He tightened his arms.

"There is nothing in this house, or outside it, to hurt you, Abbie. Not a living thing."

She lifted her head, her eyes wide. "Yes there is! That snake." She shuddered violently. "I saw it. It's out there, and it's evil."

"No, dear one. There are no snakes here, nothing to hurt you."

He managed to pull back a few inches to look into her eyes again. They were swollen with tears and dark with terror. Then he saw the welts and bloody lesions on her face.

Andrew disentangled himself from her tight grasp and took one step back, holding her at arm's length to look at her more closely. Drying rivulets of blood streaked her face, neck and hands. He yanked back the shirt sleeves and saw more. Bending, he tugged up the baggy legs of the trousers. Her calves were bloody, as well.

"Turn," he said. When she did so, he pulled up the shirt to see that her back had been scraped raw. "My God, Abbie! Come into the kitchen with me."

He took her abused hand in a gentle grasp and hustled her toward the kitchen.

"I saw it, Andrew!" she said shrilly, pointing toward the outdoors. "The biggest, most hideous snake…"

She stared at him from eyes that begged him to believe her.

"I know this sounds foolish," she continued as they entered the kitchen, "but I swear it was laughing at me, mocking me." She stopped walking and stood in the center of the room. She shivered and drew her arms close to her body, clasping her elbows. She rocked back and forward on her balls of her feet.

Andrew smoothed her brow and led her to the same chair where he had treated her head wound earlier. Brushing his fingertips across her face again, he studied her cuts.

"Abbie, listen to me." He waited while she turned her focus on him and not on her fear. It took a little while before he sensed her beginning to relax. "There is a shrub called the dementia rose. It produces tiny aromatic blooms, but it's covered with small thorns that contain a poison which can cause hallucinations. It's obvious you've been scratched by it."

She shook her head.

"No! I saw that snake as plainly as I see you right this minute. A huge, black, horrible snake, bigger than any I've ever seen. And it chased me, Andrew."

"I know it seems real, but I swear to you, Abbie, nothing lives here other than you and me and the vegetation outside. I've been here long enough to know what I'm talking about."

She sought his eyes as though looking for deceit. A violent shudder ran through her again.

"But I saw it!"

"I know." Again he brushed her cheek with his fingertips, a light soothing touch. "But it only seems real."

He held her gaze, giving himself to her, wanting to reassure her fearful mind and wipe away the terror.

"I want to show you something."

"Don't leave me!" she shrieked, reaching for him.

"I'm not leaving you. I'm just going to get a book from the shelf."

He clasped her cold, trembling hand in his and let her trail him into the parlor while he retrieved the volume. They returned to the kitchen where he settled her into the chair again. Once more he knelt beside her.

"Look here, Abbie." He opened the book, found the page he sought and handed the volume to her. With his fingertip he tapped the illustration of a small tangled shrub with tiny white blooms. Below the picture, the caption read Rosa Dementia. "Did you see this while you were out there?"

She stared at it.

"I'm not sure. Maybe. It looks like everything else that grows in that awful forest." She stared at it a moment longer, then handed the book back to him and shook her head. "I don't know."

He put the book on the table.

"I tried to eradicate that particular species from around the place." He hesitated before adding, "Things have a way of...remaining untouched. I'm sure you've come into contact with that plant, and it caused this hallucination of the snake." He paused. "Do you believe me, Abbie, that you really were not chased by a snake?"

She searched his eyes again while he waited for her answer. Her tears had finally begun to dry, and panic seemed to ebb.

"You're sure?" she asked.

"I'm positive."

A long hesitation on her part, as if weighing his veracity.

"All right," she said slowly. It seemed to Andrew she did not believe him.

He placed a soft kiss on her cheek. "I would never

deceive you."

She glanced around the room. "But tell me this: if it was all just imaginary, wouldn't I see other things that don't exist?"

He winced inwardly, wishing she trusted him.

"Fortunately, the effects of the dementia rose are fairly short-lived and, with the exception of hallucinations, relatively benign. But, these wounds need to be clean and kept free of infection."

He examined the scratches on her body again. He studied her arms for so long that she stirred restlessly.

"What's wrong?" she asked, gazing intently at him.

He deepened his frown as he once more looked at the abrasions.

"I know you wore these clothes out there. You wore the sleeves rolled to your wrists and the trouser legs rolled to your ankles, didn't you?"

"Yes. It's so cold out there. And the socks with my slippers. Andrew! Have I been exposed to something worse than that bush?"

He looked up quickly. Apprehension had rekindled on her face.

"No. You're going to be all right. It's just that…well…" He ran one hand through his hair and frowned at the shirt sleeve as he plucked it between his thumb and forefinger. "Your skin is torn and bloody, almost raw in many places. But this shirt is whole. Not a thread broken." He flicked the edge of a trouser leg. "And no harm to these trousers."

Abbie extended her arms and legs. She raised her eyes to his.

"They should be in tatters."

"Yes," he said slowly. "This is what I've been telling you. Nothing diminishes or deteriorates here."

"I don't understand."

"Neither do I," he said. "I just know it's fact that the sun never rises or sets. My garden produces with no lull in harvest. The level of oil in the lamps remains the same. The fires in the stove and fireplace never need replenishing."

Her expression betrayed extreme skepticism.

"I'm sorry, Andrew, but that sounds ridiculous."

"I know." He also knew if she stayed with him any length of time, she'd see these phenomena for herself.

NINE

Andrew went to the cabinet where he kept his herbs and other supplies and, as he had done earlier, poured hot water into a basin and cleaned Abbie's wounds.

Neither one spoke for a while, then Abbie, who seemed to have regained her equilibrium, cleared her throat and spoke.

"Andrew, please don't take offense at what I'm about to say, but, even without the episode with the snake, this whole situation, this house, the woods, the wind, everything...well, it frightens me. Something isn't right."

"I know." He paused a moment and looked into her eyes. "But you aren't afraid of me, are you?"

She pondered the question, and perhaps she was right to do so. After all, he was a stranger to her, and the place where they found themselves offered little more than shelter and certainly no cheer.

"I should be afraid," she said after a moment. "Here you are, out here living this strange, isolated existence, and I don't know you from Adam. But the truth is I'm not afraid of you—which bothers me considerably." She paused and looked hard into his eyes. "You see, Andrew, there was a time when I believed in goodness of people. I believed in honorable intentions and in the grace of second chances."

"And you no longer believe in these things?"

"I'm not sure. Three times I've entrusted my heart to the wrong men, and had it broken every time. In my work, I help give second chances that too often are trampled by repeat offenders. I used to think I was helping to redeem society, give someone who needed it a helping hand. But things don't work out as I hoped and yet I keep doing it because...well, because it's what I do. Or what I did. Bit by bit, I've changed. Maybe it's because I've looked into the eyes of bad people too much lately. I know evil when I see it. The thing is..." She reached out, touched his hand. "The thing is, Andrew, when I look into your eyes, I see something there that I've not seen before. I dare say I see actual goodness."

He stirred, smiled a bit. "I'd like to think I have a good heart," he said. "Yet you still seemed bothered, uneasy."

She nodded. "I don't trust my judgment anymore. I just..." She shrugged. "I don't know for sure, but I think the very fact that I believe you're a truly decent man scares me."

"But not me personally?"

"No. Not you personally."

There lay between them a long pause in which he continued to bathe the wounds on her arms. It seemed he could almost hear her thoughts churning. Finally, she spoke again.

"Would you please tell me why you have chosen to live this way?"

Was she wanting to change the subject, or was she wanting to reinforce her feelings of trust in him? He hardly knew how to reply. Should he tell her that he did not choose to live here, that he had no choice? Should he disclose that after what must have been years of earnest seeking he had yet to find? What would she do, if he told her what he expected was true—that she, too, was now trapped in exile.

He rinsed the cloth in warm water, wrung out the excess and put it in her hand.

"Please clean the cuts and scratches on your front while I make a poultice."

She did as he asked and worked for a while in silence. As she finished washing the abrasions on her chest and stomach, she asked, "Did something happen to you, Andrew?"

He knew her state of mind was still fragile right then and hoped his lack of response would discourage further questions.

"You aren't going to tell me, are you?" she said after bit.

He mixed a fresh batch of the poultice he had used earlier and brought the bowl of it to the table.

"There's nothing to tell. Here, let me put this on your cuts." He quickly applied the salve to her back and extremities. Setting the remainder on the table beside her, he told her, "Put this on your front scrapes. Be generous with it. I can make more if you run out. In the meantime, I'll make you tea from the leaves of the tealround bush that will help fight infection. It will also ease any lasting effects of the dementia rose. As I said, the toxic effects are short-lived, but there could be a few after-effects."

"You mean like flashbacks? I might see that snake again?" Once more fear leaped into her eyes.

"Flashbacks?" He had never heard the term but assumed its meaning. "If you drink your tea, I don't think there will be anything to worry about. It will make you drowsy. Extremely sleepy, in fact, but rest will be good for you."

He measured a small amount of coarse dark powder into a cup and poured hot water over it.

"Actually, I'm feeling better now," she told him. "And I really do need to go home."

She said this last with such a remarkable lack of conviction in her voice that Andrew felt a tiny sting of hope. Was it possible she wanted to stay with him a while longer?

Soft light shimmered briefly through the kitchen, almost like a bright shadow passing through. Andrew caught his breath and turned his head sharply toward the window. What was that? Had he imagined it? He rushed to the window and looked toward the sky. The clouds moved and roiled the same as always but…There! He saw it: a small break where light seeped through, and then it was gone.

"Oh, maybe the storm is breaking up," Abbie said, also looking toward the window.

"You saw it, too?" he asked, looking at her over his shoulder.

"A bit of sunlight? Yes."

"Excuse me a moment, Abbie," he said. "Please don't move."

He went outside, out into the soundless wind and cold. He scoured the sky with his gaze, searching for beautiful golden sunlight that he had not seen in time untold. He plunged into the forest and looked beyond the tree tops, but nowhere did he see a lightening of the clouds again. After a while, he retraced his steps. Abbie stood by the window in the kitchen, watching him. She opened the door when he reached it.

"What's wrong?" she said, clearly alarmed.

"Nothing. Not a thing. Please, Abbie, sit down. You shouldn't move about so much." He guided her back to the chair and settled her in it.

"But—"

He touched his fingertips to her lips. "Not to worry. Everything is all right. Here have your tea."

He put the cup in front of her, sat down and took one of her hands in both of his.

"You said earlier that you aren't afraid of me. I'm glad, Abbie, because I would never hurt you. And, please, don't be afraid of this place, because nothing here can hurt you, except the dementia rose. You mustn't go back into the woods until I've found that hateful bush and hacked it out."

"But what about Lefty? What about whoever it was that attacked me?"

"We'll talk about that later. After you've rested and recovered." He touched the soft skin beneath her eyes. "There are dark circles here. You're tired, and you've been through a lot. So, I repeat, you need to rest."

He pushed the cup toward her and sat back, releasing her hand. She looked at the tea, then at him.

"If I drink this concoction and do as you say, will you help me leave?"

She seemed determined to go away, didn't she? Despair dragged on his heart. He sighed and wiped his hand down his face. How could he help her do what he could not do himself? Yet how could he tell her gently there was no way to go home? He must find the words to cause her as little pain and fear and hopelessness as possible.

"If it's a deal you want," he said at last. "Here's what I propose: drink the tea, then have a good long sleep. When you wake up, we'll talk about it. I'll answer your questions to the best of my ability, and I will do everything I can to help you. If you drink this tea," he tapped her cup, "and get some rest."

She searched his face thoughtfully. He could see her struggle and finally give in.

"I am awfully tired," she admitted slowly, picking up the cup. She pinned a no-nonsense look on him over the rim. "And I'm holding you to your end of the bargain."

Andrew nodded. He hoped the right words would come to him when he needed them. He hoped he could make her understand.

Abbie stared down into the cup she held. She had not yet tasted it.

"This tea is dark red, like that other creation you had me drink earlier."

"The leaves of the mature tealround are red."

"Does it taste as nasty as that first tea?"

He chuckled at the enchanting way she curled her nose. "Not at all. In fact, it has a pleasing, rather sweet flavor."

She cautiously sniffed it. "It smells nice, a little like raspberries."

"Then drink it," he encouraged. "You'll feel better when you wake up, I promise."

"I feel better already. That first stuff you gave me was disgusting, but I admit it relieved the pain quite effectively." She tipped her head to one side, her eyes studying his face. She smiled, and he felt his heart heave in his chest. "I appreciate your help, Andrew. Thank you so, so much for everything you've done."

"It has been my pleasure to help you," he said, watching as she took a small, wary sip of the tea then eagerly finish it.

"Wonderful!" she told him with a grin. She held out the cup. "I hope there's more where that came from."

Andrew took the mug from her.

"Sorry. It's a strong sedative. A second cup would be too much."

"Ah, well." She sighed wistfully. "You would probably have given me a second cup of the bitter stuff, wouldn't you?"

He laughed at her and watched as she fought back a yawn.

"Where may I lie down?"

"Come with me."

He led her up the steep, narrow flight of stairs and into the bedroom. His bed was a large four-poster, snug and comfortable. There was not a doubt in his mind that she would sleep deeply and sleep well. With difficulty, he shoved away thoughts of lying in it with her.

"I'll draw these draperies to darken the room more for you."

"But it'll be night pretty soon, anyway," she said, not yet realizing that there was never any night time here, never any true daylight, only a gloomy, eternal grayness.

Abbie sat on the edge of the bed and watched as he closed the draperies. He turned and saw the shadowy outline of her body. She looked small and fragile, very much in need of comfort. He ached to go to her, take her in his arms, hold and kiss her as he lay her back on his big warm bed. But he would not do so. He most certainly would be overcome with desire. Indeed, he was overcome with desire for her at that very moment. To touch her, to kiss her when she was in this vulnerable state, might banish the trust she had invested in him.

He picked up the extra quilt from the foot of the bed for himself and went to the door. "Have a good sleep, Abbie."

He was in the hallway when she called him back. He stood in the doorway, saw she had not moved from the edge of the bed, a slender figure in the gloom.

"Where do you sleep? I mean, what if…" She swallowed hard. "What if that snake, somehow…that is, where will you be if I need you?"

He smiled tenderly into the darkness. She was strong, and her courage was beyond question, but he wanted so badly to hold her, to take away her fear.

"I'll be in the front room downstairs. All you have to do is call. I'll hear you."

She sat silent a moment then said, "Thank you, Andrew."

"You're welcome, Abbie. Sleep well."

***

In the kitchen, Andrew washed the dishes and set everything to rights. He wanted to take his mattock into the woods and completely destroy the rosa dementia. It was a noxious and stubborn shrub. Although he thought he had taken every bit of the root from the ground long ago, it had returned. Things had a way of surviving here. These days, he hacked at the weeds and thickets only when he felt the need of hard work, not because he desired an environment of manicured lawns and bright flower beds. He would never have those here.

Again he toyed with the idea of going into the forest and destroying the plant. He knew, though, that the lasting effects of the toxins might cause nightmares. Although he was certain the tealround would help Abbie sleep several hours, he chose to remain near. In the forest, he would be unable to hear if she called him. He hoped when she awakened, her pain would be gone, her fears relieved and her mind at ease.

The kitchen work finished, Andrew quietly went upstairs to check on her. His eyes adjusted quickly to the darker room, and he saw her curled under the cover, quilt pulled to her chin as though hunkering against the cold. He went downstairs, fetched the quilt he had taken for himself and returned to spread it over her, tucking it snugly about her body. She did not stir. Straightening, he gazed at her for a moment. Only after he made sure her breathing was quiet and even did Andrew return to the parlor.

He idly stirred the fire in the grate then sat for a time, staring into the flames. He picked up a collection of short stories by Mark Twain which had never grown stale or failed to entertain him. Settling into his chair before the fire, Andrew opened the book to the first story. He read a few lines. He read them again. When he had read them the third time, he set the book aside. His mind was totally on Abbie Matthews and her unexpected advent into his life.

What did the momentous events of this day mean? After an eternity of aloneness, would Abbie now be his companion? If his solitary existence at last had come to an end, was it possible the constant wind, the cold, the grayness and the monotony of this existence would drive her to the brink of madness as it had done him? Would she be strong enough to withstand life with him as her only companion? Was there anything more he could do or give to her?

Andrew told himself he must step outside his own dismal self and become sharper, more social, a brighter cohort. He needed to shore up his resources and offer them all to her.

What were his resources, anyway? He was still an intelligent man. Though the lack of stimulus had the power to weaken his mind, he had never allowed it to dull. He honed his brain by reading his books, by writing alternative chapters and endings, by pondering science and experimenting with his herbs.

At one time, an eternity ago, Andrew Wade had possessed a fine sense of humor. Hadn't he loved playing with his brothers and sisters, joking with his folks? Hadn't he and Matthew Levi played innumerable, good-natured pranks? Surely that drollness, that sense of fun and adventure could be renewed. Couldn't he offer humor and intelligence to his new friend? Would she accept his offering, maybe reciprocate in like manner?

Maybe she would share her life story with him. He longed to learn all about her, where she came from, and where she belonged. Recalling his own abrupt, inexplicable entrance into this world, he wondered how Abbie had made her arrival. She spoke of preparing for bed and suddenly waking in the forest. Clearly she did not know her path of arrival any more than he had known his. They were simply here.

When it was time for her to wake up and want the answers he had promised, how was he going to explain anything?

Dear God, what am I going to do?

He fixed his gaze on the ceiling as though fixed on the Almighty himself, but no answer came to him as he waited.

At last he went to the kitchen and had a cup of tea before retiring. He wished he could relax, but his mind remained on the woman upstairs. Did she continue to sleep peacefully? Was she warm enough? Hesitating only a moment, Andrew went back upstairs to her bedside. Her hand and her cheek were warm to his touch, her breath soft and regular as before.

He stood unmoving, looking down at her for a long time. In spite of the deep, angry cuts and bruises on her face, Abbie was beautiful. Her skin was neither dusky nor pallid, but a soft cream that invited his touch. Her blonde lashes were long and dense, her lips full without being thick. A part of him clung to a desperate hope that this lovely, slumbering angel could escape the life he could not. But another part of him, a deeper, more hidden section of his soul yearned for her to stay, to share with him her warmth, her words and smile, her heart and body. Could he admit, in the deepest part of his being, where his heart beat steadfastly, that her exile was his salvation?

Abbie had the power to awaken passion in him. He dared allow himself to believe he had done the same for her. But he had been in the desolate existence long enough to realize that life must be more than longing and desire to appease one's urges. A real life should be full of living and doing and purpose, of making some sense of one's place in the world.

Mere existence, he told himself, is worse than death.

"I wish had met you before this place!" he whispered to her, touching a strand of her pale hair. "I would have given you my whole self, my whole heart."

She slept on, oblivious to his words, his touch, and his presence.

Andrew stepped away, preparing to return downstairs, but found he could not leave her. Instead, he settled himself on the floor on the far side of the bedroom and rested his back against the wall. He watched her sleep. She did not move and neither did he. He had no idea how long he sat there before finally rising and going back downstairs to get warm at the fire which never burned out.

TEN

Although the room was dim and unfamiliar, Abbie knew exactly where she was when she awakened. Recent events rushed back to her in vivid detail: the cold and silent wind, the dark woods, the hideous snake and her panicked flight from it. For a moment, those memories seemed more like the remains of a nightmare. She pondered, just for the space of a breath or two, that maybe it had all been a bad dream, something created from her need to break free of a life that seemed to bind her spirit. But she knew better. Her dreams were not this detailed and focused; her dreams were usually choppy, disconnected bits and pieces events that had no substance to them, sometimes even cartoon-like.

Then she thought of Andrew Wade, his dark eyes and sensuous mouth. She remembered the pent-up passion with which he had kissed her, the feel of his hands on her body, how she had felt in his arms—as if she could not get close enough to him. An enigmatic man with a wounded soul who seemed bound by his own lonely heart into a solitary existence. Dismissing for the moment his eccentric choices, Abbie asked herself is she was ready to step into another relationship. Could she tamp down the pain old scars brought or ignore directives from her inner voice never to trust or love again? For that matter did she even want to try?

And why am I even thinking about this? She asked herself and forced the thoughts from her mind.

She had been through a lot in a very short time. Was she prepared to renew her search for the way back to civilization again? Did she have the grit to face that menacing forest once more? Was her heart ready for her to leave the enigmatic Andrew Wade? Oh, there she went again, thinking about him!

She pulled the blanket up over her head, wishing she understood everything that had transpired in the last twenty-four hours and wondering why she didn't feel the same urgent need to get away that she'd felt the night before.

Lefty was in Savannah by this time. Abbie had told her friend she needn't call, so there was little possibility the woman knew she was lost. No one from the firm knew she wasn't where she should be because she had simply left. Her parents, pursuing their own agenda somewhere in Europe were clueless and indifferent to their daughter's life at any time. It seemed useless, then, to scurry madly about, trying to get back to Lefty's house when she had a companion like Andrew Wade with whom to spend her time.

Abbie stirred restlessly and turned over on her back. She stared through the dimness toward the ceiling. Obviously she was unable to keep him out of her thoughts and finally gave herself over to them.

Although she barely knew him, he attracted her; he tempted her. More than any other man she had ever known, Andrew Wade stirred something in her both gentle and eager. No one else had ever had the ability to stir her blood the way he did. Right now, today, a window of opportunity opened itself to Abbie. She recognized it and embraced the prospect. Was this gloomy house his childhood home, or had he come from some other place, seeking solitude? What drove him to seek and maintain this private existence? Did she really need to know? She should simply accept him as she found him, and maybe she could do just that if it weren't for the fact that he seemed utterly unhappy with his life. Something, somewhere, sometime, had happened to him, and now he shut himself off from the world.

She thought of how kindly he had taken care of her. He was the only man she had ever known who demanded nothing from her, neither attention nor service, or even a touch, though touching she had done. It had been impossible not to, and she longed to kiss him again. Something inside her being swelled for a moment, then melted with a rush of warmth. She longed to be with Andrew again.

Stretching a few inches at a time, Abbie could feel the ache in her muscles, the lingering pain in her bruised and scratched body. The knot on her head had diminished, but her fingertips told her it was still tender and swollen. She pushed back the blanket, and chill air rushed to greet her. Her toes curled as she got out of bed and stood on the cold floor. She grabbed the quilt and wrapped it around her as she shuffled across the room and opened the draperies.

The light outside was unchanged from the time she last saw it leaking through the glass. It remained gray and dull, the sky continued to glower with the threat of a storm. Andrew had told Abbie that the tea she drank before she went to bed had a sedative effect. Add that to her exhaustion and injuries, and she supposed she had slept completely through the remainder of yesterday and all of last night. She had never slept so long, or so deeply.

Abbie turned. On the back of the small chair lay the clothes he had given her. Hadn't she left them in a limp little puddle by the side of the bed just before she climbed between the covers? As she pulled on the clothes she noticed everything was clean. Andrew had no electricity, no modern appliances, but he had washed and dried her clothes. No other man in the world had ever done anything like that for her. Rather, they expected her to do it for them. She looped the belt around herself and tightened it. More and more she realized the depth of Andrew's kindness.

Combing her sleep-tangled hair with her fingers, Abbie looked around in a futile attempt to find a mirror. She realized there wasn't a whole lot she could do about her appearance at this point. The bathroom was an outdoor privy, offering only the essential hole—no mirror, no vanity, no shower. Her host looked a bit shaggy around the edges, but otherwise clean, so she knew there had to be some way to bathe.

At that moment, though, she was ravenous, hungrier than she had ever been in her life. She hurried from the room and went downstairs. The scent of cooking food led her to the warm kitchen. On the stove, a large slab of steak sizzled in a skillet, and potatoes and onions fried fragrantly in another pan. Andrew was not in sight.

Abbie made a trip to the outdoor privy and when she returned, he was there, turning over the meat. Steak and fried potatoes were a far cry from her customary breakfast of yogurt and juice, but at that moment she felt hollow inside. The food looked and smelled better than any meal she had ever eaten.

Andrew looked up as she entered the room. His gaze took her in from her tousled hair to her small feet lost in his socks.

"Hello," he said.

"Good morning," she answered, returning his smile. "Or is it afternoon? I feel like I've slept for a week." She approached the stove, bent over the skillet and breathed in gratefully. "This food smells awesome."

"Good!" he said, giving her a critical glance. "Your color is better, but you're still wan. And I believe you could do with a few good meals. Fill you out a little bit. How are you feeling this morning? Let me look at your wounds."

"I'm feeling much better, thank you," she said, as he checked her cuts and bruises, gently feeling for heat or swelling. "And I won't argue with you over diet this morning. Shall I set the table?"

He smiled slightly, and stepped back. "You're healing nicely. If you wish to set the table, go ahead, but there's not much to place on it." He dipped his head toward the cupboard where he kept cutlery and plates. "It's in there."

Abbie opened the wooden doors to the cupboard.

"You're right when you said there isn't much to place," she said. "Two of everything and not a bit more. You don't entertain much, do you?" she added with a teasing note in her voice.

He jerked around to face her.

"What was that you said?"

Uh oh, she thought. "I'm sorry, Andrew. I was just joking with you. I should have been more tactful—" She broke off, somewhat alarmed by the look of utter astonishment on his face.

"Where did you get that?"

She frowned. "Get what? The table service? Out of the cupboard, of course. I thought you wanted me to."

He lifted his stunned gaze from the table to her.

"You brought the extra with you, didn't you?"

"What? I didn't bring anything with me."

"Then…where…how…?" His gaze returned to the plates and utensils on the table and clutched the back of a chair so hard his knuckles whitened. The sudden pallor of his face alarmed her.

"Andrew! Sit down. What's wrong?"

He remained where he was, his eyes fixed on the table.

"I've only ever had one of each," he said. Slowly he lifted his gaze to her. "You brought them with you."

"You think I brought a place setting? Andrew, you saw me yesterday. I had nothing but the clothes on my back."

"And I'm telling you that in all this time I have been in this house, I have never had more than one plate, one cup, one knife, fork and spoon. Where did that extra come from?"

It was as if he expected her to have the answer. She shook her head.

"I don't know, Andrew. Maybe you overlooked them

or—"

"No! I did not overlook anything! I have been over every square inch of this house a multitude of times. There has never been more than one plate, one cup, one knife, fork and spoon!"

He stalked to the cupboard and yanked it open, glaring inside as if he expected to find stacks of plates and dozens of forks. She stared at his broad back, waiting to see what he would say or do, but he stood like granite.

"Andrew. I don't understand, but is it such a terrible thing to find extras in your home?"

He turned his head slowly to meet her eyes.

"Then where...I..." He looked back at the cupboard. "I don't understand."

Abbie said nothing as he processed whatever strange notions were going on in his mind. After a bit, he turned to her. Bewilderment still colored his expression but his gaze softened and warmed as he regarded her.

"'Extras in my home,'" he repeated softly. "You are an extra in my home and that's not a terrible thing at all."

He touched her cheek, traced her lips with his fingertips. She felt lost in his gaze, her skin tingling and leaned toward him, waiting for him to take her into his arms.

He dropped his hands and turned from her to glance at the table.

"Please sit, Abbie. I know you're famished. Tealround often has that side effect."

She stood a moment longer, blood thrumming with desire, body limp with disappointment. At last she settled at the table.

"I'm starving," she admitted.

He smiled and brought her a plate heaping with steak and potatoes. It smelled warm and heavenly. She cut steak so tender it hardly needed the knife's blade. "How long did I sleep?" She put the meat between her eager lips, burning her tongue. "Mmm. Oh, Andrew. This is delicious."

Andrew stood near the stove, regarding her from eyes that seemed as ravenous as her appetite. The expression was momentary, gone in a heartbeat, when he blinked and turned away to fill his own plate.

"I don't know. Many hours. Perhaps an entire day."

She paused with a crispy chunk of fried potato on her fork. "What time is it now? What day?"

He seemed to weigh the question as if it were a mathematical puzzle then slowly replied, "I have no timepiece or calendar."

"You don't have a clock, or..." Abbie stared at him for several moments then shook her head. Another of his quirks. "Well, at least you know if a day and night have passed, and have a reasonable idea if this is morning or afternoon. I mean, I know it's cloudy outside but..." Once again her voice trailed.

Andrew settled across from her but refused to meet her eyes. Why was he acting as if she had asked him to tell her his bank balance?

She put down her knife and fork. "Well, if you don't

know the day or the time, then you just don't know it." She offered a smile. "But could you hazard a ballpark?"

He raised an eyebrow. "A what?"

"A guess."

"Oh." He shook his head. "I really have no idea."

Abbie frowned. Was he playing games, or did he really have no notion, no remote inkling of time?

He got up, took her plate and added more food.

"Eat more," he said as he set the plate in front of her once more. "You need it."

She caught his arm, looked up at him until he met her gaze. She did not attempt to staunch the flow of questions that kept churning in her brain.

"Andrew, please, tell me what's going on? Where is this place and why is it so strange? Why do you choose to stay here?"

He said nothing, but his eyes, deep brown and dark as rich earth, stayed on her steadfastly. She could lose herself in that hypnotic gaze. Her heart yearned for him, but suddenly her mind resurrected the memory of David, Robert and Michael, each with his own selfish wants that had tortured her tender feelings and left her emotionally devastated. Refusing to get caught up in that "saving the lone wolf" in which some foolish, romantically starved women lost themselves and their dignity, Abbie forced herself to take her gaze off him. No way would she ever play the bumble-headed female again, but not falling for Andrew Wade was going to be tough. Real tough.

"Andrew," she said, picking up her fork and gazing absently at it. "Remember our agreement yesterday? I drank the tea. I ate, I slept, and now I'm eating again. I have kept my half of the bargain. You said you'd help me, so now it's your turn."

He took in a deep breath, let it out slowly.

"When you've finished your meal, go into that room there." He pointed to a small, closed door. "I have a tub of warm water for you. When you've finished bathing, come into the front room. I'll answer all your questions as best I can."

Their eyes locked, and she knew he would never relent without her cooperation. She nodded and finished eating.

After her meal, Abbie went through the door Andrew had indicated and found herself in a small, candlelit room. Andrew had prepared a bath for her in a wooden tub. Steam rose from the water into the cool room. A fresh towel, a wash cloth, a bar of plain, clean-smelling white soap and a comb lay in a neat stack on a stool next to the tub. On the floor beside the stool, he had provided a container of salve with which Abbie could dress her cuts and scrapes.

She skinned out of her clothes and got into the warm water. As much as she would have loved to linger in the tub, soak some of the tenderness from her muscles, she was eager to hear what Andrew had to tell her. She bathed quickly and got dressed. She began combing out her wet hair as she walked into the warm parlor where Andrew waited for her.

Fire burned cheerfully in the grate, adding its bright

color to the room. Andrew had drawn both chairs even closer to the hearth. He stood up when she entered. His gaze took in every inch of her, returning to linger on her long, wet hair. He adjusted one of the chairs a few inches.

"Sit here and dry your hair. I'd hate for you to catch a chill."

His offer was so gallantly old-fashioned that she smiled as she settled where he suggested.

"Thank you."

She turned her head so the drying warmth of the fire could reach her hair as she gently worked out any snarls. "And thank you for that wonderful meal, and for preparing my bath. I feel much better today. You have been so kind to me, far above the norm."

He returned her smile. "You're more than welcome, Abbie."

For a while neither one spoke as Abbie continued to comb and dry her hair and he watched. The companionable crackling of the fire added an intimacy to their silence. After a minute or two Andrew cleared his throat. When Abbie looked at him, he gave her a shamefaced smile.

"Abbie, I apologize for the boorish way I acted when you first arrived. Perhaps you'll understand and forgive me after I tell you some things."

She stopped combing, reached out and laid her hand on top of his.

"I understand that you are a very kind and decent man. You've taken wonderful care of a woman who barged into your home, unannounced and uninvited, demanding your assistance. There is nothing to forgive. I should be apologizing to you, and I do."

He turned his hand over, catching her fingers with his own. He looked at her hand as though it were a precious curiosity to be studied and cherished, then raised her fingers to his lips. The kiss he planted was warm and gentle and hesitant. His lips lingered a moment before he let go, the invisible imprint of that kiss a burning reminder.

Abbie's heart beat fast, much faster than a tender touch of lips to hand warranted. She wanted him to kiss her again, a real kiss such as they had shared once before, lips to lips, tongue to tongue, his strong hands on her body. She closed her eyes, lost in the longing. When she opened them she found him gazing at her, his yearning open and vulnerable on his face. Was her own expression so easily read?

"Andrew..."

He drew his gaze away, focusing on the fire at the hearth.

"You make my home as lovely and warm and welcoming as that fire, Abbie. It has never been that way before. Although those flames always burn, this room has remained drab and chilly for me, darkly depressing. Until you came, I had no brightness, except for my books, and I am weary of them."

His words soaked into her mind, touching each point of her soul.

Dear God, she could not, would not fall in love again. Nor would she encourage him to love her. Resolutely, she banished her burgeoning desire and pulled her hand free of his. Sitting back, she focused on the immediate challenge.

"Tell me about this place, Andrew. Tell me why you're here, and why you live this way, shut off from the world. And I want to know why you can't help me leave."

She watched as the longing in his eyes faded. The smile he offered was intensely unhappy. Incredible despair filled his eyes. Abbie felt sick to her stomach, witnessing such sadness. She dropped her gaze to blink back tears then raised her eyes to him again.

"Tell me," she whispered. "Please."

ELEVEN

Andrew sighed, long and deep, shifting his gaze to the flames that crackled in front of them.

"Ah, yes. Telling you my story. That was our bargain, wasn't it? But I cannot tell you what you want to know."

"I don't understand—"

"I said I'd tell you what I could, and I shall." He ran one hand through his hair. "Will it disturb you overmuch, I wonder?"

"Andrew. Whether it disturbs me or not, you must tell me. Please."

He shifted restlessly, refusing to meet her eyes.

"I guess I should start at the beginning." For another moment a silence lay between them as Andrew seemed to gather his thoughts.

"I was born on Sumac Ridge, in the Arkansas Ozarks." He glanced at her. "Do you know of Sumac Ridge?"

She shook her head. "I'm from Ohio. Dayton."

"Ah, I see. Then you've never heard of our little mountain community. Close-knit, with big families and strong ties to the land. But Sumac Ridge is small, a poor place, quite isolated. The mountains are rugged enough to discourage visitors and deter home folks from leaving. Professional people such as doctors, teachers, and ministers are scarce, even though folks there need healing, learning, and spiritual guidance just like everyone else."

"Of course," Abbie agreed. "And most professionals seem to go where the population is. Where the money is," she added with some bitterness and self-recrimination.

Andrew lifted an eyebrow and waited for her to say more, but she shook her head, unwilling to distract him with her own.

"Please continue," she told him.

"I was born on the Ridge to parents who valued their children above everything in the world. I loved them, the ridge, and the people who live there. Even as a young boy, I knew I wanted to do something to help the folks on Sumac Ridge. Make their lives easier in some way."

He leaned forward, stirred the fire and watched sparks snap and fly before settling back in his chair. Still watching the flames, he continued, "I enjoyed learning but really didn't want to teach. That takes a special talent, I think. Likewise, I couldn't be a preacher. My temperament's not suited for a life of Godly pursuits, though I believe I was, at that time, a deeply spiritual man."

He glanced at Abbie as though he thought his confession might have offended her. She met his eyes and waited patiently for him to continue.

"When someone on the Ridge became ill or was injured, there was no one there to help them except for Granny Hodge. She was as old as the hills but still got around to treat folks." He paused again. "Do they have granny women in Dayton, Ohio?"

"There are as many grandmothers in Dayton as any

other town, I suppose."

He shook his head. "That's not what I mean. A 'granny woman' is an herbalist, a midwife, a nurse. Sometimes she's the only doctor some people know. For Sumac Ridge, it's Granny Hodge. Folks said Granny took her vocation one step further and practiced the black arts as well as the healing arts." He shrugged. "I don't know about that. For as long as I can remember, she took care of everyone up and down the ridge, even the people in the town of Smith. When I decided to be a doctor, she was kind and patient with me, let me tag along when she made her rounds to the sick folks. Granny was good to teach me herbal medicine and folk remedies. Much of what I learned from her was scoffed at by my professors. Still, her poultices and teas helped the sick and ailing."

Here he paused and smiled.

"Granny taught me those remedies I gave you."

"And did she teach you any of her 'black arts'?"

He chuckled a little, shook his head.

"No. She knew I had no interest in it. We rarely discussed it, although she did tell me once that there were times when it's the only way to deal with some people."

"There are those who believe in spells and curses and black cats and the like."

"Yes, and I suppose superstitious folks are the ones she used her sorcery on. But, as I said, I wasn't interested in it, and she understood, I think she was relieved. It was tough, getting my education. My folks had six other mouths to feed at home, so I worked with single-minded purpose for several years until I had saved enough to study medicine. I was one year away from graduating. And then this..." he made a broad gesture with one hand and looked around the room as though seeing it for the first time, "...this happened."

Abbie looked at him as silence settled around him like a heavy cloak. The silence grew long.

"What?" she prodded gently. "What happened? What is..." she made the same broad gesture he did, "...this?"

Andrew turned his head slowly and regarded her from a stranger's eyes. His gaze chilled and frightened her with its bleakness, but she did not turn away.

"I don't know," he said at last. "As long as I have lived here, I've been unable to understand this place. All I can tell you is that I was walking the two miles to the railroad depot with my valise and my books, ready to return to the university after a summer break. My memory's a little fuzzy, but I seem to recall hearing someone in the woods calling for help. I followed the voice and then...I don't know. Maybe no one was really there. Maybe I blacked out from the heat. Whatever happened, when I woke up I was here." He turned his head to face her. "You, Abbie are the first living, sentient being I've seen since that time. And it's been such a long time that surely you can understand how I had mistaken you for a figment of my imagination."

She felt as though her air had been cut off. Could the ridiculous story he just related be true? And yet hadn't something very similar happened to her, one moment going about life and the next moment waking up in an alien existence?

She fought for breath, leaned forward eagerly and managed to croak, "Andrew! Do you mean... that is... how did you...? Andrew, how long have you been here?"

He shook his head.

"I don't know. I don't have a calendar or a watch, but surely it's been many years. There are times when my stay here seems an eternity."

She swallowed hard, fighting for calm.

"Andrew. When...when did you leave home to return to the university?"

"It was late August. About the end of the month, I think."

She licked dry lips.

"What year?"

"Year? Why, 1912."

Abbie felt the blood drain from her face. She had thought he might say 2009 or 2010, but not... She sagged against the back of the chair, gaping at him.

"That's impossible," she managed to choke out. "You have to be mistaken." Or delusional.

Andrew was a young man, no older than his early thirties. There was simply no way he could have lived for more than a century. No way. Nor could he have traveled in time. Things like that happened only in books or in science fiction movies.

Again she told herself he had to be mistaken. Because if he were right, she had done some weird cosmic traveling herself. But how else could she explain her own arrival here? She had been in Lefty's house, preparing for bed; then she had been in those cold dark woods outside this house. Just that quickly.

"These things just do not happen!" she said aloud, jumping up from her chair and startling her companion. She paced the floor, every nerve twitching almost beyond endurance. "This is crazy! This is all some weird, fantastical dream, and I'm going to wake up soon." She stopped pacing, threw her arms wide open, and looked heavenward, yelling, "I'm ready to wake up now!"

But nothing happened. She remained in the fire-warmed parlor while the soundless cold wind blew through the dark forest outside and Andrew watched her from his chair.

"Abbie," he said softly. He got to his feet and went to her. Resting both hands on her shoulders, he looked into her eyes. "My dear, this is not a dream. You will not wake up. If that were possible, I would have awakened long ago."

"No!" She lashed at him with her fists, pounding his chest, his arms. "I don't believe you! This is a horrid, horrid nightmare, and you're a part of it just like the stormy sky and the cold and the snake and that ghastly silent wind outside. I will wake up. I will, I will!"

Andrew tried to calm her but she struggled and kicked against him.

"Let go of me, damn it. I want to go home!" she screamed. "I want to wake up!"

"I know you do, Abbie. So do I. So very, very much.

But, my dear, we're awake right now." He held her loosely, his quiet, reasonable voice continued to infuriate her. He said nothing more but let her shriek and flail like a tantrum-throwing three-year-old until, at last, she spent her fear and anger and wilted into his arms.

For a long space of him she rested against him, clutching the fabric of his shirt in her trembling fingers, absorbing his gentle strength. Finally she raised her hot face with its stinging, swollen eyes to him. He stood there, so strong and stalwart, patiently taking in her useless fit of temper.

"I'm sorry," she muttered, scrubbing her eyes with the heels of her hands. "I had no right to talk to you like that."

He smiled and wiped away remnants of her tears with his thumbs then enfolded her in his safe embrace once more.

"Don't you think I cursed and raved like a lunatic a thousand times, Abbie? Do you think I accepted this fate easily? But my rage did absolutely nothing to change my circumstances."

"Oh, but Andrew, listen to me. Do you know the last time I was in the sunlight and warmth?"

He shook his head.

"August 2," she said, "but the year was 2012."

Andrew looked at her wordlessly.

"Do you believe me?" she asked.

He let go of her and turned away. Standing before the hearth, he studied the fire for a moment then walked to the window. He stood there, his hands clasped behind him.

Looking at his stoic posture made Abbie want to start screaming again.

"Andrew?"

"I do not find it impossible that you came here a century after I did," he said at last. "In fact, it makes perfect sense. Why your speech is sometimes gibberish to me, for instance."

She stared at his back. "Then how can you be so unruffled? How can you just stand there? Doesn't it all just blow your mind?"

He turned to face her, his eyes oddly flat.

"I can stand here calmly because of what I told you a moment ago. I've finished with all my ranting and raving and venting my spleen. It only served to increase my frustration, and did nothing positive. I've searched for an escape from this place so many times, I can't begin to count them. I used to go outside and search until I was so done in that I fell asleep in the forest. When I would wake up, I'd just get up and search again. I must have spent decades seeking a way out of this existence, and Abbie, I'm sorry, but you have to know there is no escape. The way always ends here."

"No!" she cried. She wanted to throw something at him. "You didn't do it right! You did not mark your path, or you went in circles, or you quit too soon." She stomped one foot like a petulant child. "You didn't do it right!"

Andrew pinned a steely gaze on her then moved from the window to the bookshelf. He idly picked up and reshelved a couple of volumes. He walked to the fireplace and stood before it, hands clasped behind his back again.

"If an entire century has passed in the time I've been here, Abbie, don't you think that has been time enough for me to find a way out?"

"You didn't do it right," she repeated stubbornly.

He let it out a long, slow breath. "Then what do you suggest we do?"

"Look for a way out together." She rushed to him, grabbed both his hands in hers and squeezed hard. "There are two of us now. We can do it. It's called teamwork." She tried not to see the bleakness in his eyes. "You gave up before you found it," she said again. "You quit too soon."

He did not take his eyes from hers.

"Andrew, this place is not right. There's something here that's peculiar, maybe evil. Don't you feel it? The only time I don't feel creepy is when I'm with you. We have to get out of here. We can do it—together."

TWELVE

Andrew refused to watch this beautiful, vibrant woman waste away into a mere shell of what he saw before him.

"Please hear me, Abbie," he pleaded again. "This futile searching will break your spirit."

She stared up at him, the expression in her lovely blue eyes mutinous and stubborn. "I'll go alone if I have to. I will face down the forest, even the snake." Her voice trembled at this. "But I will find a way out of here."

Andrew gazed at her silently, fully understanding the consuming desire to cast off the dark and desolate place. He ached to bring forth the warmth and sunlight of a summer day, the absolute joy of living and share it all with her. But such strength of mind exuded from Abbie, that he felt a slow awakening of hope. Might there be a chance, as miniscule as a pinpoint, a path existed that led back to the lost world of sunlight and springtime and a renewing of expectation? If one miracle occurred—the miracle of Abbie's presence—wasn't it possible a way to freedom really did exist?

He wondered if he could summon the strength to lower his defense against hope and raise his anticipation of a new life. He decided to chance it.

"You needn't go alone, Abbie. I'll help you. But on one condition."

"And that is?" Wariness flicked across her face, and

her watchful eyes never left his.

"I'm willing to cooperate with you fully, but I will not move an inch to help you until you give your body time to heal from the lacerations during your other excursion into the forest."

As a frown settled between her eyebrows and she took in a deep breath, he saw her prepare to protest. In the short time they had been together he realized she would never give in easily. He held up one hand to stop her before she spoke.

"Many of the plants have mild poisons in them, none as severe as the dementia rose, of course." He took her hand in his and lifted it to study the angry red tear across the knuckles. "Some of these wounds are severe. If you go out, get scratched by another plant and its toxins get in your bloodstream, or if this cut or any other becomes infected, very likely you will end up in bed with fever, delirium, even gangrene. Need I go on?"

"No," she said slowly, with obvious reluctance. "I understand. Andrew, if I do as you say, do you solemnly promise to go with me and help me find our way out?"

He gently squeezed the fingers he held then let go.

"I vow to help you look until we find it—or until you are satisfied nothing is there for us."

"And if, no make that when, we find our way from this place and back to civilization, will you abandon this sad, reclusive existence?"

What a foolish, futile and beautiful dream she awakened in him: to live again as man was meant to live, with a purpose beyond mere survival, perhaps to be with Abbie in a life that held precious treasures. Dare he even entertain the notion for a moment? He knew full well there was no liberation from this dark prison for either one of them and told himself he must not let his heart and mind be duped by such recklessly desperate thinking. He feared for her brokenness when she finally grasped the truth of this situation.

"Will you continue to be my friend?" he asked with a smile.

"Of course, I will!" She paused. "So will you help me find the way out?" she asked again, and he knew he could not turn her down a second time.

He needed to be there for her, as a comrade and as a support. After all, who knew better than he how much the companionship of another could mean?

"Yes, Abbie."

"All right then," she said. "I'll let my cuts heal. But how long will it take? My friend wants me to water her flowers…"

"I'm not sure how long. A few days."

Her voice trailed, and she sagged against his chest for a moment, her hands splayed, as though taking strength from the strong beat of his heart. He pressed his lips against her soft hair. He could lose himself in those shining gold tresses.

"Andrew, it all seems unreal. I feel so…"

He held her loosely, rubbed his hands up and down her back, feeling the line of her ribs beneath his palms.

"Lost? Confused? Alone?" he prompted.

She looked up and offered a small smile.

"Lost? Yes. Confused, certainly. But not alone, Andrew, with you."

His heart bounded at her words. To be with another living being, to be needed, to have his company desired and enjoyed! He gathered her hands and kissed them ardently. Lost in her eyes, he began to believe anything was possible, even leaving this place of exile.

Abbie was warm and soft in his arms. Her sweet scent wound tendrils of longing around him, even as she entwined her arms around him neck. Breath from her slightly parted lips invited him. So close to her, he had no power to resist. He lowered his head, his lips barely touching hers for only seconds, giving her every opportunity to pull away if she chose to do so. Instead she pressed closer, melding against him, branding his lips with her own. Soft and sweet, hesitant, but he sensed an underlying passion, as if she wanted more than a simple kiss.

The heat of her body charged his blood, spurring him with urgent need. In fact, that need began to block out all reason. He wanted to tear off the shirt and britches that swallowed her small body, but something stopped him.

"Treat her special, son, that woman to whom you give your heart." His father's words seemed to echo as fresh as yesterday. "Don't make her feel second best or second rate."

The voice seemed so real that Andrew broke away suddenly, looking for his father. Had the voice come to him through time and space because Abbie Matthews was that woman? They hardly knew each other, but she had somehow found her way to him after all this time. Surely that meant something in the eyes of destiny. And if so, intimacy needed to come after love, after commitment.

His body ached to lie with this woman, to feel himself buried deep inside her, to spill his seed within her silky warmth. Although she was pliable and sweet in his arms, it would be wrong for him to press an advantage. With enormous willpower, he stepped back.

She raised her bright eyes to his, her face questioning.

"I'm sorry," he said, turning away.

"Sorry? For what? For kissing me?"

He was embarrassed that the kiss could so easily have gone so much further than it had.

"I need to get us some fresh water," he said, lamely, the only thing he could think of to get him out of her presence. "Perhaps you'd like to wash up, or go lie down, or something."

He glanced at her, saw a most singular expression settle on her face.

"Is something wrong with me?" she asked.

"Of course not," he said hastily. "It's just that..." He felt his face flame and could not meet her eyes.

She stared at him, eyes brimming with hurt, then gave a short, brittle laugh and shook her head as though fighting her own thoughts.

"Even out here in the middle of the woods with only one other living soul, a man still rejects me. Excuse me,

Andrew."

"Abbie!" he said, but her footsteps pounded up the stairs.

Helplessly, he watched her flee from him. What had he done? What had he said that made her feel rejected? He had only treated her like the sweet lady she seemed to be, with the respect she deserved.

***

Abbie fled upstairs and dashed into the first room she saw. Slamming the door, she leaned her back against it, eyes closed. Her breath heaved in and out of her lungs and blood thundered heavily in her ears. If Andrew followed her, which she doubted, she could not hear him. After all, they'd met barely a day and half ago. Why had she been so willing to kiss him and touch him? Maybe he'd perceived her willingness to kiss him as desperation. No man wants a needy woman. Her face burned at the memory.

"Dear God," she whispered in shame. What is wrong with me, acting like as foolish as a lovesick school girl, blurting out a pity party for myself in front of him? Don't I have a shred of dignity?

Abbie took in a deep breath to calm herself and blew it out slowly. After a moment, she opened her eyes. The room in which she'd taken refuge was not Andrew's bedroom. This one was more softly appointed, with pale cabbage-roses and lilacs on the wallpaper, delicate lace-trimmed ecru curtains, pillows and bed coverings. The mahogany furniture gleamed as though it had been freshly polished. A full length cheval mirror stood in the far corner, and a dressing table was nearby. On a table beside the bed, a crystal vase sat full of fresh lilacs. It was only then that Abbie noticed the flowers' delicate fragrance. Where had lilacs come from? She had seen no flowering shrubs, or blossoms of any kind.

She pushed her way from the door, momentarily stunned by the room that contrasted so sharply with the rest of the house. Why hadn't Andrew put her in this room rather than in his own the night before? Did this room belong to someone else, someone she had yet to meet? But hadn't Andrew told her no one or nothing else lived here but him?

She walked across the soft woven rug of deep purple and pale lavender as she explored the room. The cool, slippery fabric of the bedcovering was soft beneath her fingers. The thick, downy bed would make a snug place to sleep. She ran her fingers over the wood furniture finding it silky smooth and dust-free. A silver- backed brush and comb lay in the dresser, and neither looked as if they'd ever been used. Beside them a long, shallow crystal dish held hairpins and decorative combs.

Feeling snoopy but extremely curious Abbie opened the top dresser drawer. She pulled out old-fashioned undergarments, but each one looked brand new: Corsets, lace-trimmed chemises and slips, stockings and garters. The panties—she assumed they were panties—were wide-legged and knee-length. They looked a little like silk Bermuda shorts. Other drawers revealed flannel nightgowns, handkerchiefs, gloves, scarves, other clean white sleeveless garments she was sure were more articles of underwear.

She moved to a nearby door. The closet behind it was small but full of beautiful dresses made of delicate silks and fragile layers of lace. Abbie fingered the lovely pastel fabrics and the matching broad satin sashes. She saw soft kid leather shoes, with small heels and sweet pointed toes. Every article of clothing looked at least a hundred years old, yet brand new at the same time. Abbie closed the closet door quietly.

Wait a minute.

What did this room and everything in it mean?

"Abbie?" she heard him call from the hallway.

Had Andrew been expecting her? Oh, not Abbie Matthews specifically, but any young woman lost and confused, someone he could lure with sweet eccentricities and hold hostage with a crazy story of exile. Had he stalked her, drugged her, and brought her into the forest?

And then left me there for what reason? To find him? She dismissed the absurd notion. And yet...

Her gaze swept over the room, so obviously a woman's room with the soft colors and fabrics. She caught sight of her reflection in the cheval mirror: a disheveled woman wrapped in men's clothing far too big for her. With a closet and dresser full of clothes that would probably fit her, why had Andrew given her his shirt and pants? Why had he put her to sleep in his own bed yet made no move to share it with her? Was Andrew Wade a crazy eccentric who preyed on lost young women, or was he a hopeless recluse who needed someone in his life? Why had he—

"Abbie! Where are you, Abbie?"

She snapped her head around to stare at the door. He was in the hallway and the tone of his voice was one of panic, as if afraid she had left him. She fought the urge to lock the door, to hide from him. If Andrew intended to keep her a prisoner here, he went about it in a truly odd way. First ignoring her, then treating her wounds and taking care of her needs. When she had left him earlier, he had wanted her to stay, but he'd been willing to let her go.

If he wanted to imprison me, he would have barred my way, or tied me up, or locked me in...

She moved cautiously across the room, her feet making no sound on the floor. She rested one hand on the door knob, the other against the door.

"Abbie!"

She could not bear the anguish in his voice, as if his soul was being torn from his body. Despite her misgivings and the confusion about her own needs, her soft heart stirred. Turning away someone in need was impossible for Abbie Matthews. If he needed comfort, she wanted to give it. But this time, she'd react only as a friend, not as a would-be lover.

She took in a deep breath and turned the knob. Andrew stood in the hallway, staring at the door, completely unnerved. Color had drained from his face, and he looked as if he might collapse. She forgot her fear and rushed to him.

"Andrew! What's wrong?" She caught his arm in both her hands and stared at his waxen face.

"How…Where…" He continued to gape at the doorway from which she just emerged. "That door, that room…never been there before."

"Andrew, surely you've been aware of another room up here."

He shook his head. "It's like suddenly finding that extra cutlery at the table earlier…" He turned his gaze to her, grasped her hand. "It's you, Abbie…you've done something…"

She reared back slightly and tried to free herself from his grip, but he held on.

"I don't know what you think I've done, Andrew. Pulled out a hammer and nails and built a new room in the last five minutes?"

"I think you're bewitched. Magical."

"Bewitched. Magical. Are we back to that?" She yanked her hand free of his and stepped back a little. "You are too intelligent a man to believe in nonsense. Or I thought you were."

"Before you came," he continued, "nothing ever changed here. No daylight or dark, no passage of time. There was nothing beautiful here. But since you arrived, I've seen the clouds break up outside, as if they will go away at last. We have tableware for two people. There is now an extra room where before there was nothing but a blank wall. Something has changed, Abbie, and it all started with you."

The intensity of his gaze proved he believed every word he spoke. Abbie knew that there was nothing menacing or underhanded in Andrew Wade, but could she rule out delusional?

"Andrew," she said quietly, "are you positive there's never been another person in this house?"

"Yes. Positive."

"Come with me," she said, and led him into the bedroom. He stood one step inside the doorway and looked around, bewildered.

"Look," she said, opening the closet. "These are women's clothes." She pulled out a soft green gown with three-quarter length sleeves and ribbons at the elbows. Holding it up against her, and said, "This would fit me," she said. "A little long in length and way out of fashion but better than sporting your clothes."

He crossed the room to plunder through swishing silks and rustling laces.

"I don't understand! Where did these come from?" He directed his gaze over his shoulder and fixed it on her.

"The dresser is full of underwear and nightgowns," she told him, dipping her head toward it. He glanced that way but made no move other than to shake his head.

"Abbie, I don't understand…" His glance fell on the vase of fresh lilacs. "Where did you find those?"

"I didn't find them," she said. "They were there when I came in. Andrew, this room has been recently cleaned. It's been outfitted for a woman…"

He sagged against the wall, his face ashen, looking utterly lost. Something inside Abbie broke open. The remnants of her doubts and speculations about Andrew were washed away in a flood of empathy. Insecurities regarding her value as a romantic partner seemed insignificant when she was faced with a world where magic might be happening all around her. All she knew for certain at that moment was that she and Andrew had nothing to trust but each other.

"I don't understand it, either," she said, "but we both know this is a strange world in which we find ourselves. For now, Andrew, let's accept what's here. At some point, when we've pooled our efforts and diligently worked together, we'll understand where we are and why we're here." His expression told her his confusion would not be easily sorted and solved. She took his hand in hers. "Right now, let's go back downstairs and have some tea."

Together they went downstairs and slipped into a life together.

THIRTEEN

While her cuts and abrasions healed over the course of what seemed several days, Abbie realized Andrew was not delusional at all. There was no break from day into night. Storm clouds continued to hover, a constant but unfulfilled threat. The silent wind blew without ceasing. As she helped him to prepare meals, the food stock remained as if untouched although they used the stores for every meal. An eternal fire burned in the fireplace.

Abbie fit into the clothing she'd found in the upstairs bedroom. She discarded the corsets, but found the stockings and extra petticoats added warmth to her body in a house that always seemed chilly. The bedroom upstairs was comfortable and always clean, the bed as soft and welcoming as it looked.

Each night—as much as it could be measured as "night"—before they retired, Andrew paused to eye that door again as though expecting it to dissolve before his eyes.

"It's OK," Abbie said at one point, "to just accept it and stop puzzling over it."

He nodded, gave her smile. "You're right. And it's good…another room in this house, one that is so suited for you, full of clothes…"

She returned his smile. "Yes. A good thing."

She leaned forward and kissed his cheek. If he wanted a touch more intimate than that, he hid it from her. Something had happened when they'd shared the second kiss; she wasn't sure what she'd said or done that had cooled his ardor, but Abbie refused to feel more for this man than she should. Her days of nursing a bruised heart were over.

The next morning, as Abbie sliced potatoes for their breakfast, she glanced up and caught Andrew's gaze on her. It was not a gaze of indifference or speculation; rather it was a gaze full of heat and desire. The knife nearly slipped from her fingers.

"Andrew?"

He blinked as though clearing his thoughts.

"I was just thinking how beautiful your hair is, Abbie. It catches the light so that it's almost a spot of sunlight in this gloomy house."

Her fingers went instantly to hair that hadn't seen conditioner or a flatiron in days. The natural waves were pretty enough, and the mere fact that Andrew likened it to sunlight touched her. She blushed like a school girl.

"Thank you."

They held each other's eyes for a long minute, then Andrew turned away.

"I'll draw some fresh water and make tea."

She smiled as he went outside, thinking how nice it was to have a courteous, sweet-natured companion with whom to share these strange days. With his dark hair and eyes, broad shoulders and strong physique, Andrew Wade was easy on the eyes. It took considerable effort for Abbie not to spin fantasies about his touch, his kisses, spending the night in his bed and knowing him completely.

She had just put the potatoes in the skillet to brown when the door burst open.

"Abbie!" he shouted. "Look at this!"

He held up a tomato, plump and red, fully ripe and ready to eat.

"There are more!" he said. "Do you know how long it's been since I've had tomatoes? Since that morning I sat at my mother's breakfast table before leaving for the university. Biscuits, gravy, sausage, eggs, fresh tomatoes from the garden…" He set the red fruit down on the counter then holding out his hand to her, smiled broadly and said, "Come see them, Abbie!"

The pure joy on his face caused her to laugh in delight. She wiped the potato starch from her fingers onto a damp cloth.

"Show me!"

Outside, she detected something different, something softer in the air.

"Andrew, it seems less cold, doesn't it? And is the wind blowing less?"

His clasp tightened, his fingers strong, his palm warm and firm against the soft skin of her hand.

"You noticed it, too?" he asked. "I thought perhaps it was just my perceptions. I've…that is, this world seems so different now, with you in it. I thought maybe I didn't feel the cold as much as before because, well, because you tend to warm my blood, Abbie."

She nearly halted in mid-step, and then stunted her reaction. A stirring of her heart and raising of her hope—in that way lay a broken heart.

"It's not just your perception, Andrew. I'm sure it's several degrees warmer out here, and look at the trees. The branches don't twist and bend as violently as before."

He followed the direction of her pointing her finger.

He stood without moving, watching the branches lift and droop, their leaves stirring restlessly rather than violently.

They stood a moment longer, then Abbie said, "Show me the tomatoes. Maybe something else is growing."

He led her a few feet past the well, to a place clear of weeds and scrub where several lacey-leafed tomato plants grew. A few bright red globes hung heavily on the vines, while several smaller, green ones grew in abundance.

"When did you plant them?" she asked.

"I didn't. I had no seeds. Abbie, the last time I came to the well for water there was nothing here but briars and thickets. That couldn't have been more than eight hours ago."

Abbie reached down and cupped a tomato in her hand, gazing at it for a long moment.

"Andrew, what does it mean?"

"It means the world around us continues to change. And with things changing as they have been, I suspect I might actually be able to eradicate the dementia rose. After I do, we can try to find our way out with no threat to our health."

A frisson of fear crept up her spine.

"But what if it cuts you while you try to remove it? You told me the toxins can be devastating."

"Not to worry, my dear," he told her, smiling. "I have dealt with it many times; I know how to treat the abrasions."

"I want to come with you, Andrew. You show me what to do, and with the two of us working, it will be done sooner—"

"No, Abbie. Your cuts are healing well, but if you were to get another round of the poison…I'm not sure what effect it might have."

"But you'll be there! You just said—"

He rested his hands on her shoulders.

"No, Abbie. I refuse to risk your health. And you can take that pleading look out of your beautiful, if rather mutinous, blue eyes. I'm not going to change my mind, so you may as well trust me on this."

Trust him. Trust him to leave her; trust him to return. Was it too much to ask herself to trust a man who'd been nothing but kind and solicitous? A stirring in her heart encouraged her to take this small step, believing he'd come back.

"All right," she told him, "I'll stay here. But I'm not going to like it."

"Consider it doctor's orders."

She wrinkled her nose. "Go on, then. And hurry back."

Later, after breakfast, Andrew left to accomplish his chore. When the door closed behind him, an unexpected longing filled her. She wanted to be with him; whatever happened in this strange world, she wanted them to be together. Separation seemed intolerable now, as if half her soul was missing. This feeling was new and unfamiliar. It troubled her no small amount.

Abbie did not fool herself. She recognized that it was very possible, even probable, that despite her best efforts she had fallen head over heels in love with Andrew Wade. Beneath the current of her passion, she felt the uneasy stir of doubt and self-protection.

Of course, not only were the circumstances of this relationship unlike anything she'd ever known could exist, Andrew was unlike any of the men who'd taken her heart and abused it. Of all three love affairs, none had brought such an awakening of her fierce and insatiable hunger. None had brought about her instinct to care and to nurture. None had shown her the image of true kindness and compassion. Andrew had roused all those qualities in her, and more.

Abbie told herself that maybe she felt so giddy and eager because these feelings were all so newly discovered. Maybe her yearning for him would diminish as time went on. Perhaps nothing more existed in this episode than two lonely people in a bizarre environment reaching out for comfort and strength. It was much too soon to assume love could have had a hand in any of it. She would enjoy this experience while it lasted, but solemnly vowed to keep love at arm's length. Once she and Andrew were out of this situation and back into the real world, who could predict what would happen?

She straightened the kitchen, and then dozed lightly for a while on her bed upstairs, listening, hoping for his swift return. She was not tired, and taking a nap seemed a foolish goal to attempt. As she shoved back the covers and got out of bed, Abbie realized she possessed more energy at that moment than she had known in years. She wanted to do something—anything—rather than lie idle in bed.

"I'm not staying in bed like an invalid no matter what the doctor ordered," she muttered.

Downstairs, she chose a book from Andrew's full shelves, and settled down to read. But the silence of the house gave her the jitters. She longed to hear another voice, the sound of someone else's movements in the house. Just the presence of another person in this cold, solitary place was a comfort.

She had only been here a short time, and during those houses, Andrew had been with her. What must it have been like for him to be here, completely alone, these many years?

It's a wonder he did not go completely mad. In fact, she marveled now at the way he was a gracious, caring host to her after their initial meeting. And she understood now why he had treated her as an illusion. In fact, she would probably have done the same thing.

Abbie needed something to do, something active that would keep her busy until he returned. She went into small pantry just off the kitchen, and eyed the assortment of food. She was not much of a cook, had never felt the need to be, but now she was willing to try. She gathered several apples and loaf of bread and carried them into the kitchen. She sliced the bread, placed it on the stove top to toast then peeled the apples and cut them into chunks. She put these in a pan of water on the stove to cook. When the apples were partly cooked, she drained the water and added torn pieces of toast. There was nothing to sweeten or spice the bread pudding, but she remembered the sweetness of the tealround tea. Perhaps the leaves would sweeten this treat. She opened the cupboard and on the shelf she saw both sugar and cinnamon. For a long moment she stared in surprise because she knew neither had been there before.

I won't question where they came from, she thought. By now, I know this place is like no other on earth.

She measured sugar into the apples, added the cinnamon, put the mixture into a pan and set it in the oven to bake.

When Andrew returned some time later, she greeted him as eagerly as wives greeted husbands at the end of the day on those old 1950s sitcoms.

"Did you have much success?" she asked him as she handed him a cup of fresh hot tea.

"Thank you, Abbie," he said, sipping gratefully. "Actually, no. I searched the woods and saw not a single rose thicket." He sniffed appreciatively. "What smells so good? And why aren't you resting?"

"I'm not tired," she replied with a wave of one hand. "I think this dish could be called bread pudding." She made a wry face. "I'm sure it won't taste as good as what Lefty made for me, but I thought it might be a nice change from the usual fare. And if you'll wash up, I'll dish up some for you."

From the warming oven, she pulled out the pan. The result of her efforts was a sweetly fragrant dessert, brown and bubbling. Andrew gazed at it speechlessly for a minute then looked up at her, a grin breaking across his face.

While he scrubbed his face and hands in the basin, she served a generous mound of her creation onto his plate.

"So you couldn't find any of the dementia rose? You were gone a long time, it seemed."

"I searched extensively for it, but it's gone," he said through the fabric of the towel as he dried his face. He lowered it, revealing tousled hair and cheeks red from being rubbed dry. Abbie could not resist reaching up and sweetly smoothing his hair. He smiled and held her gaze. For a moment, Abbie was sure he was about to kiss her, but instead he turned his gaze to the food on the table.

"I haven't bread pudding in…well, since my mother made it for me."

They sat down and he tasted it.

"It's sweet, but I have no sugar … and cinnamon! Where did you get cinnamon?"

"I opened the cupboard door, and there it was."

His eyebrows went up, then his face relaxed and he smiled. "I suppose I should not be surprised, should I? Good things are happening because of you."

"That's a sweet thing to say, Andrew."

He shook his head. "I speak the truth, Abbie."

She ducked her head, and ate some of the pudding. His words, spoken so simply without foolish come-on lines stirred her, made her feel sweetly cherished as a friend. Abbie was happy to be his friend, but her heart longed for something more. She shoved the yearning away.

They enjoyed the treat and when they finished, Andrew said, "Let's move into the front room to finish our tea."

They settled before the fireplace and sat in companionable silence for a minute or two. Gazing into the fire, Andrew spoke.

"You were scratched by the dementia rose so severely, Abbie, that the toxin got deep into your skin and other tissue." He lifted his gaze to meet hers. "Your hallucinations were powerful, violent. And yet I found no sign of that noxious shrub. I don't understand it. Unless..." He hesitated. "Good changes have occurred around us since you arrived, Abbie...the room upstairs, the change in the wind, the tomatoes in the garden...maybe your presence has helped eradicate the dementia rose."

Something about his hesitation told her he did not fully believe this theory.

"There's another possibility, isn't there, Andrew?"

Slowly he nodded, but he said nothing. She said it for him. "It's possible that other types of thorns scratched me severely, and I was not delusional, after all."

"I hate even to think it but, yes, that's a possibility."

Abbie studied his face, noted lines of concern around his eyes and mouth.

"I know what that means, Andrew. It means if I didn't have delusions, if what I saw was real..." she swallowed hard, fighting the rise of nausea, "... it means there actually is that huge snake out there. That snake...the one that tried to kill me."

Andrew set aside his tea, got up and pulled her to her feet. He cupped her face in both of his hands, looked into her eyes.

"Shhh," he said softly, rubbing the balls of his thumbs over her lips. "If there's one thing I'm sure of, Abbie, it's that there is no snake. If one existed, I would have seen it by now."

"But—"

He bent his head and placed a sweet, lingering kiss on her lips.

"Not to worry, dear one. Nothing here will ever hurt you, because I will never allow that to happen. If there is a snake, I swear I'll search until I find it, and I will destroy it."

He searched her eyes and smiled with such reassurance that her anxiety ebbed. Her trust in his honesty and compassion were given to him. She had no reason to doubt or fear that Andrew Wade would deceive her.

He kissed her again.

"All right?" he whispered against her lips.

Abbie leaned into him, her body melding with his. She wrapped her arms around his neck.

"Yes. All right."

"My dearest one," he said, gathering her to him, his breath warm against her neck.

He lifted his head to look in her eyes. Abbie touched the side of his face with her fingertip then traced his features: the small, permanent furrow between his brows, the strong line of his jaw, his lips which she sensed had rarely lifted in a smile until recently. She spoke her thoughts aloud.

"I think it is you who are the dear one, Andrew."

Raw hunger glittered in his dark eyes. Her heart leaped in response. As blood thrummed through her veins, caution screamed at her not to lose her heart to this man. And yet she willingly gave over to him, once more lifting her face to his. As though he sensed her need to be wary, Andrew's lips barely touched hers. He raised his head and started to pull away, but she caught him and would not let go. He stared into her eyes, seeming to ask silently if she truly wanted this.

"Yes," she whispered. "Yes!"

He hesitated for the length of two heartbeats, and then bent his head, found her mouth once more. His lips were hot and greedy against hers, moving, pressing, parting. She devoured his kiss as eagerly and passionately as he offered it. Sliding her hands to caress his head, Abbie thrust her fingers into the rich thickness of his dark hair. He wrapped his arms around her and crushed her body against his. She molded herself to him while the kiss deepened, then deepened again. Abbie could joyously lose all senses and drown in that kiss.

His breath ragged and hot against her skin, Andrew

dragged his lips from hers to taste her cheek, her neck, her throat. When he began to undo the pearl buttons along the front of her dove gray silk dress, she arched her back, aching for the touch his hands on her skin.

A quick fumbling of her fingers working with his and the dress opened, sliding down her shoulders. Andrew savagely yanked loose the bow of her sash and the dress slithered down her slim body to the floor.

"Damn the shimmy!" he growled, wrangling with the slippery satin ribbons of her lacy chemise but moments later, the undergarment along with her petticoat and voluminous briefs pooled around her ankles. The chill air of the room danced across her bare breasts and down her back. She stood naked and eager in his arms.

He stared down at her, his breath stilled for the moment, as if he could not believe the beauty of what he saw and the promise of what she offered.

"Abbie!"

She smiled at him, knowing invitation lay in her eyes.

He cupped her breast, and she drew in a sharp breath as he kneaded the softness in his palm, and then stroked her hardening nipple with his thumb. With his free hand he explored the gentle curve of her back and the flair of her hips, caressed the roundness of her bare bottom.

Abbie savored his need, the proof he wasn't as indifferent to her as he would have her believe. She groped to divest him of his shirt and trousers. She parted her legs for his questing touch and sought his mouth with her own. As his fingers found and entered her, the blood singing in her ears seemed to catch fire, electrifying every nerve and cell of her body.

"Oh, my God, Andrew," she gasped against his mouth as another kiss began. Deeper than before, the kiss released the savageness in their thirst for each other.

Abbie gripped the back of his head with one hand and explored his body with the other. He growled deep in his throat as she closed her fingers around him, finding his heat and his need. She arched against him, moaning his name, begging for him to join his body with her own.

Grabbing her and they tumbled to the floor which was warm from the fire.

"Abbie!" he repeated, kissing her with heat and hunger while she gave herself to his touch, groaning with pleasure as his lips and his hands found every tender place, aching for him. When he entered her, Abbie cried out in delight and delicious fulfillment, wrapping herself about him and gave him back, thrust for thrust, the wild eagerness of his movements. As he reached his climax, she cried out his name and welcomed his seed with her own frenzied paroxysm. Perhaps it was her imagination in that moment of ecstasy that a blinding burst of light flashed above them.

As they lay spent and silent before the fire a little later, Abbie thought the room had never seemed so welcoming, so warm. The glow the fire cast over the room was brighter and more beautiful than she had ever seen it.

"Abbie," Andrew whispered against her tangled, pale hair. "Abbie, Abbie, Abbie!"

She laughed softly in delight. He raised his head and looked into her eyes.

"Your eyes seem to shine from an inner light," he said with wonder. "What a magnificent change you have brought into my life!" He cupped her cheek with one hand. "You are a sprite!" he told her. "Or maybe an angel. Are you my angel, Abbie?"

She smiled.

"If it pleases you to think so, then that's what I am."

Andrew lowered his head to hers, kissed her ardently, lingeringly, on the lips.

"Yes," he whispered in her ear. "My own dear angel."

He kissed her again, more sweetly and tenderly than she'd ever been kissed. His lips lingered on hers, kissing each corner then fully. He lifted his head, then suddenly turned and looked toward the window. He sat up, drawing her up with him.

"Look, Abbie!" he shouted. "Look! The sun is shining!"

Indeed the sunlight poured in through the windows of that room. The pair gazed in awe at the light until it waned and the gloom returned. But for a time, the new bright warmth filled the world around them.

FOURTEEN

Andrew and Abbie settled comfortably into what became a pattern of days and nights. They marked that passage with sleeping, eating, making love and inexhaustible conversation. As a team, they shared in the chores of housekeeping and cooking, of harvesting herbs and drying them. Andrew taught her which herbs were used for what purpose and showed her how to measure and crush the leaves and roots. Sunlight made its appearance from time to time, never lingering, but always returning.

Andrew coaxed her out of the house and away from it toward the forest. The first few times, she looked around warily, expecting to see the huge snake at any moment, but she never did. Along the front of the house, scarlet roses and golden marigolds bloomed, along with willowy lavender and snowy hydrangeas.

"You have brought life into this place and to me," Andrew reminded her joyously and often.

One of their favorite pastimes quickly became what Abbie grandly designated as "Evenings at the Fireside". During this time they read, either silently or to each other, from Andrew's collection of books. Frequently, as they sat in the cozy parlor before the hearth, they discussed their vastly different lifestyles and generations.

One day, though, he seemed especially pensive, gazing into the fire, speaking little.

"Andrew, is something on your mind?"

He glanced at her, nodded slightly.

"I've been thinking about my family, wondering how they fared after I left. Then for some reason, I started remembering my little sister, Hazel. She died of pneumonia when she was five and I was ten." He closed his eyes and shook his head. "That was an awful time. I stood at her bedside, watched her try to breathe and I watched her die. I guess that's when I decided to become a doctor, maybe save some other little child. But I never got the chance." He opened his eyes, met Abbie's gaze. "Do people die of pneumonia in your time?"

"Sometimes. But I think it's because they don't get treatment soon enough, since there's treatment and medication that can take care of it in a few days. My friend, Lefty—er, I mean, Linda, got pneumonia a few years ago. She went to her doctor, got her meds, went home and recovered. She was back to work in a week."

Andrew smiled, his eyes shining in wonder.

"That is truly amazing."

"Childhood diseases like measles and mumps and whooping cough? Kids are immunized against them now. Same thing with small pox. And cancer can be stopped and people who've had it can live years and years. The key there is a healthier lifestyle, early detection and treatment."

He seemed to take this all in then in an awe-filled voice, he said, "You know, that's a wondrous thing. A wondrous, blessed thing."

A few evenings later, as they sat in the parlor reading.

"I believe I'll fix us some tea and cinnamon toast," she said. "Would you like that?"

He smiled at her, his eyes shining in the firelight.

"Yes. I'd like that very much."

She fixed their snack and brought it into the parlor. Andrew helped her to arrange the food on a small table between their chairs.

"We're like an old married pair," he said, taking his hot mug of tea off the table. Before she could react, he added, "Papa and Mama used to put us kids to bed, then they'd sit together for at least a few minutes each evening before going to bed. In the summer, they sat on the porch swing, and in the winter they sat before the fire, like we're doing now. It was a comfort to me, hearing their voices, knowing they loved each other and all of us children and that we were safe…"

"That sounds lovely, Andrew. You must have had a wonderful family."

"Yes. I did. A large, boisterous, funny, lovable family."

"And you miss them."

He nodded. "Very much so. Abbie, you never talk about your own family."

"That's because I really have nothing to say about them. My mother gave birth to me; each one spent as little time as possible with me while I grew up…" She shrugged and gave him a sad smile. "I suppose that's why I invested so much of myself into my career. But now I don't want that, either." She sighed. "All I want now is simply to be happy."

Andrew gave her a warm smile, reached out and squeezed her hand.

"I want that, too." He paused, sobered, and said, "Abbie, you rarely talk about your life and where you came from. I've told you about my brothers and sisters, my parents, our home and our town, what life was like. Won't share with me?"

"Of course," she said. "But it's not very interesting, I'm afraid." She explained to him about her law career, how she'd wanted to help others and how she'd somehow fallen into a trap she may or may not have set for herself. "As I said," she concluded, "it's not very interesting. I was soul-searching when I found you, Andrew. Maybe you were what I was searching for and I didn't realize it."

"Ah, Abbie!" He reached out and brought her to his lap, settled her down in his arms. He kissed her tenderly and rested his head against hers. She snuggled down into his embrace. "My sweet darling, I'm so glad you found me. I waited so long…"

They sat quietly for a while, content, the fire burning brightly in front of them.

"Tell me about the world of 2012. Tell me what changed."

And so she told him of inventions and discoveries, advances in medicine, the World Wars and other conflicts, of space travel and modern communications. He listened without comment, his expression one of amazement, almost disbelief.

After a time, he said, "It seems to me that there is too much dependence on machines and not enough on humanity."

"I would have to agree with you," she said honestly. "In my time, we probably would not be sitting together, talking this way, reading in the evenings, simply enjoying each other's company."

"No?" He frowned. "Why not? Do lovers not like each other?"

"We'd probably be watching television, or be on our computers, enjoying the internet. In fact, most people pursue solitary activities, even in a family unit."

His frowned deepened and he shifted beneath her. "I don't think I'd like that, Abbie. I think I would never fit in your world."

An icy breath slithered down her back.

"Andrew." She swallowed hard. "Andrew, don't you realize that when we find our way out of here…you will be in my world?"

He seemed speechless for a moment, and then shook his head.

"Maybe not," he said.

"What do you mean? Of course you will," she said, almost shrilly. She did not want even to think of being anyplace where Andrew was not. She gripped his shirt front in both her hands. She dared not even to think he might choose to stay here rather than go into the modern world with her.

"When I left, there were cars and computers and jets and television and microwave ovens and…and power tools," she said in a flood of words. "You'll see them all, and you'll get used to everything, and you'll realize the twenty-first century is actually a wonderful place to live."

"But, Abbie, when I came here, I left behind horses and wagons and threshing machines and steam locomotives. Who's to say, if we get out of here, we won't come out in my time instead of yours? For that matter, what if we find the world to be a totally different place than what either of us has known?"

"Of course we won't come out in 1912. How could we? That was a hundred years ago!"

He caught her chin gently and turned her face to his.

"My own sweet angel, look at me. Do I look as though I'm a hundred and thirty years old? You must remember: something has happened to time as you and I understand it. For me, it's as if it has stood still. My hair does not grow or turn gray. My face has not aged; my body is still vigorous Time does not move here. But somewhere beyond this place, it does. And we don't know at what pace it moves, or if it's going forward or backward. So if we get out of here, Abbie, we don't know where we'll be."

She stared at him, a small hand of terror clutching her heart.

"I never thought of that," she said.

"If we get out of here, we must be prepared for anything."

She knew he was right, of course. What if they found their way out of this dark site to step into a world foreign to them both? What if they entered some terrifying future environment as hideous and alien as something from one of those old Twilight Zone episodes?

Abbie closed her eyes. Nausea churned in her belly. After a moment, she opened her eyes and reached for his hand again. It was warm and strong and firm in her grip. He was not frightened, and she took comfort in that. She clutched his hand and let his strength flow into her.

"Whatever we face, my dearest friend," she told him, "we'll face it together."

"Yes. Together."

For a time they sat quietly, the only sound was of their breathing and the fire crackling in the grate.

"Andrew? I want to go to bed now." He met her eyes. "I really need to touch you and feel you and know you are real."

Without a word, he stood and carried her upstairs to the bed they now shared.

FIFTEEN

"You know you need to lose your fear of the forest," Andrew told her the next day over breakfast. "And I think we should start working on that today."

"Oh, but I—"

"Abbie, that forest is out there. It is not going to go away. If we are to find our way out of here, you will need to be strong and courageous."

He was right, of course. Her fear of the woods, of living wild things, of being lost had crippled much enjoyment in her life. She remembered the time she had turned down an invitation to go with a friend to a lakeside resort in Minnesota last summer; she had declined the opportunity to hike the Appalachian Trail a few years ago. In her heart of hearts, Abbie had longed to go, but the thought of getting lost, of facing bears or snakes or even raccoons had forced her to stay safely in the city, away from natural beauty, away from new experiences.

It embarrassed her to remember that when she first met Andrew she had passed judgment on him, declaring him to be afraid of new experiences, afraid to leave his house, when it was she who was the coward.

Hypocrite! She scoffed at herself.

"All right," she said, "But you must help me. And whatever you do, promise that you won't leave me there alone."

She shuddered at the mere remembrance of the snake.

"Of course. I'd never desert you, Abbie. And if the time ever comes for you to face your demons on your own and venture out by yourself, you'll know it and you can tell me."

She nodded, but inwardly wondered if she'd ever be ready to go again into those dark woods alone.

Although Abbie did not enjoy the forest, she loved walking hand in hand with Andrew on their daily forays into the woods. In fact, the forest floor was not nearly as overgrown and frightening as it had been when she first arrived. The wind had died from a chill blast to a somewhat balmy whiff, only blustering from time to time. They could actually hear leaves rustle as they shifted in the breeze. He was fully convinced neither snake nor the dementia rose was a threat. He frequently pointed out the plants in the forest from which he harvested the leaves, stems and roots.

"It's foolish, I guess," he said, "to continue harvesting fresh since none of them lose their potency or flavor. It's just something I've done to keep myself busy."

He looked at her with a grin, pulled her to him and kissed her.

"I have better ways to keep myself busy now."

***

One morning after breakfast, while Andrew was out

at the vegetable garden to gather tomatoes, squash, and string beans, Abbie made sandwiches, wrapped them in clean clothes, got a couple of apples from the fragrant pantry and put everything into one of the buckets used to fetch water. She filled a jar with fresh water, capped it tightly and wedged it in the bucket between the apples. Upstairs, she took one of the quilts off the bed and folded it neatly. She carried it down to the parlor where she picked up the book of poems Andrew had been reading.

She turned to see Andrew, leaning against the doorjamb, watching her and smiling in curiosity.

"What are you doing, Miss Abigail Matthews?"

"Well, Doctor Wade, you and I are going on a picnic."

He raised one eyebrow.

"Are we?"

She held out the quilt and book to him, then turned to pick up the pail which contained the meal she had prepared.

"Yes. And why are you looking at me like that?"

He took the quilt and book from her hand and looked at her quizzically.

"I never thought of having a picnic in those woods. Are you sure you want to?"

"I'm not afraid when you're with me. Somehow, when we're together, everything feels right. You know? Safe."

"I do know," he said. "And everything is right and safe and good when we're together."

He brushed a lock of hair from her forehead and studied at every aspect of her face as though memorizing each detail. He gaze bored deeply into hers.

"You have given me back my life, Abbie. I don't know how I lived without you, here in this place or long ago on the Ridge. I love you so much."

He set aside the quilt and book, and took her into his arms.

She let the handle of the bucket slide from her grasp. It clattered to the floor. Abbie placed both hands on either side of his face and whispered near his lips, "And you have opened a new world for me, Andrew, far from this place or the life I've always known." She kissed him. "You've shown me what true kindness his, and how it's possible to be pure in heart. I..." She almost slipped and said, I love you, but caught herself. "I care for you more than I can say."

Andrew searched her eyes; she knew he looked for the truth she was unwilling to bare.

"Can't you say the words, dearest?" he asked her. "Or do you not love me?"

This was the first time he had asked her directly. She did not want to hurt him, but loving Andrew and speaking it aloud would somehow commit her to him, and what if committing to him was not the right thing to do? What if she didn't really love him but only bonded with him because they were the only two people in their world? What if, when they found their way out, he discovered she wasn't his bright angel? What if she was unable to sustain a relationship?

Abbie yearned to love him, to know and proclaim she loved him. But she could not bring herself to voice those words of decision and commitment. Not yet.

And if not now, when would she be able to admit to him what lay deep in heart? At least, maybe she could erase some of the wounded expression from his face.

"I don't know, Andrew. How can I say it, when I'm not sure what loving someone feels like? I thought myself in love before, and I was dead wrong every time. Even the love of my parents was...nothing that made me happy. I guess I'm afraid of more than just the forest."

She bit her lower lip, looked up into his eyes. He smoothed her hair, fingertips brushing the sides of her face.

"Yes. You're afraid and more than just a little bit. But it's all right, Abbie. When you're sure, and you know the time is right, I'll be waiting. Until then, you know that your tender regard will be my mainstay." Then as though banishing the moment, he kissed the tip of her nose and moved away to gather the quilt and book again. "A picnic, you say? Let's be off."

The day was lovely, with a soft breeze blowing. While the sun played hide-and-seek with the clouds, Andrew and Abbie walked hand-in-hand, going deeper into the heart of the woods than they had ever gone together.

"You're doing fine," Andrew said at one point, "walking in these woods as if you aren't afraid."

"I'm with you." She laughed self-consciously, dropping her gaze. "You know, Andrew, when I first came here, and after I met you and got to know you a little bit, my intention had been to help you overcome your fears. Instead, look what you've done for me. Nothing in my life has ever felt so good and safe to me as being with you."

Andrew stopped walking to look into her eyes.

"I think you're happy, too. Are you, Abbie? Are you happy here, and with me? If we never find our way out, and I'm the only companion you'll ever see, will you be content in this place?"

The life she'd lived before, the life of cars and computers and convenience and a career which lined her pocketbook, all of it seemed nothing more than a distant memory. Her simple life here with Andrew was real and solid and it fulfilled every dream to which she had aspired. Did this mean she loved him? And if she did, why, why, why was it so difficult just to admit it? He waited expectantly for her reply, his expression pensive and hopeful. All she could do at that moment was smile tenderly into his dark eyes.

"I want nothing more than this. If you are my only companion, Andrew, it is enough."

"Thank you, Abbie," he said so humbly she nearly wept.

After a moment, he said, "I believe there's a good place to have our picnic just over there." He dipped his head toward a small clearing flooded with sunlight. Abbie thought she heard birds singing.

They spread out the quilt she'd brought and settled comfortably on it. She lifted her face to the sunlight. Near her, Andrew stretched out on the quilt, hands linked under his head. Abbie felt his gaze on her, but she did not move.

Instead, she basked in his peaceful presence, knowing nothing bad would happen to her while Andrew Wade was nearby. Gradually, her anxiety let go, bit by bit, until her body felt nearly disconnected with the ground beneath her. She had no idea how much time had passed, but she had never felt such contentment and peace of mind in her entire life.

"Abbie?" he whispered so quietly she barely heard him.

"Hmm?" She kept her eyes closed, feeling drowsy and far away.

She felt his fingertips on her arm. Their warmth against her skin drew her out of that ethereal disconnect and slowly back to his side. She opened her eyes, turned her head and smiled at him. He gently guided her down into his arms.

He kissed her sweetly, almost chastely, his lips barely touching hers then pulled away a tiny bit so he could look at her. For a time they were suspended in each other's eyes. Abbie touched his cheek, tracing the line of his jaw and down the strong column of his neck. She followed her fingertips with her lips, brushing kisses lightly against his skin. Returning to his mouth she teased him with tiny kisses until he resolutely took over the kiss, his mouth hard demanding against hers. Weakness flooded her joints, turning her liquid and hot within his embrace. The buttons down the front of her dress presented him little resistance, yielding rapidly to his fingers. Her hands trembling with eagerness, Abbie unfastened his vest and shirt, digging her fingers into the warm, solid strength of his chest. Beneath her palm, his heart beat hard and rapid.

She lowered her head to kiss that pulsing site, cherishing the blood that thrummed through his body, keeping him alive. She stroked her hand over his flat belly and over the hardness beneath his trousers. The fire that burned in his eyes consumed her anew.

"Abbie!"

Andrew devoured her with a kiss so heated and so deep, Abbie felt herself transcend her own body and soul to merge with his.

Within moments he had torn away every stitch of her clothing and until she lay bare and reckless in his arms, fumbling with shaking fingers to open the buttons of his trousers. Her impatience matched his and seemed to fuel his need beyond control. He entered her roughly, his breath heavy and ragged.

Abbie clutched him, digging her nails into his skin while meeting his thrusts with a feral craving all her own. The renewed thrashing of the wind in the trees was mild compared to the frenzied plunging, driving force that urged them to an untamed climax that seemed to shake the forest floor. A blinding white flash of lightning seemed to set the world on fire, and then thunder rolled angrily across the darkening sky above them. So lost in the consummation with Andrew, Abbie hardly heard the thunder's ominous threat.

Andrew and Abbie clung to each other, needing to hang onto the moment and guard it as treasure. The storm stopped, as suddenly as it started. Sunlight poured down on them once more.

She lay naked in his arms as passion slowly settled

into delicious comfort. He gazed at her as though burning each detail of her face and body into his mind. With his fingertips, Andrew traced and explored every line and curve. As the dampness of their bodies began to evaporate, she shivered slightly. He kissed her face and throat, lingered on her breasts and firm nipples, and then reached for the clothes he had stripped from her body.

"Get dressed, dear one, so you don't get cold."

Ever the caretaker, the watchmen of her heart, body, and health. No one had ever cared for her as he did.

This is what it feels like to be loved, she thought. She wanted to share her joy with him, tell him how much she loved him. In fact, she opened her mouth to blurt her feelings; a sound came from the woods, a sound of movement, as though someone were walking toward them. He slid into his trousers and yanked on his shirt, his gaze never leaving the woods.

"Dress quickly, Abbie," he said.

"What is it?" she asked, peering into the forest as she slipped the dress over her head. "Is it the snake? Andrew, do you see the snake?" Abbie heard the fear in her voice and despised it for weakness. She had vowed to overcome this terror and she would.

"Stay here," he said in hushed tones. "I'll see what's making noise. If it's that snake, it won't be with us long, I promise you."

"Andrew? What are you—?"

"Shhh!" he warned. "Stay here and stay quiet. Everything will be all right."

She watched him move stealthily toward the trees, his muscular body taut and ready to spring into action. What did he plan to do? Drive it from the forest? He had no weapon with which to destroy it. Terror screamed in every cell of her body at the very notion of the giant serpent, but there was no way she would let this man face down that hideous creature alone.

"I'm coming with you," she said.

"No!" He looked at her over his shoulder, a dark scowl on his face. "Stay back."

"I will not stay back, Andrew Wade!" she said as loudly as she dared.

"You will impede me."

"No, I won't!"

"Having you with me will split my focus. I can't search for whatever is out there while worrying about your safety. Please, Abbie. If not for your sake, then for mine, stay here."

She grimaced, knowing she impeded progress at that moment, but his well-being was as much as concern to her as her welfare was to him. Let him think she stayed at the picnic site, but she would follow so quietly he would not know she was there. She planned to never to lose sight of him.

"All right then," she said, grudgingly.

When he was a few yards away but still within eyesight she moved forward as quietly as possible through the undergrowth and thick trees. Every time he paused, she did. If he turned to look around, she ducked behind a tree.

All was quiet, save for leaves rustling on tree branches and the sound of her own blood pumping in double-time.

She heard something to her left, a rumble, like wheels against a hard, hollow surface. Like the sound of a car passing over a bridge. She stopped dead still and stared hard into the forest, looking for anything out of the ordinary.

Could it be? Was it possible they had found their way back to civilization? She took a few steps in that direction almost certain something lay beyond those trees.

"Andrew!" she yelled as she hurried forward. "This way! I think I found—"

Abbie tripped over a huge tree root. She staggered, groping for anything to break her fall, but she grasped nothing. She fell. And fell and fell and fell.

SIXTEEN

Andrew heard her yell for him and he turned in alarm. He did not see her.

"Abbie?"

When she did not respond, he called louder, "Abbie! Are you all right?"

Still no reply. He rushed back to the abandoned picnic site. Abbie would not deliberately wander off. Had she been following him after all? He peered through the trees in every direction and saw nothing unusual, nothing to mark her passage or his. The sky became overcast in a moment's time, darkening the world around him. Knowing her fear of the forest, Andrew was sure the deep shadows would terrify her even more. The wind began to blow, cold and silent.

"Abbie!" he called in alarm. "Abbie, where are you?" She did not answer and he shouted, "Call out, and I'll hear you. Don't be afraid, Abbie. Just stay where you are, and I'll find you."

Still she made no reply. Had she gone back to the house? It was unlikely. She would not trust herself to find it alone. Maybe she needed to relieve herself and had hidden from his sight. Relief shot through him, and he stopped walking. Yes, of course. She merely need to answer the call of nature and was protecting her privacy. She'd come out of hiding in a minute.

"Abbie, don't be embarrassed. Just let me know if you

can you hear me."

He listened and heard only the silence of the forest respond him.

"Abbie! Abbie, answer me!"

The woods were soundless. The silent wind now blowing its cold breath against him made Andrew want to curse, and he did so, uselessly.

"Damn it, Abbie, you're scaring the hell out of me."

He looked around in near-panic, hoping to see her emerge. He would forgive her for frightening him like this, and he would apologize for swearing at her, but she never appeared. The dark, cold forest offered no sound to comfort him.

Andrew crashed through the trees and thickets, calling for her ceaselessly. He ignored the thorns and briars which clawed at him as though trying to hold him back. He told himself that maybe he had irked her when he demanded she stay alone at the picnic site instead of going with him to look for the source of the sounds in the forest. She'd become more familiar with the woods, less fearful. Maybe in her irritation, she had flounced away and found her way back to the house. Once there, she probably would not come into the woods again, not alone. He cursed again, this time at himself for insisting she stay in the picnic area. He'd thought was doing the right thing, protecting her from whatever creature crept or slithered around nearby, but obviously he had erred.

Fueled by the hope she was home safe, Andrew raced back to the house, willing her to be there when he arrived. He leaped up the steps and flinging the front door wide open, shouted, "Abbie! Answer me, sweetheart!"

Silence greeted him. He sought every room, every nook, moved the chairs and looked under the bed, in the closets and cupboards. He went outside to the privy and looked inside.

"Abbie! Abbie, where are you?" His voice was hoarse, his throat burning and raw. "Abbie!"

His gaze landed on the well. In an instant, his mind conjured the image of her returning to the house for a drink and tumbling into the well. Reason told him this was a foolish notion because she had a carried a jar of water in the pail with their food. Right then, though, he could not, would not listen to reason. He peered down into the depths of the well and saw nothing but his own murky reflection.

Quickly Andrew lowered the bucket and watched it sink out of sight. He hefted himself to the edge of the well, grasped the pull-rope with both hands and lowered himself along its length and into the cold water. His feet touched soft ground and gravel where the water was about waist high. Letting go of the rope, he dunked beneath the surface of the water and sought the area with his hands. His open eyes saw nothing in the darkness, and he knew she was not there.

Gasping from the cold, he shot out of the water and clutching the rope, pulled himself up, hand over hand, the length of the well and clambered out of it and onto dry ground.

By that time, his wet skin and clothes, the wind and his fear had chilled him to his very marrow. But he did not go inside to the comfort of the fire. Instead, Andrew plunged once more into the forest, calling for her. At their picnic site, he grabbed up the quilt and her clothes, telling himself she would be blue with cold wearing only that thin silk dress.

Andrew covered the familiar territory of the forest twice, shouting for her until his voice was nothing but a weak rasp. At the edge of the small clearing, exhausted, he looked across at the house once more.

"Please be home," he pleaded, willing her to be there. But inside himself, in the depths of his very soul, he knew she was not there. Whatever mystical, magical event that had occurred to bring her to him must have swept her away again.

"Abbie," he managed to call one last time. "Abbie."

He tried to run toward the house, but the cold, the damp and the despair had drained the last of his strength. He stumbled and fell hard on his knees, unable to go forward.

"Come back to me, Abbie. Dear God in Heaven, let her come back to me."

***

Abbie tried to wake up. The hideously slow process terrified her, as if she were awakening from the sleep of the drugged.

Someone spoke, the voice far away, much too distant

for her to understand the words or recognize the speaker. She attempted to open her eyes but the lids refused. Her body remained inert in spite of her best effort to move. Within the fog of her mind, Abbie's thoughts grappled for reality. What was the last thing she remembered? A storm? Not exactly, but there had been a brilliant light and crash of thunder.

She tried to turn her head on the pillow to see if he slept soundly beside her.

"She moved!" someone said suddenly. "Get the doctor."

The voice was familiar, but not recognizable, not the voice she wanted to hear.

"Andrew?" she managed to whisper.

"She's trying to speak. Get the doctor! Abbie! Abbie, can you hear me?"

Movements by the side of her bed, rustling, someone grasping her hand. An unfamiliar voice, an unfriendly one, spoke.

"He's gone for the day."

Abbie felt something brush her arm, then it squeezed, squeezed, kept squeezing until her arm ached. She groaned. A rhythmic huff-huff then a soft hiss and the force eased.

"Her pressure's good, one-oh-two over seventy-eight."

Where am I?

"She's trying to speak and open her eyes. I saw her lips move!"

That voice. It was as familiar as her own but she couldn't remember...

"Try to keep in mind that she's been doing that off and on since she's been here. It means nothing."

"It does mean something! And I'm telling you, Fran, she's waking up. If you're not going to get Doctor Rhyss in here right now, I will."

Her hand was freed of the tight grip and she sensed movement from the owner of the voice.

"I'm telling you, he's gone for the day," said the other one, snappish and unfriendly. "Doctor Stuart's on call and I can get him, if you insist on it. But you're a nurse, Linda, and you know as well as I do all this mumbling and twitching is normal in a coma patient. It means nothing."

"I'm not listening to you," the first speaker responded angrily. The voice was near Abbie once more. "I'm going to believe the best. Abbie. Abbie, can you hear me? Honey, it's Lefty. If you wake up now, I'll let you call me Lefty in front of the administrator, and every doctor, nurse, and patient in this entire hospital. But you have to wake up. Let us know you're all right."

Abbie felt her hand being encased gently, lifted to a soft, warm cheek. She heard a sob, felt tears wet her fingers.

With extreme effort and more willpower than she thought she possessed just then, Abbie forced her eyelids to part. Only a slit, but she saw a fuzzy image peering into her face.

"Abbie!"

"Where…" Her voice came out a mere papery rasp. She tried again. "Where's Andrew?"

"I can't understand you, honey. Let me get you some water."

Her heavy lids closed without permission. She gathered her strength and tried once more. This time she was able to keep them open for a longer than just a few seconds. She saw a plastic cup with a flexible straw near her face.

"Take a sip, real slow."

Abbie drank just enough to moisten her lips and tongue. Anything beyond that would have taken more strength than she could muster. She closed her eyes again, and felt herself slipping close to unconsciousness.

"Andrew," she managed to say.

"Someone has gone to get the doctor for you," Lefty told her. "He'll be here in a jiffy."

The doctor. Good. Someone had gone to get Andrew. She managed a weak smile and let sleep overtake her again. Andrew would be here when she woke up, so everything was fine.

The effort to awaken and open her eyes the second time was much easier. Blearily she glanced around, found herself in a dark, cool room. Good. She was home with Andrew, in his bedroom, and all that hospital nonsense had been nothing more than a dream. She must have been scratched by the briars of the dementia rose again. She wondered how long she had been asleep.

Abbie turned her head to look at Andrew in the bed

beside her. He was not there. In fact, she was not lying in his bed; she was not even in his bedroom. Instead of Andrew's sleeping face, she encountered the soft, blinking lights of a machine and the awkward profile of an IV pole. She tracked the length of the tube with eyes and saw it connected to her arm.

A modern day hospital. Why was she here? And where was Andrew? Her stunned gaze probed the shadows of the room. She saw someone in the chair in the corner.

"Andrew?" Her voice was little more than a hoarse croak.

The person sat up suddenly then leaped out of the chair and hurried to her side. A soft light next to her bed flickered on. Lefty smiled down at her.

"You're finally awake! Thank God! How are you feeling, honey?"

Abbie stared at her friend. How did Lefty get here? How did Abbie get here? And where was Andrew? She looked beyond her friend, around the room, toward the open door, seeking him but not finding him.

"Where is he? Is he all right?"

"Who?"

"Andrew. Where is he?"

Lefty gave her an odd look. "Who's Andrew, honey?"

"Andrew Wade. Is he in another room? Is he all right?" She reached for Lefty's hand and clutched it weakly. "Tell me he's all right!"

Lefty seemed at a loss for words. She turned, picked

up the plastic cup from the rolling bed tray and offered Abbie water. Abbie turned her head away from the straw.

"I don't want a drink. I want Andrew!"

Slowly, Lefty set the cup back on the tray. She picked up a folded white washcloth and wet it from water the gray plastic pitcher. She gently patted its coolness against Abbie's forehead. Abbie weakly batted it away.

"Where's Andrew?" she pleaded. "I need to know if he's all right." She tried and failed to sit up. "Has something happened to him? Tell me, Lefty!"

Lefty carefully shook out the moist cloth and just as carefully refolded it. Her studied movements frightened Abbie.

"What has happened to him?"

Lefty looked at her.

"Abbie," she said slowly, quietly, "who is Andrew? I don't know him."

"But he was with me! We were together all this time. In that house, in those woods. He said there was no way out, but…but there must have been because here I am, and he was with me, and I would never have left without him." She reached out and grabbed the other woman's hand. "Where is he?"

Lefty took a deep breath. In the shadowy room, worry etched lines into her face. She seemed to ponder her words before she spoke.

"Abbie, you've been here in the hospital, comatose, for several weeks."

The words seemed to come from some far planet.

"That's impossible." Abbie tried to sit up and found that weakness kept her prone. "I have been with Andrew, in a strange place. I've been with him for weeks."

Lefty said nothing but Abbie saw clearly her friend did not believe her. She felt betrayed by the woman, angry that Lefty chose to doubt the truth. Maybe Lefty was jealous.

"We were together. Inseparable, except when he went into the forest to look for the dementia rose. We talked and laughed and made love..." She broke off, realizing that nothing she said would penetrate Lefty's skepticism. "We were together and I want him with me now. Something must have happened to him. He must not have followed me here."

At Lefty's silence Abbie burst into tears of frustration.

Lefty sat on the edge of the bed and put an arm around her. "Honey, I don't know what to tell you. Where did you meet Andrew? Is he someone from Dayton that you didn't tell me about? Or did you go into Tomville while I was gone and meet him? Abbie, please don't carry on like this. You're going to make yourself sick."

"His name is Andrew Wade. He lives in an old house in the woods..." She looked at Lefty, digging her fingers into the woman's hand. "Find him for me. Please!" She began crying again, head turned against the pillow, her body shaking.

She barely heard her friend say, "I can't let you continue to carry on like this, Abbie. I'm getting the nurse."

A short time later, a short gray-haired nurse with a face like the dried hull of a walnut entered the room. Without a word, she grimly gouged something into the IV. When it invaded Abbie's bloodstream, deep sleep swallowed her effortlessly.

The next time Abbie woke up, daylight streamed through the window. She was alone in the hospital room. The memory of Lefty's words trickled back into her mind: had she really been lying in this room, in a coma, for weeks? Had she been separated from Andrew for that long? Had they actually found their way out of that imprisoning world but somehow been separated, he into his world and she into hers? Surely God would not be cruel enough to let that happen! She closed her eyes, struggling to recollect anything after that but try as she might, she could not remember leaving him. She would never have left him of her own freewill. Never. Something else must have happened.

A rather short man with curly salt-and-pepper hair, round glasses, and heavy dark eyebrows came into her room.

"Good morning," he said crisply. The greeting seemed perfunctory, as if he was far busier than he wanted to be. "I'm Doctor Rhyss, in case you don't remember me." He checked her pulse, her heart and breathing, took her temperature and looked into her eyes. He made notations on the small computerized tablet in his hands. "So how are you feeling? Mind fuzzy, any anxiety, odd dreams?"

She gave him a sharp look. "Did Lefty say something to you?"

He raised his eyebrows. "Lefty?"

Abbie winced inwardly, remembering her promise never to reveal her friend's nickname. "Linda Richardson."

A small smile played across his stern features.

"Ah. That Lefty."

"Yes. And please don't tell her I let that old nickname slip."

"It'll be our little secret. Now, tell me about these dreams you've been having."

"So she did say something to you. You may rest assured, Doctor, that I've not been having dreams. Andrew and his world are as real as you and I."

"Um hmm," he said, entering the data in his small computer. He looked up. "Tell me about 'Andrew and his world.'"

As Abbie told the man about Andrew, the old house, and the creepy forest that surrounded him, she heard a story that, if she had not been so thoroughly convinced of its reality, would have been preposterous. She saw that very notion reflected in the doctor's eyes although he kept his face impassive.

"I see," he said as she finished. "And tell me again how you arrived in this strange place."

"I…I don't know. I just woke up with no memory of how I got there."

"I see. And you don't think it's a little strange that you don't remember arriving in those dark woods?"

Doctor Rhyss's blunt bedside manner left a lot to be

desired and she resisted his words.

"There are a number of reasons I wandered off and woke up in the woods. I'd been under a lot of stress on my job. I'd been driving for hours. I was exhausted. I was a little scared..." She broke off, knowing she sounded foolish and thinking she'd probably said too much, but added, "Stress causes a person to sleepwalk. I read that somewhere."

Surely a smirk hadn't just flickered across his expression, had it? She bristled even more.

"Yes, there are many articles online," he said, "but no amount of stress, or sleep-walking, is going to lead you into a...well, an alternate world where someone has lived for a century and where things 'magically' appear. These are called 'dreams,' or 'delusions' if you continue to believe in them when you're awake and lucid."

"So you're saying I'm delusional."

"Or perhaps you're not lucid, right now."

Abbie gave him a hard stare. "Doctor Rhyss, I assure you am fully awake, perfectly lucid, and completely without delusions. What I experienced really happened, and I will find Andrew again, whether he lives in the woods here in Arkansas, or in some 'alternate world' as you suggest."

He kept his face impassive and typed in something.

"All right, then," he said. "Your BP is good, temperature normal, eyes good and clear." He glanced up. "A nurse will be in shortly to draw blood." And with that, he went out of the room.

Later, a plump young woman with rosy cheeks and snug pencil skirt trotted into the room in three-inch heels. Her dark hair escaped whatever attempt had been made to give her a professional updo. Right then, she looked like a teenager playing at being an adult. With a bright smile, she effusively announced herself as Doctor Kirk from "upstairs." Abbie soon learned "upstairs" was Psychiatric Services.

The woman read questions from her own computer tablet, smiling merrily the entire time. When Abbie gave her the same information she'd given Doctor Rhyss, the woman nodded, made notes, acted as if she believed every word, though something told Abbie this young doctor believed nothing.

"I'm going to put you on a regime of meds. We'll start with Zyprexa and see—"

Abbie sat straight up in the bed. She felt a little lightheaded but figured that was because she'd had nothing to eat but clear broth, four crackers, and Jell-O as if she were on a diet for a weak stomach.

"You most certainly are not putting me on medication!" she said. "There is nothing wrong with me."

The smile never slid from the face, but it did take on a frozen quality. She met Abbie's eyes.

"But the meds will help control the—"

"If you say delusions or hallucinations, I'm going to scream. Andrew is not a delusion. He is real!" She swung her legs off the side of the bed. "I'm feeling just fine, and I see no reason to stay here. I want to go home."

"Where is home?" Doctor Kirk scanned through the screen, eyes darting back and forth in their sockets as if she were the one needing medication. "Ah. Dayton. Dayton? Ohio?"

Abbie said nothing.

"How did you get to Arkansas from Dayton, Ohio?"

"I drove."

"And you plan to drive back there?"

"I plan to find Andrew Wade, and the sooner you let me out of here, the sooner I can find him."

"Actually, we need to keep you here for a few days—"

Abbie shook her head as she got out of bed and began looking around for her clothes. "I'm leaving."

"Mrs. Matthews, I must advise you that you are in no condition—"

"It's Miss Matthews. And I must advise you, Doctor, that I am an attorney, so I'm well-schooled about my rights. I'm neither a danger to myself or anyone else. I have the right to refuse medical treatment—and that includes whatever medication you want to use on me. I have the right to leave this hospital against medical advice, and that's what I intend to do."

She picked up the telephone, punched number nine to get an outside line, and then called Lefty to come pick her up.

SEVENTEEN

As Abbie waited for Lefty to arrive, her agitation gradually gave way to something darker, something far more grim. What if the doctors had been right? What if the entire time she'd been with Andrew truly had been a sometimes frightening but magnificent dream as she recovered from stress-related exhaustion in a sterile hospital bed. What if Andrew Wade did not exist? Then he did not know her; he did not love her. Abbie had spent no joyous hours in his arms, neither in his home, nor in the terrifying forest. They did not witness the world around them change in sudden but often subtle ways.

It makes more sense than waking up in a forest on a cold day in August and finding a young man who had lived alone for over one hundred years, she thought, with a sudden deep sickness in her heart. It makes more sense than a cold, silent wind or a pantry that never depleted or a fire that never burned out.

As she stared outside the window at the parking lot glaring in the brittle sunlight, truth seemed to settle in heavy, relentless strokes. Andrew Wade, who had yearned for sunlight for decades, could not possibly exist. Everything she thought she had found: real love, honorable purpose, fulfilled life—none of it was real. It had been a dream. Every minute detail of it.

Abbie was sure her heart bled out its life with every slow, painful beat.

Behind her a man cleared his throat. She turned, saw

Doctor Rhyss. His face was as coldly impassive as ever.

"I understand you're leaving?"

"AMA."

A small upward tilt of his lips seemed less of a smile than a sneer.

"Against medical advice, yes, so Doctor Kirk informed me. Physically, you're still very weak. We don't know what happened to you, whether you fell and hit your head, or if you passed out and hit your head. Or if you went on a sleep-walking jaunt, as you cleverly surmised. It could happen again. Will you not reconsider staying for a few more days; let us keep an eye on you?"

"I want to go," Abbie murmured, but said nothing more. Right then, she feared she might break down in front of this man who had been instrumental in stripping away the loveliest moments of her life.

"Then I'll sign off on your case, and you're free to leave as soon as your ride gets here."

She nodded once and he left.

***

Lefty seemed to think Abbie was made of glass and drove toward home accordingly. Any other time, the constant stream of inane chatter which issued from her friend's mouth would have made Abbie feel like screaming. Today the words pounded against her depressed mood and fell hopelessly unheeded. She sat quietly and stared out the side window, noting the sun, the dancing heat waves ahead on the highway, listening to the sound of hissing tires on the hot pavement.

Through the buzz that was Lefty's cheerful voice, Abbie spoke her thoughts aloud.

"There was a time, not long ago, Andrew and I yearned for the heat and the light and the sound."

Lefty stopped talking abruptly.

"What did you say?"

Abbie continued, taking no notice of the question.

"It was cold when I got there. Dark and cold and windy, and Andrew said it was always like that. But inside the parlor the fire in the fireplace burned bright and warm. Andrew's bed was warm, too, and being in his arms..." Her voice broke.

Lefty shot a quick look at her then directed her attention back to the road. She slowed the car to a crawl.

"Are you feeling all right, Abbie? Do I need to stop?"

Abbie rose from her grief long enough to say, "I suppose I'm fine."

Lefty stared hard at her.

"Really," Abbie added. "Fine. Please just drive. You're holding up traffic."

Lefty glanced in the rearview mirror. "There's not a single car behind me."

"Well there will be if you don't drive. Please, Lefty, just...go. I'm fine."

The other woman kept transferring her attention between Abbie and the road, but finally settled her gaze ahead and increased their speed. Abbie closed her eyes against the brightness of the sun, loving it and hating it at the same time. She would have loved it thoroughly if Andrew were with her to enjoy it; she loathed it now because he was not here. She gladly would embrace the dim chill of his world if she could be with him once again.

"How about a root beer float?" Lefty's voice cut into her thoughts. "I remember how you used to love 'em."

"No, thanks."

"C'mon. You've had nothing but a feeding tube, then hospital's bland food diet. I'm losing weight just watching you. Let's have a root beer float."

Abbie heard the underlying worry in her friend's tone. She made an attempt at courtesy. "If you want."

"I want."

They stopped at a drive-in on the main drag in Tomville. Lefty ordered two extra-large floats. Abbie drank about a fourth of hers, then put it in the cup holder. She felt nauseous. Lefty, happily sipping her own, drove blithely toward home.

"When we get to my house," she said, "I want you to lie down."

"OK."

"And I'm going to fix some of my auntie's famous chicken soup. She swore it cured everything from pneumonia to prickly heat."

"That'll be nice."

Lefty hesitated a moment before continuing, "I have to be at the hospital tomorrow, so I got the new John Grisham novel for you to read, and a couple of magazines. And I bought a TV Guide in case you'd rather watch television. Oh, and I rented some DVDs, if that's what you'd rather do."

In spite of the dull ache in her middle, Abbie tried to respond with the gratitude her friend deserved.

"Thanks, Lefty. That's fine."

Again they rode in silence. Lefty turned off the secondary highway and onto the gravel road leading to her house.

"Say, you didn't drink much of your float, Abbie. Didn't you like it?"

Abbie picked up the big Styrofoam cup and took an obligatory sip.

"Yes," she said. "It's good."

"You all right? You hurt anywhere?"

How could she hurt anywhere when she was hollow inside? There was nothing left to feel but this extreme emptiness.

"I'm fine. Stop worrying and fussing."

They jounced along the gravel road.

"Well, I do worry about you, Abbie. That's what friends do."

Lefty steered the car into her driveway and stopped

beneath the huge maple tree.

"I'm sorry," Abbie said.

Lefty turned off the engine and looked at her for a long time. Abbie turned from the probing eyes. The nearby woods trapped her gaze. The memory of Andrew, of that last time they made love ascended into her mind with such swiftness and force that she reeled back in the seat.

"Abbie!" Lefty gasped. "Are you all right?"

Andrew's touch still seemed to linger on her skin; his kiss still burned her lips. She closed her eyelids and could see his dark eyes, full of love and passion and honor. She clutched her hands to her chest to halt the shattering of her heart. She bent forward, keening inside herself like a lost child.

Lefty touched her shoulder. "Abbie. Oh, Abbie."

"I miss him," she sobbed. "Oh God, I miss him so much!"

"Cry it all out, honey," she counseled, rubbing Abbie's back.

Abbie knew she could never cry out all her grief, but sobbing seemed only to underscore the wretchedly hopeless state of affairs. She sat up and tried to dry her tears.

"Feel better?" Lefty asked.

Abbie nodded, though she did not feel better. She was in love with a delusion, an imaginary man. Feeling better seemed impossible.

"I'm fine." She wiped her eyes with the heels of her hands. "I'm sorry. I'm sorry I'm such a crybaby."

"You have nothing to apologize for. I just wish there was something I could do for you."

Lefty got out the car then opened Abbie's door.

"Come on, honey," she coaxed, taking her arm as if Abbie was in invalid. "Let's go inside."

Abbie realized just how lucky she was to have such a friend. How many people would give their time and open their home to someone as foolishly sad as Abigail Matthews, yet expect nothing in return?

"Thank you for being such a good friend."

"You know if the shoe was on the other foot, you'd do the same thing for me."

She hugged Lefty hard then allowed herself be steered toward the house. In the living room, the blue-checked sofa was ready with a soft, fat pillow and a cool sheet. A fan sat on an end table and the breeze it created fluttered the flounced edge of the crisp white pillowcase. The quiet white noise it hummed was comforting.

"I thought you might prefer not being alone right now," Lefty said, "but if you'd rather lie down in the bed upstairs, I have it ready."

"No, this is fine. Thank you."

Abbie wearily lay down without coaxing and closed her eyes. She ached all over, as if she had run a great distance. She awakened to the odor of cooking food. She heard and smelled these things with the same indifference that she saw daylight dwindle into dusk beyond the window and felt the fan stir air across her face. At that moment, she could have been lying in a stark room with no sound, sight, smell or feel in it. She closed her eyes again.

In the darkness behind her lids she clearly saw Andrew. She noted his quirked brow and quizzical smile, smelled the clean, masculine scent of his skin, heard the soft rumble of his voice, felt the caress of his fingertips against her cheek.

"Here you go! Good for what ails you." Lefty's voice broke into her thoughts, shattering them.

Abbie opened her eyes just as Lefty settled a food tray on the coffee table in front of the sofa. The tray held a blue goblet of ice water and a bowl with a generous serving of fragrant chicken soup. She had no desire to eat; she felt no thirst, but when she glanced up at her friend, saw the deep concern that continued to fill in Lefty's expression, Abbie tried to cast aside her despair.

She sat up and did her best to give her friend a cheery smile.

"It looks good, Lefty. Thanks."

Lefty's face relaxed. "Great. I'll get myself a bowl of it and join you."

Abbie nibbled a chunk of gently seasoned chicken and forced herself to swallow. The food was tasteless in her mouth. She sipped the water, took another bite. A minute later her friend returned, carrying her own soup bowl.

Lefty's voice rose and fell as she chattered. In spite of her best efforts, Abbie once again found herself unable to center on the smallest thread of conversation. She could only think of what she had lost by simply waking up. Why had her brain conjured such a futile dream?

She reminded herself only weak or confused people indulged in tender emotions. She had hardened herself, and being tough and unbreakable enabled her to defend miscreants and predators without a second thought. But that wasn't accurate, was it? Abbie Matthews had harbored weakness, an inability to decide what was best. She'd had qualms and tender feelings just like anyone. When that innocent child lost her life to one of Abbie's freed villains, Abbie had chosen to seek a new path. Somehow, in the wending way of destiny, the new path included love. What destiny failed to understand was reality.

She would never love anyone but Andrew Wade, but he wasn't real.

An unexpected mirthless laugh erupted from her.

"The day I met him, Andrew staunchly declared that I was unreal, some kind of delusional vision, a product of 'brain fever.' He emphatically told me to vanish! I believe his exact words were 'You do not exist. Begone!'" Again she laughed without happiness. "And all that time it was he who was a product of my imagination." She met Lefty's somewhat bewildered gaze. "How ironic is that?"

"I...I don't know what to say, Abbie," she murmured. "I wish I could do something...I just feel so responsible for all this."

Abbie's spoon clattered into her bowl. "How could you be responsible for any of it, Lefty? You've been nothing but a good friend to me."

"You came to me for help. You were a guest in my house. I should have been here for you instead of at the stupid conference in Savannah—"

"You had a commitment! And you'd made it long before I came crying to you."

"But still...I saw how distraught you were, Abbie. I should've stayed and been here for you, as a support and comfort the way friends are supposed to."

"So let's assume you cancelled your commitment. You stayed here and played mother hen to me. How could you have stopped whatever it was that happened?"

"I would have been here with you when you passed out instead of you lying there, alone, in a coma. I could have gotten you to the hospital as soon as it happened. My God, Abbie. You could have died!" She shuddered. "I'd asked you to call me if you needed anything and when you didn't, I assumed you were getting that much needed respite we had talked about. I didn't want to interrupt you with a call...especially as you had asked me not to." She looked up, eyes swimming, expression agonized. "I thought it was best to leave you alone. I never once imagined you might be sick or injured. My little home here is so safe and quiet and peaceful—I just never considered it." Her voice broke. "I'll never, ever forgive myself." She covered her face with her hands.

Abbie felt something stir inside her, something living and viable and precious. Her friend's pain was so strong in the room she could feel its echo in herself. She put aside her nearly untouched bowl and knelt on the floor beside her friend's chair. She laid one hand on Lefty's arm.

"It's all right," she said. "I don't blame you. Not for a second! You didn't know. You couldn't know."

"But I should have—"

Abbie squeezed the other woman's hand. "No, you shouldn't have. It's all over now, and I'm fine."

"You're not fine!" Lefty's voice cracked. "I can see plain as day that you're heart-broken and despondent. Even more than when you first arrived. Maybe if I'd been here and got you help sooner, you'd not have slipped into that world—"

"I'd never have met Andrew."

Lefty hesitated then nodded. "If you want to put it that way."

She forced herself to smile. "Besides, I had the best... dream I've ever had while I was out. It's something dear and wonderful that I'll carry with me all my life."

Abbie knew how foolish the words sounded; she knew that no one, not even Lefty whom she loved like a sister could ever understand the love she'd felt for Andrew Wade, real or imaginary. At least now she knew what the love of a man for a woman should be.

"I want you to let go of your guilt, Lefty. I don't regret a moment of that dream."

"Even the frightening parts?"

Abbie smiled. "Even those."

For the next few days, Abbie rested. She pondered her life; she meditated the state of her heart and spirit. One thing she had learned from her dream was to forgive her foolish choices and grave errors in judgment. She had learned from those mistakes; she could move forward into a life that had meaning and hope. In addition, she discovered she was a woman capable of great tenderness and passion, two traits she never knew she possessed. She also knew criminal law practice was not in her future, but right then, she didn't know what was. She had much to think about. Memories of her time with Andrew kept returning but she resolutely shoved them back. She must move forward, not wallow in a dream.

One evening she and Lefty took a walk along the dirt road that cut through the nearby farms and neighborhoods.

"Exercise is good for the body and soul," Lefty told her, and Abbie agreed. The walk was more of a stroll than a brisk jaunt, but it elevated her heart rate and brought the sweat just the same. It was nice to watch dusk gently sweep away daylight and feel the cool change night brought to the air.

"We must do this every day," Lefty declared when they returned.

"It was nice. But now I'm dusty and sweaty and need a shower."

"I'll fix us some sangria, and after we've gotten cleaned up, we can enjoy it on the front porch."

"Lovely," Abbie said, going up the stairs. Nice how her fear of night beyond the walls of the house no longer kept her indoors.

Upstairs, after her shower, Abbie slid into a thin, cotton nightdress, but the evening air was cooler now and she needed a robe, something lightweight and comfy. She pilfered through the large closet, hoping to unearth something Lefty or even Lefty's Aunt Sally might have hanging there and discovered, leaning against the back wall of the closet, the painting she had bought at the Lost Treasures Shop. She had completely forgotten about it until that moment.

Lefty must have banished the murky depiction out of sight. Certainly there was nothing bright and inspiring about the painting to encourage the woman to display it in her lovely, cozy home. Abbie pulled it from the closet, wanting to see all its shadowy details again, see if she could figure out what had drawn her to buy the thing in the first place. She laid it flat on top of the bed and looked down at it.

She eyed the lowering, threatening storm clouds, the overgrown forest and tangle of bushes bent in the wind, the dark, dismal house. It was all there, all familiar.

"Oh my God!"

She stared at Andrew's home, the place where she had lived and loved him, the place she yearned to be. The dream, held at bay for the past several minutes, came crashing back into her mind with a force that buckled her knees. With a clarity unknown until that moment, Abbie realized her dream really had been just that, nothing more than a fantasy her mind had woven, using this grim painting as its genesis. With a cry of anguish and despair, she fell across the painting.

"Andrew! Oh God, I've lost you. I've really, really lost you."

Lefty's footsteps pounded up the stairs and down the hallway.

"Abbie! What's wrong? Are you all right?" She sat on

the bed next to her. "Honey, what...?"

"There really is no hope of it being real," Abbie said in a strangled voice. "I know it's all over."

She remained prostrate across the painting, sobbing until her throat was raw while a worried Lefty sat helplessly beside her, rubbing her back.

Lefty's voice was as soft as if she spoke to mourners at a funeral. "Is there anything I can do?"

But Abbie couldn't respond right then. She lay, wilted and defeated, tears leaking silently. At one point she actually thought she heard his voice calling her. She cursed such a foolish imagination. It was her ability to imagine things that had created the amazing man in the first place.

After what seemed an hour of agony she began to gather her emotions and temper her heartbeat. How many more breakdowns must she endure before they went away? She sat up with tortuous sluggishness and stared down at the painting, at her teardrops on the cracked paint, feeling as though her very soul had shattered.

"I know it's over," she repeated. "My brain conjured the whole thing because of this...this painting." She shoved it off the bed and it thudded to the floor. "In my heart, in the deepest part of it, I hoped that, maybe, somehow, somewhere, I'd be able to find that gloomy old house again. I'd find that it was real, that Andrew was an actual living, breathing man, and that I had lived with him. But now...now I know for certain this house does not exist... and neither does Andrew."

She drew in a deep, shuddering breath "I made the whole thing up because..." she glared down at the painting and through clenched teeth, finished, "because of this damned picture!"

She gave the frame a hard kick and the painting sailed under the bed, out of sight. She squeezed her eyes shut for a minute then opened them and looked at her friend still sitting quietly on the edge of the bed.

"I just had to have that horrible old painting," she muttered. "Then I dreamed about the blasted thing. Made it all up in the longest sleep of my life. I could've just as well watched something like it on the television and saved myself a lot of pain." Her voice cracked and she cleared her throat. "Damn!"

"I'll take it," Lefty said, getting down on her hands and knees to pull it out from under the bed. "In fact, I'll throw it in the trash."

"No," Abbie told her. "I need to work through this, so I'll keep the painting for a while."

EIGHTEEN

A week later Abbie loaded her suitcases into the Lexus just before sunrise. Lefty would be leaving for her shift at the hospital soon. The morning air was sweet with just the hint of the promise of autumn in a few weeks.

The two women stood in the dim greenness of the front yard as daylight inched its way across the landscape. Lefty wore pink scrubs; she was working in the NICU that day. Abbie was in a pair of white cotton shorts and a blue tank top. No more designer dresses and heels for traveling. She decided she liked dressing down.

"I wish you would stay longer," Lefty told her. "We spent so little time together."

Abbie closed the trunk and smiled wistfully at her friend. "I know. Me, too. But I need to get back and start my job search."

"And you're sure you want to leave criminal law?"

"I already have, up here." She tapped her temple. "And here, where it counts." She placed her palm over her heart. "All I need to do when I get back is put it on paper and make it official. You and I both know I can't go back to what I was before. Life is too short and too precious to live in pursuit of disastrous decisions and the almighty dollar."

Lefty grinned. "You don't know how good it sounds to hear you say that."

Abbie smiled back. "Ah, well. I know what's important now, and I won't soon forget it. And I'll tell you something else. All this time I thought it was that job that gave me power, but it didn't."

"Of course not. You're a strong woman, Abbie, you always have been. So...do you know for sure what you'll do when you get home?"

Abbie took a deep breath and let it out slowly. The sun silently scooted above the horizon. A soft breeze lifted a tendril of her pale hair and tickled her face with it. She brushed it back.

"I'll find something. I have money set aside, and if I get a less expensive apartment and be satisfied with the closets full of clothes I have already, I'll do all right. Who knows? Maybe I'll start my own practice. Or maybe I'll do something totally unrelated to law."

Lefty seemed to hesitate a moment before she said, "What about...?" Her gaze drifted to the painting Abbie had placed in the backseat. "Are you sure you—"

"I'll be fine," Abbie interrupted. She did not want to think about the painting, Andrew or her dream. She wanted to get on with reality. "It's just going to take some time, like everything else."

"Don't let anything get you down, Abbie."

Abbie smiled again and hugged the woman.

"How can anything get me down for long when I have a pal like you, huh? Thanks for listening to me, for taking care of me. I appreciate you more than you know."

"As Aunt Sally would have said, 'Pshaw, what are

friends for?'"

Abbie got into her car. She slid on smoky sunglasses and looked at her friend through the open door. "You will come to visit me in Dayton, won't you?"

"Of course. And you better come here again, too. Three years is too long."

"It is, isnt it?"

"E-mail me more often, would you?" Lefty said.

"I will. I promise."

Abbie closed the car door, waved a final good-bye to Lefty and pulled out of the driveway. As she drove along the dusty gravel road to the highway, she asked herself how many people were lucky enough to have a good friend like the one she just left.

She turned east onto the highway, lowered the sun visor against the glare and adjusted the rearview mirror. As she did so her glance fell on the reflected image of the painting in the backseat. She decided at that moment she was going to get rid of it at the first opportunity.

Her first opportunity happened about two hours later when she detoured off the main highway into the small town of Gemstone to find a restroom. As she drove back to the highway, she spotted a red and white hand-painted sign in front of a large, red barn-like structure. The sign announced that the building was the Gemstone Thrift Store. Below, in small, uneven black letters that seemed to have been added as an afterthought, were the words "donations accepted." Abbie assumed donations meant food, clothing or money. She hoped the request included dark, depressing paintings.

Ten minutes later she had persuaded a large, red-faced woman into taking the painting, although the woman had gruffly told her, "Ain't nobody in their right mind who'd want that thing."

Back on the main highway, Abbie told herself that getting rid of the painting was a good move. As far as she could see, keeping it would serve only to remind her that the time she spent Andrew had been merely a by-product of a concussion. Maybe its absence, please God, would bring her some relief.

But it did not. Instead, within a few minutes she felt worse than ever. A peculiar sense that she had left something crucial undone haunted her like a restless spirit. Three times she slowed the car and almost u-turned to go back to the flea market and retrieve the painting. She told herself over and over that to even think of returning was both foolish and futile. What possible good could be served by having that painting where she could see it day after day, reminding her of what she would never have?

"It was just a dream, all in my head," she muttered.

She turned on the radio and fiddled with the buttons in an unsuccessful search, trying to find a station that played anything other than country music. Blast it all, she needed something to listen to so she wouldn't have to think for a while, but she sure didn't want to hear anything to make her sadder than she was already. She didn't even have any disks for the CD player. Sighing with resignation, Abbie punched off the radio.

She knew the sooner she overcame her dream, the

sooner she could get on with her life. After all, she was intelligent and resourceful; she had a sense of humor and playfulness. She thought she was reasonably attractive and tried to take good care of herself.

I sound like an ad for the personals: SWF seeking love with the mysterious man of my dreams.

As the morning progressed, Abbie felt the first drags of sleepiness begin to settle into her brain. Her early departure seemed to be catching up. Maybe she wasn't fully recovered from whatever had landed her in the hospital. When she spotted a small roadside café/convenience store, she pulled into the nearly empty parking lot. Inside the building, the air smelled of a poorly ventilated kitchen and stale air conditioning. Somewhere a radio pricked the air with bluegrass music. With a lively fiddle and banjo, at least it wasn't depressing.

Abbie bought a cup of coffee and a bagel at the counter and sat down in a worn vinyl booth. She was one of three people in the store. The clerk behind the food counter paid scant attention to her and the tubby, dark-haired man behind the cash register near the door seemed intent on cleaning his fingernails with the blade of his pocketknife. Abbie looked away, repressing a shudder.

She finished the coffee and bagel and for a few minutes she sat where she was, allowing the resurgence of energy to hit her bloodstream. After a bit she got up to leave, but as she walked toward the door her glance fell on the display of hand-made candles and soaps. The simple white label read Sumac Ridge Natural Products.

Her heart leaped like a trout, and a shiver skimmed down her spine. Sumac Ridge was where Andrew had said he lived. Until Abbie met him, she had never heard of the place. Was it a weird coincidence that she conjured it in her dream?

She turned to the girl at the food counter and dipped her head toward the soaps and candles.

"Is Sumac Ridge a real place?"

The girl shrugged. "I dunno. I never heard of it."

She looked past Abbie at the fat man who still whittled cheerfully on his fingernails.

"Hey, Leo, is there such a place as Sumac Ridge where these soaps are from?"

Leo looked up, scrunched his face in thought and held the knife blade unmoving in his fingers.

"Not sure," he said. "Haven't lived here but a coupla years, but the candle maker is a native. She could tell you."

A fire lit in Abbie's belly.

"Does she live nearby?"

The man shook his big head and started shaving his thumbnail. "Lives back in the hills somewhere, but I don't know where exactly." He looked up, squinted his eyes at Abbie. "Whyn't you call her? Phone number is on the label."

Abbie grabbed up a bar of lavender soap, paid him for it, thanked him for his help and hurried to her car. She punched in the numbers on her cell phone, mentally rushing the candle maker to answer. Abbie was so breathless that when the woman did answer, she practically gasped out her question.

"Is Sumac Ridge an actual place, or is it a name you made up for your company?"

The woman's laugh was sweet and soft.

"Well, hello, to you, too," she said in a quiet drawl, then added. "And yes, Sumac Ridge is real. As real as Little Rock or Fort Smith, and if you ask me, a whole lot more appealing."

"Would please you tell me where it is?"

"Of course, honey, why do you want to know? There's not a blessed thing up here but me and Granny and my little factory."

"I…I've heard about Sumac Ridge. I need…I want to see it."

There was a brief pause.

"Well, you're more than welcome, of course. And I'll even give you a tour of my business." She laughed again. "I don't get many visitors, so it will be nice having you here. I'll give you some sweet tea, and we'll visit. Tell me where you're coming from, and I'll give you directions how to get here from there."

Abbie told her the name of the roadside store, and with a shaking hand, she wrote down directions the woman gave her.

***

Sumac Ridge Natural Products was run by Grace Ethridge who lived on a rutted dirt lane that made Lefty's gravel road look like a superhighway. Grace's driveway climbed and curled up a steep hill then leveled as it reached her place at the summit.

An abundance of bright red zinnia, golden dahlias and orange marigolds surrounded a weathered gray little dwelling. Beyond the house sat another weathered building, shady and just as flower-banked as the house, but with a decidedly commercial air about it. Beside the door a carved wooden sign read Sumac Ridge Natural Products Welcome, Visitors! It was to that building Abbie drove. She parked in a small, graveled space near the door.

A comfortably warm breeze met Abbie as she got out of the car on the tree-studded hilltop and walked to the door. The welcome thrum of a noisy air conditioner promised coolness inside, but the brightly lit interior proved to be uncomfortably warm as Abbie walked in. And no wonder. Several vats, apparently full of hot wax and fat, sat on two industrial sized stainless steel stoves. The scents of cinnamon, patchouli, rose and lavender mingled with the scent of wax and oil. Soap and candle making was not only a warm business but fragrant as well. Abbie inhaled deeply.

"Welcome!" called the slender woman who approached from the back of the building. She wore a thin camisole of white eyelet, a flowing red skirt and wide-strapped leather sandals. Her long, gray-streaked blonde hair was pulled back neatly into a low ponytail, and she did not wear a dot of makeup. Abbie thought her understated appearance carried a beauty all its own.

The other woman wiped her perspiring forehead with her arm and smiled at Abbie.

"Welcome to Sumac Ridge Natural Products. I'm Grace Ethridge." She held out her left hand.

Abbie introduced herself and shook hands, charmed by the direct simplicity of this woman.

"Everything we make here is all natural," Grace told her, sweeping her hand toward her little factory. "We use essential oils and vegetable fat, nothing animal. Would you like a tour of the place?"

Abbie glanced around.

"This is very unique," she replied. "And I'd like to see it, but maybe you can show me around a little later. Right now, I need to ask you about Sumac Ridge."

Grace quirked one eyebrow, a gesture that clutched Abbie's heart with memory. How many times had she seen Andrew lift an eyebrow in just that way when he was curious or skeptical?

"All right. Ask me anything."

"Is Sumac Ridge really real?" Abbie blurted. The expression on the other woman's face caused her to rephrase her question. "I mean, is there an actual place, a town or something, called 'Sumac Ridge', or did you just make up the name for your company?"

Grace spread her arms, her expression still a mixture of curiosity and kindness.

"This is Sumac Ridge. That is, this range of hills through here. It's always been called Sumac Ridge—at least as far as I know. There's no town of Sumac Ridge. There used to a town down the road a piece called Smith, but the trains stopped running through there, so it's just a ghost town now."

"But Sumac Ridge had people living here a hundred years ago?"

"Oh, sure. Even longer ago than that. Listen, hon, it's so hot in here. How about I get us some sweet tea? I have some in the back."

Without waiting for a reply she took off toward the back the building, the soles of her sandals hissing against the cement floor and her red skirt flowing around her calves as she walked. Abbie waited impatiently the two minutes it took Grace Ethridge to bring the tea, but she accepted the tall, cold glass gratefully and swigged from its icy contents.

"That's wonderful! Thank you. You were saying that people lived on Sumac Ridge many years ago."

Grace nodded. She wiped the beads of tea off her upper lip with the tip of her index finger.

"It's not much of a community now, as you can see. Folks left the Ridge years and years ago, to find work in the towns or other parts of the country. We're pretty remote and isolated, as you could tell just by driving up here. Industry never came this close, and I can't say that I'm sorry. I like it wild and untouched like this. There are the lakes and resorts and tourist attractions, but if you want the real Ozarks, Abbie, this is it."

Abbie nodded, but she wondered how anyone could prefer living as far away from civilization as Grace did.

Unless, of course, that person had a companion like Andrew Wade. In which case, she could live on the moon, and happily. But only if Andrew was with her.

"Have you been here long?" she asked and politely sipped the tea.

Grace nodded and laughed. "You could say that. Six generations of my family were born on the Ridge. I left to do that popular thing in the 'seventies: 'find myself'. After about twenty-five years, I realized I'd left myself right here so I came home."

Abbie stared at her. "You left, and came back?"

Grace offered a beatific smile. "So many people ask me that, and with that same I-can't-believe-it voice. But, yes, I came back to my home. And I started my own business."

"My goodness," Abbie said faintly. She had thought Lefty lived in the back of beyond, but her friend lived in the middle of Times Square compared to Grace Ethridge. "Six generations, you said?"

"Yes. And unfortunately, I'm the only descendant of my family still living on the Ridge. Here, let me show you around the factory."

She put down her empty tea glass on a nearby table and took Abbie's arm, steering her toward the inner workings of her industry. "I do most of the work myself, but I have a couple of girls from Peace Valley to come in a day or two a week. Peace Valley is a little town about twenty miles from here."

Although Abbie found the factory both unique and

interesting, her mind was not on the tour Grace seemed intent on giving. She tagged along with her hostess—she had no choice, seeing that Grace kept a friendly arm linked through hers. The other woman clearly loved her work and loved to share it. Abbie forced herself to take an interest, but she waited for the right opportunity to ask the question that burned inside her. Finally, back at the table where the tour had started, Abbie sat down the sweating tea glass. In her hands she held a fat, smooth sandalwood candle Grace had given her.

Nervously stroking the smooth wax and feeling both foolish and hopeful, Abbie cleared her throat and asked, "Have you ever heard of a man from Sumac Ridge named Andrew Wade?"

Grace, who had been lovingly but sadly examining a candle with a crack in it, laid it in a basket with other broken pieces. She looked at Abbie in some surprise.

"Why, yes. He was my great-great uncle."

NINETEEN

The fragrant candle she held slipped from Abbie's hand and hit the cement floor with a dull thud. She stared wordlessly at Grace who retrieved it and put in back in her nerveless hands.

"How did you hear about our mysterious ancestor? Granted his story was the talk of the Ridge a hundred years ago, but I didn't know anyone outside the family had ever even heard of him. Unless..." She grinned broadly, clasped Abbie's upper arm in a friendly clutch. "Unless you're a cousin. Oh, what fun! I thought our clan had just about died out with only Susan Wade McLeod and I left and both of us without a child."

Grace's words seemed to run together senselessly.

Abbie licked dry lips and managed to say, "Tell me about him."

"About Great-uncle Andrew?"

Abbie nodded.

"Well, I suppose you know what happened to him, so what else do you want to know?"

Abbie closed her eyes and took a deep breath, trying to quiet her thrumming, pounding blood.

"All of it," she said, opening her eyes. "Everything you know about him. What he looked like, the kind of person he was, did he have children...anything, everything."

"You do know the legend, don't you?"

Abbie thought her heart was going to jump out of her chest and her brain would explode. She wanted to scream from her need to know, but she forced her voice to remain quiet and calm as she replied.

"Tell me. Tell me everything."

"So you don't know the legend?" Grace asked. "I would think that, since you're family, you'd have heard the story."

Here Grace paused. In Abbie's impatience to know the truth, she did not want to deceive the woman, but she felt the rise of desperation.

"Will you tell me about him even if I'm not family?"

"Of course! But aren't you a relative?"

"No," she replied faintly. "Please. Tell me about him."

Grace's happy expression slipped a little. "I would have loved to meet a long lost cousin," she replied wistfully. "We could have—"

Abbie had to bite the inside of both lips to keep from screaming.

"Grace, what is the legend? I want to know all about Andrew."

"Are you a writer or journalist or something?" Grace asked, narrowing her eyes slightly. "Because I don't want my family exploited for some story."

"No. I'm just a…" What could she say? Just a friend, just a lover of a man who may have been your great-uncle? "I'm just interested."

"A stranger who is more than just a little interested in an old family legend? Seems odd to me," Grace said, tilting her head and gazing at Abbie. "But," she said, after a moment and throwing her arms wide, "it's not a deep, dark, secret skeleton hidden away in the closet. Just a peculiar story. And it probably isn't true." She smiled. "By the way, would you like more iced tea? It's so hot today—"

"No!" Abbie barked. "I mean…please, just…that is…" She forced herself to take a deep breath. "No, thank you. No more tea. I just want to know the story." She offered a smile. "Please?"

Grace looked at her for a moment longer, as if she thought Abbie wasn't quite altogether in her right mind, but finally she shook her head and blinked.

"All right, then." She leaned her backside against the table and loosely folded her arms across her chest. "Well, the legend goes that my great-uncle was something of a paragon in the community. He was smart and kind and he loved the people here on the Ridge. In those days, hardly anyone around here had money, but he worked from daybreak to dark for anyone who'd hire him so he could earn enough to go away and study medicine. He had only a year or so left in his training when, one day in August, he left home, heading for the train station and never arrived. They looked for him for weeks, but he had vanished without a trace."

As Grace related the same facts Andrew once shared, Abbie felt the blood drain from her vitals. A high-pitched hum buzzed in her ears as the room shifted and dimmed.

Grace, still happily chattering about the possibility of Andrew simply going for pastures far greener than the Ridge offered, noticed Abbie's face and broke off in mid-word.

"You're white as a sheet, hon! Here, sit down quick."

She dragged an old wooden chair across the floor just as Abbie's legs buckled.

"Oh, my goodness!" Grace looked toward the back of the factory and called, "Granny! Quick, bring a glass of water and a cool cloth."

Her long, full skirt made a bright puddle of fabric against the gray floor as she sank to her knees next to Abbie. Gone was the bright smile and laughing eyes, replaced by genuine concern and careful watchfulness. She patted Abbie's wrists gently.

"Breathe deeply, darlin'. If you feel like you're going to faint, put your head between your knees."

Abbie breathed deeply and blew it out noisily, just as she had learned in her stress management class a few months ago. She leaned back in the hard chair and took another deep breath. How had she known all these details of Andrew Wade's life to dream about him when she'd never been here before today? She knew, without a doubt, she had never heard this family legend from anyone other than Andrew. Was it possible her dream had not been a dream, after all, but a very real encounter with the legend himself? More importantly, did Andrew Wade continue to exist somehow, somewhere, still young and vibrant and alive as she had last seen him?

Grace had ceased to pat Abbie's wrists and now stroked

her hands. She looked anxiously into Abbie's eyes.

"It's this awful humidity," she said. "And sometimes the smell of the essential oils can get so strong in this damp air...Granny, can you hurry with that water?" She half-stood and looked toward the back of the building then turned back to Abbie. "Are you feeling any better, hon?"

Abbie tried to take slow, deep breaths, but her heart raced like a runaway train. She moistened her dry lips.

"Andrew is...was real?" she asked, searching Grace's wide eyes. "Did you ever see him...I mean a picture?"

Grace puckered her forehead, tilted her head slightly and asked, "Why are you so interested in him? It's just a story, you know."

When Abbie just looked at her, pleading with her eyes, the other woman gave her a half-smile and lifted her shoulders.

"Well, it's not my place to judge another. I think there's a photograph of him in an album back at the house."

Abbie leaned forward and clutched Grace's hand. "I have to see it. That picture. Please."

"I can get it for you, but I don't understand—"

"Please." She squeezed the other woman's fingers tightly. "Please."

Grace patted the hand that gripped hers. "All right. Don't get yourself all worked up again. I'll run to the house and get it." She stood up, glanced toward the back of the shop. "Here comes Granny with some cold water and a damp cloth. You sit right there, and I'll be back in a jiffy."

Abbie leaned back in the chair, closed her eyes.

She asked herself again if it could be true. And what would she do if the man in the picture turned out to be the Andrew Wade in her dream? Check herself into an institution?

"Because I must be insane," she muttered. "Totally and completely out of my mind."

Dimly she registered approaching footsteps, a dragging, shuffling sound of an old person. When the steps halted, she opened her eyes and saw a tall, icy glass of water being offered to her. The hand holding the glass was worn and gnarled with age. On it was a scarlet crescent-shaped birthmark, a mark Abbie had seen before, and not so long ago.

She raised her eyes and met the rheumy gaze of the old woman from the Lost Treasures shop.

"You!" She stared at the old woman whom Grace had called Granny, probing the old eyes for some unspoken knowledge. "You sold me the painting!"

Granny simply looked at her.

"You know about that house in the painting, don't you? You know where it is; you know where Andrew is, don't you? Tell me!" She grabbed the old woman's forearm. "Please, tell me where he is!"

"Have this water," the old woman said, unconcerned that Abbie held her arm like a vise. "You're overheated. Come now, and drink this. And I have a nice damp rag for your face." She held up a snowy white cloth. "You'll feel better."

The door to the shop opened and closed noisily, and Grace rushed to them.

"Thank you, Granny," she said. She took the glass and held it nearer to Abbie. "Here, hon."

Abbie took it without shifting her gaze from Granny.

While both women watched, she sipped the cold water, felt the wetness refresh her parched lips and mouth. Granny offered the cloth and Abbie accepted it wordlessly. She patted it against her cheeks, and then buried her hot face in the cool, damp cleanness of it. It smelled of sweet fresh air.

"Thanks," she murmured as she straightened and patted the back of her neck with it. "Thank you," she said again as she handed the cloth back to the old woman.

"Do you feel better now?" Grace asked.

"A little."

"Thank goodness. The heat in the factory can be overpowering sometimes." Grace glanced at Granny. "Thank you for helping." She turned to Abbie. "This is a photo album, full of pictures of my family." It was quite old and bound in dark green leather. "And here is the only photograph of Andrew Wade that I've ever seen." Grace released it to Abbie's eager hands. "This was taken the summer he disappeared." Grace rested her long index finger on a small, yellowed photograph.

With her heart nearly bursting from her ribcage, Abbie stared down at the familiar face of the man she loved.

She pressed her fingers against her lips to keep from crying out. He had posed without smiling, but Abbie saw the depth of compassion in his eyes, the underlying humor. There was his dear rumpled hair that always seemed in need of combing, his straight nose and firm chin, the finely chiseled lips that had caused her to burn for more than just his kisses.

She snapped her head around once more to face the old woman who held the answers.

"You sent me to him in the first place, and now you know where he is," she asked again. "Please, please! Take me to him!"

"What?" Grace squawked.

Abbie ignored her. "Please! You have to take me to him."

"Now listen!" Grace said, her friendly tone replaced with anger. "I can't have you coming in here and raising your voice to Granny. She's old, and she's fragile."

Granny did not give a moment's notice to Grace's protests. Instead she said to Abbie, "The painting holds the secret. You must go to the painting. You must hurry."

"But I can't go to the painting! I got rid of it!"

She watched alarm flicker across the aged features. "Then you have to get it back, as quick as possible." Granny's eyes lost their dimness and seemed almost to glow from within as she stared at Abbie. "As quick as possible," she repeated. "Here is what you must remember:

Passion spurned; hatred burned.

A curse of thirteen hundred moons must pass.

Then death will come, unless love breaks the curse to set the prisoner free."

Granny's gaze was steely, frightening in its intensity. "His time is almost gone."

"I don't understand. Where is he? Tell me how to find him."

"Go to the painting."

"I told you I don't have it!" She clutched the album to her chest, holding it so tightly her hands hurt. "Just tell me where that house is, that house in the painting. He's there, isn't he? Then tell me where it is!"

"You must hurry. His time is almost gone."

The old woman turned and shuffled away, her misshapen figure seemingly more bent than ever, exuding despair and pain. Abbie shot up from the chair, shoving the photograph album back into Grace's hands and grabbed Granny's arm, stopping her retreat.

"Here now!" Grace shrieked, rushing to Granny's aid. "She's an old woman!" She tried to wedge herself between the two women and break Abbie's grasp. "Stop hurting her!"

"I'm not trying to hurt her. I'm sorry, Granny—"

"You leave her be, Grace," the old woman said, fastening her flinty glare on the candle maker. "This is none of your concern."

"Well, Granny, if you think I'm going to let a strange young woman come in here, yelling and manhandling you—"

"She ain't hurting me, and this don't concern you. You leave us be." Granny pinned her with a look until Grace stood aside, helpless and jittery, her agitated gaze flitting from one woman to the other.

Granny turned to Abbie. Gone was the glow in her eyes, replaced by what seemed unbearable regret.

"I can't help you, child. I've..."

"I'll give you anything. All my money, my car, everything I have. Please, just tell me where he is."

Granny's mouth worked pitifully. Her eyes were full of desperation.

"Do you love him?" she asked. "Do you love him more than your own life?"

Dear God, the very emotion Abbie never wanted to feel, never wanted to acknowledge. But she knew she loved him. She loved him enough to lay down her life for him. Her foolish vow never to love again had been banished to dust.

"Yes!" she said fiercely. "Yes, I love him!"

A small beam of hope kindled in the old woman's dim eyes. She took both of Abbie's hands in hers and gripped them with gnarled fingers.

"I knew you were the one! I knew finding you was the one good thing I've done. Now, you must rush, rush like the wind. Find that painting, and you will find your love."

"But—"

"I can't tell you more. Remember the words. Remember time. Remember love!"

TWENTY

Abbie stared deeply into the old woman's eyes and in that moment knew she had one, and only one, chance to be with Andrew again. From that look she also recognized that her failure to reunite with him would be devastating beyond belief. She did not understand how she would be able to reach him, but she had been with him before and she knew it was possible to do so again. She was ready to believe anything, and right now, she would seize any chance.

"I'll go," she told Granny. "I'll find the painting. And I will find Andrew."

Granny said nothing, but in her gaze, Abbie read pleading, desperation and hope, as if finding Andrew meant as much to her as it did to Abbie.

She reached one hand toward Granny, but the old woman dropped her gaze, turned and walked away, urging as she left, "Go. Go now!"

Taking the woman at her word, Abbie rushed to the door and flung it open. She turned to look once more at the bent form of the old woman.

"Thank you," she said.

Granny responded in neither word nor action.

Abbie heard Grace spluttering and calling to her, but trusting Granny's urgency as an indication for single-minded haste, she chose to waste no time explaining what she did not understand herself. Perhaps Granny would enlighten the woman. Or maybe, if good fortune was with her, Abbie would find her love and bring him here, to meet his great-great niece.

Abbie drove recklessly over the rutted dirt road leading back to the highway. She barely slowed when she reached the stop sign at the intersection. Spewing gravel from her squealing tires, she pulled onto the highway. The car skidded sideways. She knew a moment's panic, but controlled the skid then mashed the accelerator to the floor.

The narrow, twisting Ozark mountain highway offered sharp curve after curve and steep hill after steep hill. Abbie, whose nerves were as tight as a guitar string, exhausted herself keeping the car under control in the abundance of such obstacles. She entered the town of Gemstone at dusk and located the flea market. The parking lot was empty, and the door to the building was securely locked when she tried to enter.

Abbie refused to accept defeat. She rattled the knob. Maybe someone was in the back, or sweeping the floor. She pummeled the door with both fists.

"Hello!" she shouted. "Is anyone in there? Hello!"

She pounded the door, yelling until a woman came out of a house next door and hurried across the parking lot. A heavy-set woman with a deep frown etched on her broad forehead, she wore a flour-streaked red apron, and in her hand she carried a hefty, floury rolling pin.

"Here now, stop that!" she hollered, brandishing the rolling pin. "You want me to call cops?"

Abbie turned to her in relief, dismissing the threat. She

recognized the volunteer who had taken the painting from her that morning.

Ignoring the woman's thunderous expression and tense posture, she said, "Oh, thank goodness you're here! I need to have my painting back. You have to let me inside so I can get it."

The woman stood at the foot of the rickety steps, feet wide apart, arms crossed and rolling pin clutched menacingly to the forefront.

"I'll do no such of a thing!" she bellowed. "What in the world are you doing at this time of day, screaming and hollering like a fool and trying to break into the store?"

Abbie ran down the steps toward her. The woman tensed, drew herself up even larger and her glare deepened. Abbie halted.

"Don't you remember me? I was here this morning. I donated a big, dark painting. Don't you remember me?"

An expression of recognition crossed the woman's face, but she hung on to her defensive stand. She ran a critical gaze over Abbie's length.

"Now that you mention it, yes. What do you want?"

"I want the painting back."

The woman's eyes rounded. "Do what?"

"I'm sorry to bother you, but I made a mistake. I have to get my painting." In the dim evening light, Abbie could not see the other woman well, but she was willing to bet the broad, florid face was three times redder than its usual color.

"You mean to tell me you're doing all that wild hollering and carrying on over that picture? Come back tomorrow in the morning 'bout ten o'clock. And for mercy's sake, stop all this racket. You got my mother-in-law ready to have a runaway."

She turned to leave. Abbie lunged and caught the fleshy arm, not caring if the rolling pin came down on her head.

"Please, ma'am! I must get that painting back. Right now. Tonight."

The woman looked down at her as if she really might offer a clout from her doughy weapon. She studied Abbie's face, and something flicked across her features. Her expression softened just that much.

"Can't you just come back in the morning like everybody else?"

"No." Sensing a weakening of resolve, Abbie pressed her advantage. "Please, ma'am. I have to have that painting back as soon as possible."

"And I reckon 'soon as possible' just can't be in the morning?"

"No, I'm sorry. Honestly, under normal circumstances I wouldn't do this, but…please, I'm begging you. Open the door and let me get my painting. I'll buy it back; I'll pay what you ask. But please, let me have my painting."

The big woman stared at her another minute, a bit like a scientist might examine a peculiar specimen under the microscope. Heaving a sigh that must have come from the very depths of her beleaguered soul, her animosity seemed to ebb as resignation took over. She lowered the rolling pin to her side.

"Well, I need to go get the key and make sure Mama Ernie hasn't collapsed from nerves. You...now you just settle down and wait here. Set on them steps. I'll be back directly."

Abbie could not sit. She could not relax, and it had been foolish of the woman to recommend it. She paced the small area in front of the building and repeated Granny's words in her mind a dozen times: His time grows short.

What did that mean? It sounded so urgent, so...ominous, as though his life was in danger. This thought, fully formed and recognized in her mind, brought such a rush of exigency she felt sick. She started across the parking lot toward the house when the woman stepped out her door and came toward the flea market, sans rolling pin. She held up a wad of keys on a heavy ring as she approached and shook them noisily. Abbie eagerly followed her up the steps to the door.

As the old door yielded to the woman's push, she muttered, "I sure as shootin' hope we don't get a gaggle of folks coming in here, thinking we're open in the middle of the night." She flipped on the lights, then closed and locked the door behind her.

It was hardly dark outside, but Abbie thought it best not to mention it. At this point she didn't care if it was eight in the evening or two in the morning. She wanted the painting and she would have it.

"Well, let us find that thing so's you can quit your faunching and fuming. If it was such an all-fired important painting why'd you leave it here in the first place?" She squinted her eyes. "I bet you talked to some hotshot dealer down in Little Rock, didn't you, and he offered you a wad of money for it, didn't he?" She shook her head. "People!"

Abbie did not respond. If she told the woman the truth that the painting held the secret of a 130-year-old man with whom Abbie was in love, Abbie would probably be hauled off the premises by the aforementioned cops. She began searching the market with her reluctant companion, looking at every table and shelf, above and below them, in the corners and behind the counters. After several minutes she was close to tears. The woman gave half-hearted assistance by standing in the middle of the room and glancing around, muttering about her mother-in-law's nerves and voracious appetite.

"As you can see, it obviously ain't here," she finally announced, walking to the door.

"Wait!" Abbie said frantically. "We haven't looked everywhere. Isn't there a room where you sort donations, or store them, or something?"

The woman, facing the door, sighed loudly and turned around.

"Back yonder," she said, pointing. "But I'm pretty sure that picture was put on that table over there where all them books are."

Abbie glanced where the older woman indicated, but of course she had already searched that area, as well as under the table on which the books sat. The painting was not there. She followed the woman into a windowless, airless backroom crammed to capacity with castoffs. She began riffling through piles of clothing, old shoes, threadbare sheets and curtains, dog-eared books and worn-out magazines. The only pictures she found were two faded landscape prints in cheap, plain frames.

Rather than help Abbie look, her reluctant companion weaved her way through the merchandise to a wall telephone with an old-fashioned rotary dial. She dialed a number.

"Edna Lou?" the woman said into the mouthpiece. Abbie listened to her side of the conversation. "It's Rochelle. I've got some woman down here at the store looking for that picture she gave us earlier today...yes; of course I'm with her. You think I'd let someone prowl and paw around in here alone...well, she was yelling and banging on the door like she was here to get her baby outta jail, and Mama Ernie was convinced it was the Second Coming and she'd missed it...Oh, you remember it, that ugly old black picture of a old house and a storm...yeah, that's the one, and we can't find it for love or money...what?... Oh for heaven sake, no wonder we can't find it then."

Abbie froze and stared wild-eyed at the woman.

"What? What? Is it gone?"

The woman waved an impatient hand at her and kept talking to Edna Lou.

"Well, I know that, but what would you have done with all her carrying on? And what could Jimmy have done if I had called him?...Well, I'll tell you the honest truth, Edna Jean, I ain't gonna vote for him for sheriff again next time, and I don't care if he is your cousin. He don't know his head from a bucket of rocks…well, just let me tell you something, if he put as much effort into being a sheriff as he did running for the office of sheriff—"

Here Abbie grabbed the woman's hand that held the telephone. "Is my painting gone?"

Rochelle tried to murder her with a look. "Let go of me! Yes, it's gone. It sold this afternoon."

"No!" Abbie sagged against the wall, feeling as though she might pass out. The painting held the key to finding Andrew and it was gone.

"Oh, lordy, Edna Lou, she's going crazy again. You sell that painting to someone here in town? Oh, her. I shoulda known…listen, I gotta get off the phone before this gal starts foaming at the mouth. I'll talk to you in the mornin'."

She hung up the phone. For the moment she lost her annoyance and appeared genuinely concerned.

"You better set down, 'fore you fall down."

She shoved a pile of yellowed underwear and stiff-looking shoes from a vinyl chair, and Abbie sank into it, feeling as though her head was about to explode.

"Now, you just calm down, missus. That picture is still in town, but it's been sold to Nancy Salem over on Parkview Drive. She might sell it back to you, though, if you was to ask her. She's a real nice woman, even if she is rich."

Abbie looked up, buoyed by new hope. She bounded out of the chair.

"She lives here? In this town? How do I get there?"

"Well, now, you can't just so running off to folks' houses in the middle of the night and expect them to give you what you want. Someone a little less nice than me will sure enough call the law—"

"Ma'am, excuse me, I don't mean to be rude, but right now I don't give a gigantic flying rat's ass what time of day it is. Tell me how to find Parkview Drive, and I'll find Nancy Salem if I have to knock on every door on that street."

Rochelle's mouth flew open. "Well, merciful heavens, after me opening up this store outta the goodness of my heart and you talking to me that way, why, I'm half-a-mind not to tell you Nancy's address or her phone number." She crimped her lips together as though she would never speak again for the rest of her life, then she said, "You know where the park is?"

"I've never been to this town before today. And I apologize for offending you…I…just…." Her voice trailed. There was no explanation she could give that would make sense to anyone. "I'm sorry."

Rochelle pinned her with that scientist's scrutiny again.

"Well, never you mind," she said, suddenly generous with her compassion. "Let's close up the store, and I'll tell you how to find Nancy's house. It ain't hard, and you can't get lost in Gemstone."

She sounded almost pleasant. As she turned out the light in the storeroom and led the way back to the front door, she gave Abbie directions to Parkview Drive and concluded her instructions with, "You can't miss the Salems' house; it's the nicest one on the street."

Abbie thanked Rochelle and ran down the steps to the car. She stopped and looked over her shoulder. The other woman turned the key and rattled the door to be sure it was locked and tight.

"Wait, please, before you go home," Abbie said.

Rochelle puffed up. "Now, listen, I ain't gonna—"

"Just a minute."

Abbie got her purse out of the car and grabbed every bit of cash from her wallet. This she offered to the woman, saying, "I'm sorry I bothered you, and I'm sorry I was so boorish. I want you to take this for your trouble."

The woman looked at the wad of bills in Abbie's hand. This time, in spite of having very little light, Abbie saw a flush steal up Rochelle's ruddy cheeks. She shook her head.

"No. You keep your money. I didn't do anything, really."

"Yes, you did." But when Rochelle backed away a couple of steps, she added, "I see by your sign near the door that this thrift store helps to buy food for needy families. Take this for that fund."

At the suggestion, Rochelle relented. "That's right kind of you, missus. And I'm sorry I was so rude, too. It's just that Mama Ernie...she gets me all tense and then my tension slops out on everyone else. Well, good luck in finding your picture."

"Thank you," Abbie said. "And thank you so much for your help."

TWENTY-ONE

She had no difficulty in finding the Salems' house. From the brightness of the streetlights it was easy to see that the large Victorian house was indeed the loveliest one on a street full of beautiful homes. Lamplight blazed in the numerous mullioned windows, and walklights illuminated the broad, curving brick sidewalk leading to the front porch. Abbie ran up the steps and to the front door. She rang the bell, paused about five seconds and rang it again.

"Hurry, hurry, hurry," she muttered.

The door opened, and she faced a pleasant-faced, chunky man standing in his stocking feet. He wore dark slacks and a white shirt with his tie loosened and top button open. In his hand he held a newspaper. He gave her a tired, mild smile.

"Mr. Salem?"

"The one and only," he said. "But I have to tell you upfront I don't take care of bank business at home after hours. I learned that lesson the hard way."

"I'm not here on bank business, Mr. Salem. My name is Abigail Matthews." She stuck out her left hand. Gazing at her curiously, he shook her hand as she continued, "I understand you bought a painting today from the Gemstone Flea Market. It was donated by mistake, and I need to retrieve it."

Mr. Salem drew in the corners of his mouth, either in

humor or annoyance, Abbie wasn't sure which. He stood back, holding open the door with one hand and gestured an invitation with the hand that held the paper.

"Come in, Miss…Matthews, was it?"

"Abigail Matthews. Abbie. Thank you."

She stepped inside the air conditioned, well-lit interior of the home that smelled of lemon oil and bee's wax. An eclectic mix of refurbished antiques with some pieces in a state of natural distress created an appealing, homey atmosphere. Abbie surprised herself by liking what she saw, although her taste ran more to sleek lines and polished steel. Or it did at one time. She wasn't sure what her taste was these days, but cool and cosmopolitan starkness had begun to ebb from her preference. At that moment, however, she was not thinking about home decorating.

"If I could just buy back the painting…"

He shook his head. "I don't know what to tell you other than come in and sit down."

"You did buy a painting today at the flea market, didn't you? Rochelle at the thrift store said you—"

"I didn't buy a thing, but my wife undoubtedly did. Have a seat, Ms. Matthews. Would you like something cold to drink? Or maybe some coffee?"

"No, thank you. Could I please speak to your wife?"

"Surely. I'll just go get her. But are you sure you wouldn't want something to drink?" He walked to the liquor cabinet on the other side of the room. "Maybe a glass of wine?"

"Not just now, thank you." Abbie tried to give him a patient smile, but she felt as stretched as a well-used rubber band around a too-large bundle. At this point, Abbie had already lost precious hours backtracking, searching and talking. Now she was so close, so close. The last thing she wanted to do was sip wine and make pleasant, inane chitchat with this very nice man. He poured himself a generous shot of whiskey.

"I really, really need to see your wife right away, please," she pressed as graciously as possible.

Mr. Salem nodded. "I'll get her."

He padded silently from the room and climbed the stairs to the second floor. Abbie could not stand still. She did not want to roam the room like an investigator looking for clues, but she had no capacity to sit and wait. She paced the tiled foyer, back and forth, the soles of her sneakers squeaking on the hard surface.

"Well, I have to tell you, Ms. Matthews," Mr. Salem drawled as he descended the stairs, "my wife is a doll. Don't know what I'd do without her. As you can see, she's made us a nice home here. She entertains friends and family as if she were poured from Miss Emily Post's mold. She's a wonderful mother and my best friend." He stepped off the last stair and smiled at Abbie. "But I don't understand her. She likes flea market finds, God knows why. She can buy whatever she wants, brand-new, and not have to clean it and fumigate it and strip it and restore it, but there you are, that's Nancy for you." He stretched out an arm toward the living room. "Please, come in and sit down."

Abbie glanced up the stairs.

"Is your wife coming down soon? I really need to speak to her."

"Oh, sure. Please, have a seat." He ushered her into the other room, dipped his head toward a soft, inviting armchair.

Abbie remained standing, clenching and unclenching one hand while fiddling with her purse strap with the other.

He said, "God bless you, Ms. Matthews, I was born and raised Southern. Good manners are instilled in us, and I can't, in good conscience, sit until you do, and I'm very, very tired. Please, have a seat. Nancy will be down directly."

"Oh, I'm so sorry," Abbie said and quickly sank onto the edge of the nearest chair. "I'm just so nervous, you see, and when I'm tense, I can hardly sit still."

"Ahhh," he said as he settled into a recliner and elevated the footrest. He drank his whiskey and sighed. "That's better. Well, you know, I'm not as young as I used to be, and there's a great deal more of me resting on these feet nowadays. I just have to sit down in the evenings. If you need to, please fidget all you want."

"Your wife will be down soon?" she asked again, as if the first twelve times had been inadequate.

"Well, 'soon' is a relative word in this house. She's taking a bath, one of those bubbly, candle-lit aromatic adventures with New Age music on the CD player and a glass of wine. Say, you want something to drink now?"

He thunked down the footrest, picked up his empty

shot glass as he got up and went to the liquor cabinet.

"Scotch?" He held up the bottle. "Steady your nerves a bit."

Maybe a stiffener would do her some good.

"Yes," she told him. "Thank you. But not much. I'm driving."

After several minutes, in which Abbie surprised herself by being able to converse intelligently with Mr. Salem without shrieking from frustration and impatience, a plump, pretty woman in a silky pink robe came down the stairs. Damp curls from the careless pile of dark hair on her head framed a face rosy from her warm bath. Abbie detected the subtle fragrance of lavender.

"Hi, I'm Nancy Salem," she held out a hand and shook Abbie's gently. "You must be Abigail?"

"Yes. But please, it's Abbie."

"Of course. Abbie, it is." She turned to her husband, comfortably situated on his recliner. "A nice brandy, Mark. And you might want to freshen Abbie's drink."

Abbie looked at her empty shot glass. "No, thanks. Actually, I'm not here on a social call."

Nancy settled onto the sofa and curled her legs under her like a child. She accepted the drink her husband offered and smiled her thanks.

"That's too bad," she said to Abbie. "You'll have to come back when you can stay and visit." She took a sip of her brandy but before Abbie could speak, she continued, "How long have you been in Gemstone? Are you settled yet?"

Abbie shoved aside the peculiarities of these friendly strangers and fought the irritation of participating in niceties, but it was obvious that these people lived and behaved by a certain code. No amount of trying to breach it would succeed. She stifled the urge to wail for her painting like a spoiled kid.

"Actually, I've never been to Gemstone before today. Just passing through, which brings me—"

"I know who you are!" Nancy said suddenly, leaning forward and laughing. "You are one of the Greenbriar Matthews, aren't you? I went to the University with Alice Ann. Are you related? You know, you do look a lot like her!"

"Umm, no. I doubt we're related. I'm from Ohio, actually."

"A Yankee!" Nancy laughed again, with obvious delight. "I should have known from your accent." She turned to her husband. "Mark-honey, when was the last time we had a Yankee in our living room?"

Mark looked thoughtful, but only for about five seconds because Nancy answered her own question.

"Oh, I remember! Two years ago last Christmas. Danielle Ramsey's fiancée was from New Jersey. Remember him, Mark?" She turned a merry expression to Abbie. "That was not a match made in heaven, believe me. You'd have to know Danielle." She sipped her brandy and gazed at Abbie. "Sweetie, you are just fit to be tied, aren't you, hon? What's wrong?"

Her question was so unexpected that Abbie was momentarily wordless. She had been casting about in her mind for a way to short circuit all this talk when Nancy pulled the plug on her own chatter.

"The painting," she blurted. "I want to buy back the painting."

Nancy blinked. "What painting is that, sugar?"

"The one you bought at the flea market this morning. You see, I foolishly donated it, and I desperately need it back."

Nancy stared at her. "You don't mean that hideous picture of the storm and old house?"

"Yes," Abbie said eagerly, twitching on the edge of the seat. "I want to buy it back from you."

Nancy drained her brandy before she answered. "Why, honey, I'd be more than happy just to give it to you—"

"Oh, thank you." Abbie went limp with relief. "You don't how much this means."

Nancy made a little face of pain. "Let me finish, sweetie. I'd be more than happy just to give it to you, but I don't have it."

Abbie felt the breath leave her. "But...but you just said...but you...oh, my God. Where is it?"

Nancy set the snifter down on the old trunk she used as a coffee table and sat forward.

"Well, it just never occurred to me that anyone would want the picture. I bought it for the frame. That frame is at least a hundred years old."

"I don't care about the frame; you are more than welcomed to that." Abbie felt the threat of tears burn her eyes; her voice shook. "But where is the painting?"

"Why, I'm afraid it's gone for good, honey. Destroyed. I put it in the incinerator this afternoon."

"The incinerator?"

"Yes." Nancy bit her lower lip, apology etched deeply on her features. "I never dreamed someone would want that painting. It was so dark and disturbing, almost as if it was alive. It really gave me the willies. Oh, honey, don't cry. I'll buy you another painting, or give you one of mine…oh, dear. Mark, what'll we do?"

Mark had a strange smile on his face.

"Mark?" His wife stared at him. "You did burn the trash after dinner, didn't you? There was that awful thing from the refrigerator that Marie pitched in the garbage this morning."

He looked both happy and abashed. "Well, actually, I thought I'd just burn the trash tomorrow…"

"You didn't burn it?" Abbie shrieked, ready to cover his face with kisses and bow at his feet.

"If Nancy threw your picture in the incinerator, it's still there."

"Oh! Oh, my God. Thank you, thank you!" Abbie rushed to the man who had his recliner upright by now. She hugged him hard as he stood. "Tell me where the incinerator is, and I'll go get the painting."

"Why, it's liable to covered with that gooey, fuzzy,

gray-green stuff from the 'fridge."

"That's OK. I don't care about gooey green stuff as long as I can have my painting."

"Let me find my slippers." He shot a vague glance around the room.

"Upstairs in your closet, where they should be when not on your feet, sugar."

"Oh. Well. Just a minute, then, Abbie, and let me go put them on."

Abbie thought she would burst out of her skin waiting for him to return, but he did come back, about ten minutes later. He wore a pair of tattered sneakers and had changed from his good slacks and shirt to a pair of sweat pants and a T-shirt.

"Well, Mark-honey, what an outfit to wear in front of our guest!" Nancy said, laughing.

"I'm just going to the incinerator. Not likely to see anyone I know between there and here." He gave a wry grin to Abbie, adding, "I'll be back directly with your painting."

No way was she going to sit around and wait while he strolled to the incinerator and sifted leisurely through garbage. Who knew how long that would take?

"I'll come with you."

"You'll get dirty," he warned.

"I can wash."

"Well."

She followed him down the marble-tiled hallway, through a large kitchen and out the back door.

"Incinerator's at the back of the property," he said as they crossed the considerable back lawn. "Now, normally, Marie burns the garbage, but she was in a snit today because Nancy had her clean out the 'fridge." He chuckled. "You don't want to cross Marie when she's in a snit. Just lucky this isn't Tuesday. Tuesday is the garbage pick-up day. But Nancy has a real sensitive nose. She can smell a fire before you light a match; so when she says take out the garbage and burn it, I take it out." In a whisper, he added, "But I don't always burn it."

"I'm glad you didn't burn it today."

"Me, too, since your picture is in it. Did you paint that picture your own self?"

"No, but I treasure it, and I need it back."

"Well, here we are. Now you just stand there and let me poke around in here and find it. Peuw! That does reek! I think it was something with broccoli in it. Things with broccoli always stink, have you ever noticed? And Brussell sprouts. Why God ever created either one of them is beyond me."

Gingerly he plucked the top layer off the trash. Abbie could not stand by and watch. She plunged both hands into the offal, ignoring the wetness and the odor. Once she thought she had the painting and pulled it out of the rubbish only to find a thick clump of damp paper towels. She thrust her hands in again, clutching and feeling, rejecting what must have been eggshells and peelings.

"Here now!" Mark said. "You're getting right dirty."

"I think I found it. Help me, please. Clear away the stuff on top."

Mark pushed away the rubbish and Abbie pulled out something large, slightly stiff and crushed, made of fabric. She squatted and smoothed the canvas out on the ground. By the illumination of the back yard security light, she saw Andrew's house.

"Oh, thank God, thank God," she cried, gathering the painting to her chest. "Thank God."

Tears flooded her eyes and flowed freely down her face.

"God bless you, Abbie," Mark said. "I know those are tears of joy. But, look, you're getting nasty stuff all over you. Come back inside and clean up. We'll try to clean off that picture, too."

Now that Abbie had retrieved the painting she did not know the next step, but one thing was certain: she needed to be alone so she could think. She doubted her reasoning power could work very well with this wonderfully kind but far too chatty couple hovering around her.

"Thank you, no. I'll take care of it." She got to her feet, the crushed painting still pressed against her bosom. "I can't thank you enough. I'll never forget your kindness."

"You're sure you won't stay a bit longer? Have you had dinner?"

"It's nice of you to ask, but I really have to go now." She was already walking, almost running across the back yard. "Thank you, Mr. Salem. Thank you both so much!"

Once inside the Lexus, she put the painting on the

seat beside her, started the motor and backed out of the driveway. On the street, however, she realized she had the painting but no place to tend to it. No place to go. She recalled seeing a small, nondescript motel on the edge of town. Abbie mashed down on the accelerator, driving as fast as she thought she could without getting pulled over in that small, southern town.

TWENTY-TWO

Inside the dingy, beige room she had rented, Abbie switched on both lamps and the overhead light. Beneath their blaze, she lovingly smoothed the battered painting on the bed. She recognized every aspect of it: the ominous dark sky, tree branches bent in the wind, the tangled growth of brush and briars, and the dismal house where she had found Andrew. Somehow it seemed even darker and bleaker now. The trees branches seemed to droop from more than the wind, almost as if they were dying. The house seemed more run down, as though it was long abandoned. And hadn't there once been a light in the upstairs window?

That would have been his bedroom window, she realized as she brushed her hand gently across it. Beneath her fingertips, the paint was stiff and cracked. Tiny bits flecked off. She stared down at her fingers, then at the painting. She had obeyed the old woman's admonition to find the painting. Here, at last, it lay before her, bringing bittersweet memories into her mind. Having made the breakneck trip back to Gemstone, nearly having had the police called on her, disrupting a couple's quiet evening and plunging her arms elbow deep in garbage to retrieve this painting, she again wondered what next step she should take. There lay the painting, abused, cracked, filthy and she was not an iota closer to reaching Andrew than she had been when she woke up in the hospital. What good was the painting if she could not find the actual house?

Maybe, said a part of her mind not overcome with raw

frustration and sheer nerves, maybe there is a map on the back, or directions to the house.

"Yes, that has to be it!" she said.

Gingerly she turned over the precious, fragile canvas. Her heart leaped when she saw writing through the stains. The writing was dim, almost illegible. She held the table lamp over it as she bent and examined what she saw.

"Passion spurned, hatred burned," she read aloud. It was the same words the old woman had told her in the junk shop when Abbie bought the painting, and the same words she had quoted earlier today as she urged Abbie to find the picture.

She frowned, read the poem, examined it line by line, word by word, but it scarcely made sense.

A curse of 1300 moons. Moons as in months? How did that translate into real time? Math never being Abbie's strong point, she put down the lamp, rummaged through her purse and pulled out the small pocket calculator she always carried. She punched in the numbers. Thirteen hundred moons equaled one hundred years, if she had done the math right, and she was pretty sure she had. She read the poem again, substituting 100 years for thirteen hundred moons.

A curse of 100 years must pass.

A century had passed from the time Andrew found himself lost in that awful place to the time Abbie arrived.

One hundred years. A curse. Could it be possible? Did such things as spells and curses really exist? In a world where a man could live without aging for a century, where she had awakened in an alien setting, anything was possible—time travel, curses or spells, magic or witchcraft.

Abbie put the lamp back on the bedside table and sat on the edge of the bed next to the painting.

She recalled Andrew speaking of Granny Hodge who had lived on Sumac Ridge and practiced black arts. Had she put a curse on him, maybe because he was going to be an actual doctor and the people would turn to him instead of her? But that seemed foolish. Andrew spoke highly of the old woman and how eager she had been to teach him her ways. Considering a curse was nonsense.

As she thought about it, though, Abbie realized she could not dismiss any notion as being too irrational or impossible. Had she not met a man from a previous century, in a place neither he nor she could understand nor escape? She stared down at the bleak painting, at the dismal house and stormy skies.

Slowly a notion formed in her mind and she allowed herself to let it grow. Day and night did not exist in Andrew's world. Storm clouds had hung over his home without breaking. Wind, silent wind, ceaselessly whipped the trees and bent their branches. Until Abbie showed up, nothing ever grew, or ever changed, or died. It was almost as if he lived…in a painting.

Could it be possible that someone had cursed Andrew to live in a painting? Cursed him to an exile of one hundred years?

She grabbed the lamp and read the words on the back of the canvas once more: A curse of thirteen hundred moons must pass, then death will come, unless love breaks the curse and sets the prisoner free.

"That means," she said aloud, "if one hundred years pass and the curse is not broken, Andrew will die." She looked down at the painting. "He will die, alone, in that awful, awful place."

Unless love breaks the curse to set the prisoner free.

Abbie pressed her palms to her face, staring at where she was now convinced Andrew lived imprisoned.

"No!" she cried. "No, he will not die. I will go to him again, and this time he will leave with me."

But how? How could she return to him and bring him back with her? She jumped up, pacing, clenching and unclenching her hands, feeling as though she would fly into a thousand pieces any moment if she did not find the answer.

She had been there with him. Somehow she had entered his world, and somehow she had made her escape.

"If I did it once, I can do it again," she muttered, chewing on the knuckles of her bent thumbs as she paced. She pivoted and returned to gaze at the painting.

How had she traveled there? What had she done, what words had she spoken? What port of entry had she found?

Abbie sank to her knees by the side of the bed, once again moved the lamp and held it steady so that every aspect of the painting was illuminated. She studied the house, the windows and doors. She examined the porch, the lawn, the trees and bushes. As she examined each point, her skin prickled with the familiarity of what she saw. There, just beyond that point of the house, but out of sight, was the well that never went dry. And there, that tiny brown dot on the door was the tarnished doorknocker shaped like a gargoyle.

Eagerly she looked at the windows. She was sure she could make out the shape of the two chairs before the hearth, though she saw no infinitesimal cheery glow. Upstairs, the bedroom windows, she saw...nothing. Andrew had drawn the draperies to help darken the room so she could sleep. Were they drawn now, limiting her view?

She examined the forest. Somewhere, in there among all those trees she had made love to Andrew; it had been there that she last saw him. They'd heard something moving, even thrashing in the forest. She'd thought it was that horrible, huge snake with evil, intelligent eyes. Andrew had gone to search; she'd heard the sounds, sounds like wheels against a road, coming from another place in the forest. She had called out to Andrew, taken a few steps toward what she was sure was civilization and...and she had awakened in a hospital room, torn from him in the blink of an eye.

If she had stumbled upon a way out once, she could find it again. But first, she had to return to Andrew.

"Oh, God," she said as the separation slammed full force into her once more.

Deep inside, she felt as though her heart bled, draining her life. She pressed her face against the cracked, painted surface as tears slid from her eyes and onto the canvas.

"Andrew," she murmured into the stained fabric, "be strong. I love you, and I'm coming for you."

She closed her eyes, fighting the sense of futility that

surged from the center of her body.

"I'm coming for you," she said again. "I will never give up."

She remembered then, for the first time, what had happened that night at Lefty's house. She had taken a shower and dressed for bed. She had brought the painting inside to clean it. As the elusive memory finally returned, she raised her head. She had wiped off the dust, and a piece of paint had fallen away. She found where she thought it would fit and when she placed it there.

She sat straight up and looked at the lower left corner of the painting. There! It was there that the chip of paint was missing. The paint was still gone, but something, perhaps a bit of Marie's spoiled food from the Salem's refrigerator had soiled it.

Abbie scrambled to her feet, ran into the bathroom and dampened a wash cloth. She dabbed away the dirt and uncovered what she had seen before: a swirling, dizzying blue. How could she have forgotten something so unusual, so significant?

There lay her threshold to Andrew.

She tossed aside the cloth, placed her fingertips on the blue, watched them disappear then felt her hand, her arm, her whole self, slide, slide gently back into Andrew's world.

TWENTY-THREE

This time Abbie's journey did not end with a violent landing. She seemed to float, ethereally in the gauzy blueness. As she looked around, she saw nothing, heard nothing.

Serenity enfolded her. Her very being was filled with a light and hope as she had never known. In this strange crossing she knew all things were possible. Andrew's exile would soon pass away; his liberation was at hand.

As the blue became darker, grayer, her body took its weight again. Cold seeped into her pores. The light slipped away, and Abbie realized saving Andrew might not be as easy as she believed only a moment ago. She recalled how difficult it had been to convince him to look for a way out. Of course, there had been no proof of an exit then, but surely he would believe her now. She was evidence that escape was possible.

She sensed something solid nearby, prepared herself, and a moment later felt ground beneath her feet. She stood, strong and unharmed, a cold silent wind whipping against her, shaking and bending branches of the surrounding thick forest. The tranquility that had been her companion as she entered this world now slid away completely as urgency took its place.

"A curse of 1300 moons," echoed in her brain and instinctively turned her toward the house.

Her master plan was to take him away from this dark

prison and back into a world of light and warmth, where they could be together, in love, always.

"Please God," she prayed and left the rest of her petition unspoken as she took her bearings. She had studied the painting closely and now understood exactly where she was in relationship to other portions of it. She would not get lost again.

She set out for the house, taking note as she went that the flora was not as lush as it had been. In fact, parts of it were quite brown, as though it were dying. Her trek through the forest was easier because the resilience of the vegetation had diminished and crushed easily beneath her feet. Nearby she heard the distinct, sharp report as a tree branch cracked. It broke free and crashed to the ground. Leaves, edged in brown, swirled from the trees as if in the throes of an autumn wind.

The painting was changing, and Abbie knew she had to move fast.

Reaching the tangled clearing in front of the house, she staggered and jerked to a halt when she saw that much of the roof had blown away. Urgency shook her out of her shock and spurred her onward. As she ran toward the house, she saw broken numerous windows. The steps leading up the porch sagged, and so did the porch roof. One of its supports had buckled and looked ready to give way completely.

"Andrew!" she cried. "Andrew, I'm here!"

Heedless of danger from the ruined environment, she rushed up the broken steps and across the deteriorating porch floor, fully expecting him to joyously fling open the door and welcome her into his arms.

"I'll never leave you again, Andrew, because I'm taking you with me!"

She opened the door and froze on the threshold. Inside, the house was dark and cold, giving off the aura of emptiness and neglect. Although the house had been dismal and chilly before, it carried within it the heartbeat of life: a fire always burned in the grate; the fragrance of a simmering stew or sizzling meat welcomed their appetites. The sense that someone lived and moved within had always lingered in the air.

Abbie felt nothing of Andrew's presence now. She looked in the parlor, hoping to see him in his chair before the fire. The parlor was vacant. The grate stood empty and cold.

"Andrew! Where are you?"

She dashed across the small passage and ran upstairs into the bedroom they had shared. It, too, was deserted. The lovely room across the hall that had been Abbie's was gone as if it had never existed.

"Andrew!" she screamed as panic rose. "Where are you?"

Was she too late? Had the hundred years of the curse passed? Was he gone, was he...dead?

Not yet, not yet, she screamed in her head. One hundred years cannot be over yet.

"Andrew!"

She ran back downstairs and into the kitchen. There

he sat; slumped over the table, head turned from her and resting on his arms, silent, cold and unmoving as if dead.

"Oh, God, don't let him be..." She approached him. "Andrew? Can you hear me? It's Abbie."

He groaned then, a weak sound, barely audible. Abbie's relief buckled her legs so she could hardly move.

"Oh, my love!" she cried. "I'm here, and I'll never ever leave you again."

She dropped to her knees beside him, brushed back his hair from his face and stifled a gasp at what she saw. He was thin, almost emaciated and gray-faced. His eyes burned bright with fever. When he looked at Abbie, it was if he saw right through her.

But he did see her. With obvious effort he turned head from her and muttered, "Go away. Do not do this to me again."

"I'm not going away. Andrew, look at me."

"Let me die in peace."

She shook him. "I will not! You come with me now."

Andrew roused himself enough to peer at her through eyes that seemed to grow dimmer with each passing moment.

"A witch," he mumbled. "A sprite."

"No. I'm real."

He groaned and started to turn from her again. She cupped his face and forced him to look in her eyes.

"Listen to me. I know where we are and how to get

out."

"There is no getting out of Hell."

"Andrew, listen to me. I know what happened. A hundred years ago someone cursed you into a painting. This is a painting you've been living in; that is why you've not been able to leave. But I know how to get out."

He stared at her, eyes dark with hopelessness. His cheek burned beneath her touch. Whether he heard, understood, or believed her, Abbie had no time to ponder. She knew she must to get him to safety. She had to do it now.

"Andrew, I got out. That time in the woods, our last time together, I stumbled through a portal, a passage we never found because the picture frame had all but hidden it in darkness. But the important thing at this moment is that I found my way back to you, and now you must come with me."

He gazed at her, blinked slowly. "I don't believe you. I'm sick and don't believe you're really here. Go away, Abbie, and never return."

She wanted to scream.

"Andrew! We've been through this before! How can I make you understand that I'm real?"

Then she remembered what she had done that first time. If it worked once, maybe it would work again.

She placed both hands on either side of his head and kissed him. She kissed him with all the passion and love she possessed. At first he seemed apathetic to the touch, but after bit he wrapped his arms about her. As weak as he was at that moment, her lips against his awakened a response in him. He returned the fiery kiss with his own.

He pulled away, looked into her eyes.

"Is it really you?" he whispered, lifting one hand to her cheek. "Have you really come back to me?"

"Yes," she said, "yes, yes, yes! Not only come back to you, but come back for you."

"And do you love me?"

"More than anything, Andrew. More than life."

"Truly?"

She smiled gently, kissed his feverish brow.

"Truly, passionately, forever. And I refuse to be without you ever again."

He said nothing as his gaze caressed her face, memorizing every movement, every detail.

"Then my prayer has been answered," he told her. She kissed his lips again, lingering only a moment.

"We won't be parted again, I promise you." She stood, tugged on both his hands. "So now you must come with me."

He hardly moved. "Abbie, I'm very sick. I fear I'm dying."

She tamped down the terror his words brought. Instead, she said in her briskest, most demanding voice, "Come with me this minute."

"I don't think—"

"Andrew! Do you love me?"

"Of course, I do. You know I do."

"Then enough of this nonsense. You must help me to help you. This world in this painting is collapsing, and we must go. Now."

While every nerve in her body screamed with a frantic urgency that bordered hysteria, Abbie stared at him. Still, he did not move. She thought he might never move or speak again.

"Andrew," she said, cupping his face and looking into his eyes again. "Sweetheart, if you want to live, if you want us to be together, you have to come with me. You need to get up and walk out the door with me. We need to get to the portal before something happens to it."

He blinked slowly, as though taking in her words.

"All right, Abbie," he said at last. "I will go with you, if I can."

"Thank God! Now get up from your chair and let's go."

He stood up with some difficulty. His slow movements were weak yet determined. If only she had known about and understood the curse, she would have come back to him sooner, before everything had degenerated to this state. If only…who could have ever believed a cursed painting existed? No one from the world Abbie Matthews had inhabited most of her life. She had done what she thought was right; she had truly believed Andrew was no more than the memory of a most excellent dream. They had each other at this moment, right now, and she must concentrate all her efforts on their escape.

She slipped her arm around his waist, pulled his arm across her shoulders.

"Lean on me if you need to, Andrew."

They got to the front door, which she had left open in her haste to reach him. He halted in the doorway. His eyes moved across the landscape.

"There is no more water. The food has spoiled. I've been hearing the trees fall. And something happened to the house. It's all dying around us, isn't it?"

"Don't think about, sweetheart," she said encouragingly. "We'll be all right. Just be careful where you step as we cross the porch and down the steps."

They moved cautiously but as quickly as Andrew could maneuver.

"We are truly leaving, aren't we?" he asked as they crossed the clearing toward the forest.

"Truly and absolutely."

He was silent for just a moment. "I shall not miss this place, except for those days you were with me."

She looked up at him. He gave her a smile, his fingers pressing into her shoulder. She said nothing, intent on making good their escape while the possibility still existed.

Once they were in the woods, however, movement became dangerous. Tree limbs fell at an alarming rate. Many crashed dangerously close. A branch missed them by mere inches. The groundcover beneath their feet gave way to their steps so that they tripped and stumbled, over and over, slowing their movements even more. It was as if the painting was trying to impede their progress.

"Are you positive you know where we're going?" Andrew asked at one point, his breath quick and shallow.

Looking at him, Abbie saw his unspoken need to rest for a moment, but she knew there were no moments to use. They could not afford to stop.

"We're almost there."

A thunderous crash almost deafened them as one of the largest trees in the forest upended itself across their path, bashing into other trees and breaking them, pulling them down in its wake.

Forward motion ceased to be an option.

"We have to go around this," Abbie said.

"Or climb over it."

She looked at him. He seemed weaker with each step.

"Can you?" she asked.

"Can you?"

"Yes."

"Then so can I."

Abbie hesitated, and in that moment of indecision another tree crashed. There was no longer time for self-doubt or second guessing. Abbie Matthews had to trust herself.

"We must move quickly," she said.

"I understand. I can do it." The determination in his expression belied his deteriorating physical vigor, and her heart swelled with love.

Climbing over the fallen trees, fighting against the branches that snagged their arms, legs and clothing, stumbling, falling, standing and continuing on, all of it consumed much of their precious time. When they cleared the last of the fallen timber, Abbie was breathless and soaked with sweat, even in the cold wind. Andrew was white-faced and shaking from thirst, hunger and fatigue. But Abbie knew exactly where they were, and the knowledge gave her strength.

"A few more steps, Andrew," she encouraged. "We're almost there. I can see it from here."

They were within three yards of their escape when Andrew collapsed.

She knelt beside him, shook him.

"Andrew, a few more steps, darling. We're almost there. You're almost free."

He did not move, and she realized he was unconscious. She must drag him out. To do so, she only needed to clear the path. She looked at his dear face, loving him and knew nothing was impossible.

"You will have your second chance at the good life you deserve, I swear it."

She set about clearing away the limbs and dead briars between them and the escape portal. She worked a single-minded quickness, methodically, stooping to pick up and toss the litter. When she finished she straightened and started to turn back to Andrew.

The snake lay coiled across the threshold of the painting, a guardian of this cursed prison and the world of freedom beyond. Coiled and alert, the serpent seemed in no way to be weak or diminished like the rest of the milieu. Abbie's heart stopped beating. There was no way they could get past that huge, hideous creature. It would kill them both before they had a chance to gain liberty.

As if the serpent had read her thoughts, its evil reptilian face seemed to gloat, knowing it had won: Andrew was cursed and would forever be cursed, dying in a barren, collapsing world.

In the distance another tree fell. Its reverberation shook the ground where she stood. In a few minutes, only desolation would remain. She must act now, this moment.

The snake never took its lidless gloating gaze off her as she picked up the heavy limb she had just pitched aside. She hefted it, got the feel of it in her hand, moved it a little to understand its weight. She thanked Lefty who had taught her to swing a ball bat with power and purpose.

She fixed the snake with her own cold glare. It tensed as though probing her mind again then flexed its huge body, the tongue flicking and lashing.

Heaving the club, Abbie approached the vile guardian of Andrew's world. It began to tighten itself into a hard coil, ready to spring. She looked directly into the glittering tiny eyes, knowing this serpent was not what it seemed. She ignored the raging fear that threatened to take over and lay waste to everything she stood for, everything she tried to do. Her very insides shook with terror, but she would not fail to obliterate this final obstacle.

"Nothing," she said to the reptile, "not you or this vile, dying world will stop me from saving Andrew. If it costs my life to save him, I gladly give it, because I love him more than myself, more than my own life. You will not have him!"

The serpent lunged at her, its mouth gaping like the entrance gate to Hell. She saw the fangs and leaped sideways. The snake missed its mark, striking the ground with an ominous thud. It lashed its body sideways, curled back enough to ready itself for another strike.

Abbie raised the club.

"I will fight you to the death," she said, preparing to bash in the sleek, triangular head, "because even if you kill me, I will still love him."

The snake froze in its place. Abbie knew then this reptile was the embodiment of evil. It heard and understood her words. She knew no foolish notion, no restrictive prison, no hideous evil in the form of a serpent was enough to stop her from loving Andrew. Nor could it stop her from saving him.

"You have no power here," she said. "Fear was your authority but I'm not afraid anymore."

As she spoke these words, Abbie felt her terror ebb away.

The snake began to lose its power. The light in its eyes dimmed. The tight coil of its body turned flaccid and dull. It shrank, falling in on itself, bit by bit, until nothing remained but dried skin.

Abbie prodded the membrane with the club, wanting to rid every vestige of the serpent from this place. It crumbled to dust and was blown away by the wind.

She stood only a moment, relishing her relief and her victory. But that moment was short-lived because the forest continued to fall around them, decimating itself. She knelt beside Andrew, feeling for his pulse. It was weak. His chest barely rose and fell with each shallow breath.

With few trees to block her view, Abbie could glimpse the house from where she stood. It appeared on the verge of total collapse. Another minute lost, and she would have to clear the path again. There was no time for that. Grabbing Andrew under his arms, she hefted his head and shoulders from the ground and pulled backward. Stumbling over the tree limbs, she had to stop long enough to toss them aside. At that moment, her greatest concern was that a limb would fall on Andrew as she dragged him to freedom.

Please, please, God. Help me. Help me save the man I love.

At that moment she took a big step backward, and felt the ground beneath her feet gave way. She knew a moment's panic then realized she no longer stood on the forest floor. The stormy dark sky steadily grew brighter and bluer. As before, tranquility quietly filled her and she knew the struggle to free the man in her arms was over. In this ephemeral blue that seemed to have no substance, she was able to lay him down gently. She sat next to his inert body, weak from exertion and giddy with relief.

Abbie no longer needed to fear for Andrew's life or his well-being. This moment was what she had wanted for him from the first time she met him. To take him from the awful prison in which he lived and bring him into the light of a new day was her heart's pleasure and desire.

"Andrew," she said gently. "You will be fine. We will be fine. Wake up now. Open your eyes and see where you are."

When he did not respond, she knew another moment of fear. Had she been wrong? Was it too late for him to survive? Would traveling into the twenty-first century age him abruptly and snuff out his life?

She had broken the curse, hadn't she? Hadn't she?

"Andrew!" she cried, shaking him. "Please don't let it be too late for us!"

As she stared down at him, her eyes wide and swimming, she watched as he stirred. Just a twitching of his eyes beneath their lids, then a weak flutter of eyelashes. Slowly, very slowly, he opened his eyes but immediately closed them against the unaccustomed light. Her heart began to beat again.

"Look, Andrew!" she encouraged softly. "Look, my love, and see where you are."

With studied and deliberate slowness he again opened his eyes slightly, then wider, gazing with awe into the gentle swirling blue light that surrounded them. After a long moment, his gaze searched until he found Abbie next to him. He stared at her as one who has been handed a long-sought and elusive treasure. He took her hand in his, kissed it ardently, fingers tight around her own.

"I knew it was so!" he said in an excited whisper. "This

is Heaven, isn't it?"

She clasped his hand to her heart and smiled down at him.

"I don't know," she told him. "It may be a part of Heaven."

"Yes," he said, looking around them. Color was beginning to return to his cheeks. The fever seemed to have left him, and his eyes grew bright with life.

"Yes," he repeated as he sat up and drew her into his arms. "This is Heaven. And you, Abbie, you are my own dear angel."

EPILOGUE

10 years later

On a cool afternoon in early May, Granny Hodge watched the family in their backyard. She blended into the dappled shade of ancient maple tree, but even if she had not, they would not be able to see her. Granny still possessed the power to control some aspects of her life. Remaining unseen when she wished it was one of them.

Abbie knelt by a flowerbed, working the soil, preparing it for the pansies she purchased the day before. There had been a time in her life when she never would have dreamed of working in dirt, planting flowers, pulling weeds. Never, in her wildest imagination, had she thought she would live in an old refurbished Ozarks farmhouse, five miles from the closest town, sixty miles from the nearest city.

"Hey, my angel," Andrew said as he approached.

She glanced up, squinting in the bright sunlight of the spring morning. He smiled down at her, his dark eyes warmer and more loving than ever in a face that grew more handsome as it aged. The warm breeze tousled his unruly hair.

"Hey, sweetie," she answered, grinning up at him. "What brings you into the wilds of your backyard when you should be sleeping in?"

He held a glass of milk in one hand, and with the other helped Abbie to get to her feet.

"Drink this," he said as she brushed the dirt from her knees. "You know I'll plague you 'til you do."

She made a face at him, took the glass and sipped.

"Cute as you look in shorts and T-shirt," he continued, "isn't it a mite chilly out here for you?"

"Nag, nag, nag," she said and quickly finished the milk. "Need I remind you, my dear sir, how pregnancy always affects my inner thermometer? I'm sure several of your expectant mothers have told you the same thing."

He grinned at her.

"Ah, but I'm not married to them. I just deliver their babies. They have their own husbands and significant others to nag them into taking care of themselves."

"Uh huh," she said skeptically. Then twisting a bit on the balls of her feet, she batted her eyes and asked, "Am I really cute in my shorts?"

"Flirting with me again, are you?" He leered at her. "My dear young woman, this behavior is what got you in this condition." He patted her rounded tummy.

She threw her arms around his neck. "And don't you love it?"

He wrapped his arms around her, crushing her to him briefly and kissed her hard on the mouth.

"Don't I, though?" He cupped her face tenderly. "You are happy, aren't you, Abbie?"

"Beyond measure, Andrew. Beyond anything I ever hoped."

"And this life…do you ever regret—"

She placed her fingertips on his lips.

"If I ever choose to return to a law practice, I shall. But right now, this is all I could ever want."

"Cooking and cleaning and being a wife and mother?"

"Yep." She kissed him slowly, loving the feel of his lips, the warmth of his skin beneath her hand, the slight roughness of his unshaven cheek. "A dozen years ago I thought housewives and stay-at-home moms were fools. What did I know back then?" She smiled into his eyes. "Andrew, this is living."

"Dad!"

The plaintive call broke their moment, and they watched the slender, long-legged ten-year-old run toward them. Born less than nine months after they had escaped the painting, their daughter had Abbie's silky blonde hair and Andrew's liquid, dark eyes.

She stopped and looked at them both, arms crossed on her chest.

"Dad. Will you puh-leeze tell Matthew and Levi to stop teasing Callie? Her whining is driving me crazy!"

He grimaced. Since when had "Dad" replaced "Daddy"? He supposed soon she'd be calling him "Father", in that bored adolescent tone girls seemed to adopt.

He let go of his wife and looked down at his daughter. Her silvery blonde hair shimmered in sunlight as she looked up at him expectantly.

"What's going on, Angela?"

She pointed across the yard at her seven-year-old twin brothers and four-year-old sister.

"They keep teasing Callie, the brats."

Andrew lifted his left eyebrow.

"So…you're suddenly concerned for your sister?"

"Dad. My birthday is tomorrow. Callie promised to leave my friends alone and not be a pest if I make Matthew and Levi give her back Victorian Barbie."

"Ah. And are the boys playing with her doll? Did they have it first?"

Angela rolled her eyes.

"They are using her as an alien from the planet Badok. Victorian Barbie does not come from the planet Badok. I should know. I played with Barbies when I was child."

Behind him, Abbie choked and turned her giggle into a cough. She patted Andrew's shoulder and in a somewhat strangled voice she said, "Go ahead and rescue Barbie, sweetie. I'll just return to my pansies."

He shot her a look over his shoulder, grinning.

"Ah, Saturdays at home. I love it." Turning to Angela, he held out his hand to this beautiful child. "Let us reason with those boys. And if all else fails, let us brave the planet Badok and rescue Miss Victorian Barbie from their evil clutches."

"Dad." She gave him a stern look of reproof which evaporated a moment later when she smiled. A smile like her mother's. A smile that melted his heart all over again. Taking his hand, she said, "OK, Daddy. Let us go reason."

A half-second later, she added, "You know what? You're the best dad in the whole world." She cast a look back to Abbie who was kneeling by the flower bed again but watching them fondly. "And Mom's the best mom. I'm glad I was born."

***

Granny Hodge, hearing the child's the words, let them soak into her tired old soul. Love had changed one deed done by her hand, a deed that had been too cruel. Out of that dark, desolate place in which she had cast Andrew Wade, a miracle had been conceived, and now it grew and flourished in the warmth of a sunlit world.

Maybe it was not too late for her. Maybe there were others she could help free from the fetters that bound them to unhappiness. Perhaps, one day, she could even redeem her own broken soul.

Clinging to that hope, Granny turned and walked away.

The End

CPSIA information can be obtained at www.ICGtesting.com
Printed in the USA
LVOW10s0637040813

346169LV00001B/11/P